# BEST DETECTIVE STORIES OF THE YEAR—1978

## 32nd Annual Collection

# BEST DETECTIVE STORIES OF THE YEAR 1978

## 32nd Annual Collection

Edited by
Edward D. Hoch

E. P. Dutton | New York

For Connie DiRienzo

For information contact: E. P. Dutton, 2 Park Avenue,
New York, N.Y. 10016.

Library of Congress Catalog Card Number: 46-5872

ISBN: 0-525-06437-0

Published simultaneously in Canada by Clarke, Irwin & Company
Limited, Toronto and Vancouver

10 9 8 7 6 5 4 3 2 1

First Edition

# Contents

# Introduction

What was the first mystery magazine ever published? Oddly enough, that's a question with two answers, depending upon how one categorizes the early dime novels. The first dime-novel weekly devoted exclusively to detective stories was *Old Cap. Collier Library*, which began publication with an issue dated April 9, 1883. That's one answer to the question. Still, dime novels were essentially novels, or even serials, with only an occasional shorter work to fill out the pages.

Street & Smith's *Nick Carter Library* (August 8, 1891) was the first dime-novel weekly to feature the exploits of a single detective hero, and here we are on the trail of the first real mystery magazine. *Nick Carter Library* became *Nick Carter Weekly* in 1897, and *Nick Carter Stories* in 1912, tending more toward the combination of serials and shorter works with each name change. Finally, with the issue of October 5, 1915, it became *Detective Story Magazine*—truly the first periodical devoted exclusively to mystery and suspense tales. That first issue of *Detective Story* (a magazine that was to continue publication until 1949) actually ran the next chapter of a Nick Carter serial that had been appearing in *Nick Carter Stories*. The new magazine's editor was even listed as Nick Carter, though in truth he was Frank E. Blackwell, a staff member of Street & Smtih.

Although there were a number of important mystery writers on the magazine scene in 1915, none of them appeared in that first issue of *Detective Story*. Sax Rohmer's series about Morris Klaw was running in *All-Star Cavalier Weekly* during 1915, and some of Melville Davisson Post's classic Uncle Abner stories were appearing in *The Saturday Evening Post*. But readers of the semimonthly *Detective Story*, priced at ten cents for its 128 pages, had to content themselves with such writers as Arnold Duncan, R. Norman Grisewood, and Scott Campbell, a dime novelist who authored a number of the Nick Carter stories.

A competing publication, *Mystery Magazine*, made its appear-

ance two years later with an issue dated November 15, 1917, and
again the authors were drawn from the ranks of dime novelists.
It was not until H. L. Mencken and George Jean Nathan
founded *Black Mask* in 1920 that a major mystery magazine
appeared among the pulps—and even here the mystery content
was sometimes diluted with western and adventure stories.

In the ensuing years scores of mystery magazines appeared,
with varying degrees of success. Among the best were *Mystery
Book Magazine, Manhunt,* and *The Saint Mystery Magazine.*

A comprehensive historical survey of the mystery magazine is
yet to be published (though some excellent histories of the science
fiction magazine already exist). When it does appear it will no
doubt trace the decline of these genre publications in the decades
since World War II. Today there are only three regularly published mystery magazines—the lowest number at any time since
the early 1920s. Plans for one new magazine were abandoned
early in 1977 due to distribution and financing problems. *Mystery
Monthly,* which had been launched in 1976, suspended publication following its ninth issue, but there was talk of its possible
revival under a new name. One new publication, *The World of
Sherlock Holmes Mystery Magazine,* bowed with a December
issue, but it carried virtually no new fiction.

Still, short mysteries kept turning up during the year, some in
unexpected places. In the pages that follow you'll find stories
that originally appeared in a leading general magazine, in a
literary quarterly, and in a four-part newspaper syndication—as
well as stories from the three mystery magazines. And in the
Yearbook section you'll find further proof that the publication
of mystery anthologies and single-author collections continues at
an unusually high rate.

My thanks to all who helped in the preparation of this volume,
especially to Fred Dannay, Eleanor Sullivan, John D. MacDonald, Bill Pronzini, Mike Nevins, Jim Leachman, and—more than
anyone—my wife, Patricia.

EDWARD D. HOCH

*Thomas Walsh is one of the very few* Black Mask *contributors from the 1930s who is still active in the mystery field. His career can roughly be divided into three parts: frequent magazine appearances during the thirties and forties in both pulp and slick publications; a successful career as a novelist in the fifties and sixties, beginning with the Edgar-winning* Nightmare in Manhattan; *and a return to short stories in the seventies. This fine tale shows he has lost none of his old touch. In fact something new has been added. This moving portrait of a fallen priest is one of the best to be found outside the works of Graham Greene, and it earned a second Edgar Award for Thomas Walsh when the Mystery Writers of America voted it the best short story of 1977.*

# THOMAS WALSH
## Chance After Chance

Padre, everybody in Harrington's called him. Year after year he dropped in from his furnished room about seven at night, then drank steadily until three in the morning, closing time; and one Christmas Eve, very drunk, he curled both arms around his shot glass, put his head down, and began chanting some kind of crazy gibberish. Nobody in Harrington's knew what it was—but maybe, Harrington himself thought later on, maybe it was Latin. Because little by little, from remarks he let drop about his earlier life, it became rumored that he had once been a Roman Catholic priest in a small New England town somewhere near Boston.

He was perhaps in his fifties and in youth must have been a lusty and physically powerful man. Now, however, the whiskey had almost finished him. His hands trembled; his face was markedly lined, weary, and sunken; his shabby alcoholic's jauntiness had a forced ring to it; and he was almost never without a stubble of dirty gray beard on his cheeks.

One night Jack Delgardo on the next stool inquired idly as to why they had kicked him out of the church. Was it the whiskey,

1

Jack wanted to know, or was it women? Did he mean to say they never even gave him a second chance?

"Well, a chance," Padre admitted, always a bit genially boastful in man-of-the-world conversation. "They found out about a certain French girl over in Holyoke, Massachusetts, and because of her and the booze they told me I'd have to go down to a penitential monastery in Georgia for two years. But bare feet and long hours of prayerful communion with the Lord God would be the only ticket for me in that place, not to mention the dirtiest sort of physical labor day after day. They had no conception at all, however, about the kind of man they were dealing with. So naturally, when I told the monsignor straight out where to go, since I discovered that I had lost the faith by that time, there was no more point in discussing the matter. A long time past, Jack—twenty-odd years."

But Jack Delgardo was not much interested in the Lord God. Besides which, he had just seen his new girl bob in, very dainty and elegant, through Harrington's front door.

"Yeah," he said, rising briskly. "Can't blame you a bit, Padre, for getting the hell out. See you around, huh?"

"Very probably," Padre said, blessing him with humorously overdone solemnity for the free drink. "Always here, Jack. Could you spare me a dollar or two until the first of the month?"

Because the first of the month was when his four checks arrived. In Harrington's he never mentioned that part of his life, but he came from a large and very prosperous family of Boston Irish—Robert the surgeon, Michael the chemist, Edward the engineer, and Kevin Patrick the businessman; and three married sisters and their families who had all settled down years ago in one or another of the more well-to-do Boston suburbs.

But Padre had eventually found himself unable to endure his family any more than he had been able to endure his monsignor. He never failed to detect a slight but telltale flush of shame and apology when they had to introduce him to some friend who dropped by, and he could all too easily imagine the sly knowledge of him that would be whispered from mouth to mouth later on—the weakling of the family, the black sheep, the spoiled youngest of them, and now the drunken, profligate, defrocked priest.

Although having been the spoiled youngest, Padre occasionally thought, might have been the beginning of all his troubles. Like Robert he might well have been the surgeon, or, like Michael the chemist; but as little Joey, always too much loved, always dearest and closest of anyone to the mother, he seemed never once to have had his own life in his hands. As far back as he could remember anything, he could remember Mama and him in a church pew, with sunlight streaming in over them through a stained-glass window, her face lifted up to the high dim altar before them, her lips moving silently, and the rosary beads slipping one by one through her fingers.

Only three or four years old then, Padre had been young enough to believe anything he was told; young enough, in fact, to have believed everything. Only in seminary days had come his first questioning, his first resentment, his first rebellion. So he had written a long letter to his favorite uncle, Uncle Jack, and announced dramatically that he was unable to take the life anymore. So if Uncle Jack could not get Mama to see some sense, he had made up his mind to run away, or even to kill himself.

But in the end he had done neither. He had gone on, and he could also remember, if he ever wanted to, a winter night soon afterward in the kitchen at home, with Uncle Jack and his mother shouting angrily at each other from opposite sides of the table.

"Don't try to make the boy do what he has no inclination at all for," Uncle Jack had cried out at her. "Damn it to hell, Maggie, can't you understand there's nothing half so contemptible in this world as a bad priest? Where in God's name are your brains? It's his life, don't you see? It's not yours. Then let him do what he wants with it, or you'll have to answer for that yourself. It's just the pride you'd feel at having a son in the church—that's why you're bound and determined on it! Why, you're forcing him to—"

Leaning forward shakily, his mother had rested both hands on the table in front of her.

"He'll do what I say!" she had cried back. "He'll have the only true happiness there is in this world. He'll have the collar, I tell you! And you daring to come here tonight and lead him on like this when you never once had the faith that I do, and you never will! What were you all your days but a shame and disgrace to yourself and to the Holy Roman Catholic Church? I know what he wants and what he needs, and better than you. I've prayed to the Blessed Lady every night of my life for it—and she'll answer me! And you'll change that, will you, with your mad carrying on here tonight, and your cursing and swearing at us! Then I take my vow on the thing here and now. From this day on I swear to Almighty God that you and yours will never again enter this house, as I swear to Almighty God that I and mine will never again enter yours! Is that the answer you want? Then there it is. Never again!"

But after that had come the sudden horrible twist of her whole face to one side and her clumsy lurch forward halfway across the table. And after that, Padre could also remember, there had been the family doctor hurriedly summoned, and old Father O'Mara, and up in her bedroom a few minutes after, all the family down on their knees, with Bonnie and Eileen and Agnes all crying, and Father O'Mara leading them on solemnly and gravely in the Litany for the Dying. But Padre had been closest of all to her, as he knew from the day of his birth he had always been, and holding her hand. So . . . .

So. He had gone on. He had done what he had promised her in that moment, if without words. He had got the collar at last. But now, on the first of every month, what he got were the fifty-dollar checks mailed in, one apiece, from the surgeon and the chemist and the engineer and the businessman. To earn them, tacitly understood, he had only to keep himself well away from the city of Boston for as long as he lived. So Harrington's, as the finale of all; so his regular stool at the end of the bar, nearest the rest rooms; so Padre, now hardly more than a shaky and alcoholic shadow of his former self, at the age of not quite fifty-three years old.

There, year after year, he troubled no one and bothered no one, making no friends and no enemies. So he was rather surprised when he was invited up to Jack Delgardo's apartment on Lexington Avenue one January night to meet two of Jack's friends, with a promise that the whiskey would be free and liberally provided for him. And it was. They all had a lot to drink, one after another—a lot even for Padre; and then in half an hour or so, surprisingly enough, it appeared that the conversation had turned to theology.

"But at least you have to believe in God," Jack argued, refilling the glass for him. "You can't kid me, Padre—because a guy has to believe in something, that's all, no matter what he says. And I can still remember what they taught me in parochial school. Once a priest always a priest, the way I got it."

"Quite true," Padre had to agree, smacking his lips over the fine bourbon. "Although I believe the biblical terminology is a priest forever, according to the order of the high priest Melchizedek."

"Yeah, I guess," Eddie Roberts grinned—Steady Eddie, as Jack often referred to him. "Only how do you mean high, Padre? The way you get every night in the week down at Harrington's?"

At that they all laughed, including Padre, although the third man, Pete, did not permit the laugh to change his expression in any way. He had said little so far. He appeared to be studying Padre silently and intently, though not openly, dropping his eyes down to the cigarette in his hand every time Padre happened to glance at him.

"No, not quite like me," Padre said, very jovial about it. "In seminary we used to paraphrase a poem about him, or at least I did. 'Melchizedek, he praised the Lord and gave some wine to Abraham; but who can tell what else he did is smarter far than what I am.'"

"Oh, sometimes you seem smart enough," Steady Eddie put in. "Almost smart enough to know the right score, Padre. I wonder, are you?"

"Classical education," Padre assured him. "Only the best, Eddie, Latin, Greek, and Advanced Theology."

"Yeah, but I thought the theology never took," Jack said, exchanging a quick glance with Pete. "That's what you're always claiming around at Harrington's, isn't it?"

"Well, yes," Padre had to agree once more. "At least these days. Years ago it just happened to strike me all of a sudden that the Lord God Almighty, granting that He exists at all, isn't what most of us are inclined to believe about Him. Look at His record for yourself. Who else, one by one, has killed off every life that He ever created?"

"Yeah, but Sister Mary Cecilia," Jack objected, "used to tell us that no human being ever died, actually. They were transported."

"No, no," Padre corrected grandly. "Transformed, Jack. Into

a higher and more superior being, into the spirit; or else, conversely, down into eternal and everlasting hell. And very useful teaching too, let me tell you. Nothing like it for keeping in line everyone who still believes."

"Only you don't believe it anymore?" Pete asked softly.

Padre finished his drink, again smacking his lips over it with great relish. He was very cunning in defending himself at these moments. He'd had much practice.

"I believe," he said, indicating the glass to them, "in what a man sees, hears, tastes, touches, and feels. That's what I believe, gentlemen, and all I believe. Is your bourbon running out, Jack?"

"Yeah, sure," Steady Eddie grinned. "But of course lots of guys talk real big with a few drinks in them. Sometimes you never know whether to believe them or not, Padre."

"So you don't believe in nothing," Pete said, while Jack hurriedly refilled Padre's glass. "Nothing at all. How about money, though? You believe in that?"

"Oh, most emphatically. And in God too. Or at least," Padre amended, trying his new drink, "at least God in the bottle. Which of course means God in the wallet too."

"Yeah, but old habits," Pete said, even more softly. "Hard to break, Padre. Let's suppose somebody ast you to hear a guy's confession, say—and for maybe five or ten thousand dollars? Your specialty too. Right up your alley. Only it wouldn't bother you even one bit?"

"Shrive the penitent," Padre beamed, knowing that he was somewhat overdoing it, as always in discussions of this kind, but unable to restrain himself. Why? He did not know. He did not, as a matter of fact, want to know. It simply had to be done, that was all. Someone had to know the kind of a man He was dealing with. "Solace the afflicted and comfort the dying. I've heard many a confession in my day, and for nothing at all. Very juicy listening too, some of them. You wouldn't believe the things that—"

Pete and Jack exchanged quick glances. Steady Eddie inched forward a bit.

"And then tell us," he whispered, "tell us what the guy said to you afterwards?"

Padre, hand up with the refilled glass, felt an altogether absurd

catch of the heart. He had broken many vows in his time, but
there was one he had not. He looked over at Eddie, as if a bit
startled, then up at Jack, then around at Pete. But this was not
fair, something whispered in him. This was active and deliberate
malevolence. All his life he had been tried and tried, and beyond
his strength; tested and tested; but now at last to betray the only
thing he had never betrayed. . . .

Yet he managed to nod calmly. There had to be considered,
after all, the kind of man that he was, and what five or ten
thousand dollars would mean to him. Could he admit now
that he had lied and lied even to himself all these years, and
lied to everyone else too? Never! It was not to be thought of for
one instant.

"I see," he murmured. "And tell you afterwards. So that's
the condition?"

"That's the condition," Pete said. "You still got a priest's
shirt and a Roman collar, Padre?"

"Here or there," Padre said, still smiling brightly at them,
which was very necessary now; nothing but the bold face for it.
"Only it's been a very long time, of course. As the old song has
it, there's been a few changes made. So I don't know that I
could quite—"

Jack Delgardo rubbed a savage hand over his mouth. Steady
Eddie replaced his grin with a cold ominous stare. But Pete
proved much more acute than either of them. He understood
at once why the protest had been made by Padre—not out of
strength, but from sudden shrinking weakness; the hidden and
unadmitted desire, probably, to be persuaded now even against
himself.

"Easiest thing in the world," Pete remarked quietly. "Guy you
know, too—so no question about you being a priest, Padre. All
you'd have to say is that you've gone back to the church and
he'd believe it. Remember Big Lefty Carmichael?"

And Padre did—four or five years ago from Harrington's—but
not clearly. He was trying to get the name straight in his head
when Jack Delgardo leaned forward to him.

"Well, they let him out," Jack whispered, resting his right
hand on Padre's arm, then shaking it, as if to give the most perfect assurance of what he said. "He got sick up in Dannemora
Prison, Padre, and now he's dying in a cheap little furnished

room over on Ninth Avenue. They can't do a damned thing for him anymore now. They can't even operate. He's just sick as hell and ready to holler cop, see? A friend of his told us. He said that Lefty asked him to bring a priest tomorrow night. So where's any problem?"

That time Padre decided only to sip from his glass. He had begun to feel all drunkenly confused.

"Because what happened," Pete drawled, apparently observing that Padre could not quite place the name, "is that Lefty and two other guys got away with a potful of money three years ago— only they piled up into a trailer truck on Second Avenue, and no one but Lefty got out alive.

"Then the cops grabbed him that night, soon as they identified the two dead guys he always worked with. Grabbed him, Padre —but not the bank money. Well, he couldn't have spent it, of course. No time. And he wouldn't have given it to anyone to hold for him, because he wasn't that stupid. He must have stashed it away somewhere real cute, and wherever he put it, it's still there. They only let him out of Dannemora yesterday morning and he ain't left the house on Ninth Avenue since he got there. He couldn't have. We've been watching it. We'd have seen.

"OK. So now he wants somebody like you, old Lefty does. No more of the old zip in him, Padre. So if we have the friend tell him about you rejoining the church and all, he's gonna believe it. You're the kind of a priest he wouldn't mind telling his confession to, you know what I mean? You're just like him, the way he'll look at it. You're both losers. Then when he confesses about the bank holdup, all you have to do is tell him he's got to make restitution for what he stole. That's what you'd do, anyway, isn't it? Only this time, of course, soon as he tells you where the money is hid—"

Padre picked up his drink from the coffee table and this time he emptied it. His mind still worked slowly, which irritated him. He could not understand why. So he took good care to conceal whatever he felt, and to smile back at Pete even more arrogantly than before. He reached over to the bourbon bottle with his right hand, lifted it, and solemnly blessed the assembly.

"*Absolvo te,*" he announced then, and in a tone that successfully gave just the right touch of derisive priestly unction to what he said. "'Blessed is he that comes in the name of the Lord.' If it's as simple as that, gentlemen, then I think we're just about agreed on the matter. Let's say somewhere about nine o'clock tomorrow night, then. What's the address?"

Pete was behind the steering wheel, Eddie beside him. Jack Delgardo was crouched forward in the middle of the back seat. It was 9:30 the next night and they were all watching the entrance to a tenement house directly opposite.

About fifteen minutes later Padre came out of the house. He was now shaved cleanly; he wore the black shirt and the Roman collar; and Steady Eddie at once reached back to open the rear door.

"Hey, Padre," he called guardedly. "Over here. We decided to wait for you."

It was a cold January night, with misty rain in the air, but Padre removed his hat a bit wearily in the vestibule doorway. They could see his gray hair then, and the thinly drawn pale face under it—the alcoholic's face. He glanced about, right and left, but did not move until Pete impatiently tapped on the car horn.

Even then, when Jack Delgardo had made room on the back seat, there was a kind of funny look on his face, Steady Eddie thought—a look, for a couple of long seconds, just like he had never seen them before and did not know who they were.

"So how did it go?" Jack Delgardo whispered. "Come on and tell us, Padre. He make his confession to you?"

But for another moment or so Padre only fingered the black hat on his knees, lightly and carefully.

"Yes," he said then. "Yes, he did. He made his confession."

"Then open up," Steady Eddie urged. "What did he tell you? Where's the money, Padre?"

"What?" Padre said. He appeared to be thinking of other matters; like in some damn fog, Jack thought furiously. He did not answer the question. All he did was to keep smoothing the black hat time after time while looking down at it, as if he had never seen that before either. "But first," he added, "I decided that I'd better talk to him a little—to get him into the right mood for the thing. And I had to think up the words to do that, of course—only pretty soon they seemed to be coming out of me

all by themselves. Father, he kept calling me—" and he had to
laugh here, with a kind of shakily nervous unsteadiness. "It's
almost thirty years since anybody called me that, in that way.
With respect, I mean. With a certain kind of dependence on
me . . . Father."

Eddie got hold of him by the throat angrily and yanked his
head up.

"You listen to me, you old lush! Jack asked you something.
Where's that money?"

"What?" Padre repeated. He did not seem to understand the
question. He was frowning absently. "I had to tell him I'd be
around first thing tomorrow morning with the Host," he said.
"I think I may have helped him a little. When I gave him
Absolution afterwards, he kissed my hand. He actually—"

Pete, who had been staring fixedly ahead through the windshield, his lips compressed, started the car. Nothing more was
said. It must have been all decided between them, just as they
had decided to wait for Padre while he was still in the house.

They drove onto a dingy street farther west under the shadows
of an overhead roadway that was being constructed, and there
they drove up and around on a half-finished approach ramp.
There was a kind of platform at the top of it, with lumber and
big concrete mixers scattered about; before them a waist-high
stone parapet; and beyond that the river.

No other cars could be seen, and no other people; no illumina-
tion except the intermittent gleam of a blinker light down on
the next corner. Red, dark, red, dark. Padre found himself thinking with a curious and altogether aimless detachment of mind.
Bitter cold cheer this night against the January rain and against
the cluster of faint lights way over on the Jersey side—or not
cheer at all, really . . . Father.

"Padre," Pete said, and unlike Eddie in a calm, perfectly controlled manner. "Where's the money?"

Padre might not have heard him at all.

"I had to—comfort him," he said. "But the only thing that
came to me was what I had read once in the words of a French
Jesuit priest—that a Christian must never be afraid of death,
that he must welcome it, that it was the greatest act of faith he
would ever make in this life, and that he must plunge joyfully

into death as into the arms of his living and loving God. Then I led him on into the Act of Contrition—after I remembered it myself. And somehow I did remember it. Hoist by my own petard, then—" and once more he had to laugh softly. " 'Oh, my God, I am heartily sorry for having offended Thee—' That's how it starts, you know. And once I'd repeated that for him—would any of you have a drink for me?"

Pete got out of the car. So did Eddie. So did Jack Delgardo. One of them opened the door for Padre and took his arm. He got out obediently and then stood there.

"Padre," Pete said. "Where's the money?"

"What?" Padre said. The third time.

There were no more words wasted, just Eddie and Jack Delgardo closing in on him. They were quick about it and very efficient. They got Padre back against the stone parapet, which was some eighty or ninety feet above the river at this point, and there Eddie used his hands, and Jack Delgardo the tip of his right shoe.

There were almost no sounds, just the quick scrape of their feet on the paving, then a gasp, and then Padre falling. After that they allowed him to sit up groggily, muddy brown gutter water all over his black suit, his hat knocked off so that his gray hair could again be seen, and blood on his mouth.

"Now you just come on," Steady Eddie gritted. "We ain't even started on you. You ain't getting away with this, not now. We didn't make you come in with us. You promised you would. So do what we tell you, you phony old lush, or we'll—*Where's that money?*"

By then Padre had straightened against the parapet, supporting himself by his two hands, and breathing with shallow and labored effort.

"But it was never fair," he cried out. "Never fair! I was tempted not in one way during my life but in every possible way—and time after time! And now tonight, up in that room back there, I had to listen to myself saying something—whatever kept coming into my head. And not for him either—but for myself, don't you see? That it didn't matter how often we failed. That we only had to succeed at the end! That it wasn't trial after trial that was given to us. That it was chance after chance

after chance! And that if only once, if only once and at the very
finish of everything, we could say to Almighty God that we accepted the chance—"

Pete gestured Eddie and Jack Delgardo off and then moved
back himself into somewhat better light so that the knife in his
hand became clearly visible.

"You know what this is?" he said. "This is a knife. And you
know, if you want to go ahead and make me, what I can do with
it?"

He proceeded to say. He spoke in a clinically detached manner
of various parts of the human body, of their extreme vulnerability
to pain, and of what he could do with the knife—if he was forced.
Very soon Padre, still hanging onto the parapet, had to turn
shuddering away from that voice, and in blind panic. But on
one side there was Steady Eddie waiting for him. On the other
was Jack Delgardo.

"We'll even give you a square count," Steady Eddie urged, obviously thinking that part important, and at the same time offering a pint bottle of whiskey out of his overcoat pocket. "Honest
to God, Padre. Just take a good long drink for yourself—and then
think for a minute. Nothing like it, remember? God in a bottle."

And Padre needed that drink. He was beginning to feel the
pain now—in his face, in the pit of his stomach, in his right
knee. Which would be nothing at all, he realized, to the pain
of the knife. Yes, then, he would tell. In the end, knowing himself, he knew he would have to tell.

But was it test after test that had always been demanded of
him, venomously and to no purpose? Or was it, as he had found
himself saying earlier tonight, chance after chance after chance
that was offered—and the chance even now, it might be, to admit
finally and for the first time in his life a greater love which, being
the kind of man he was, or had insisted he was, he had always
denied?

He still could not say. But how queer, it came to him, that the
last denial of all, the only promise he had never violated, was
now being demanded of him. But as proof of what? Of a thing
he believed in his heart even yet, or of a thing he did not believe?

His hands were shaking. He looked at them, at the pint bottle
they held, and then at the jagged cluster of rocks almost a hundred feet straight down that he could see at the very edge of the

river. He had not drunk from the bottle yet. Now he attempted to and it rolled out of his hands, as if accidentally, onto the parapet.

He wailed aloud, scrambling up desperately for the bottle, and before Steady Eddie could lose his contemptuous grin, before Jack Delgardo, turning his back to the wind, could light the match for his cigarette, and before Pete, now more distant than either of them, could move, Padre was standing erect on top of the parapet.

Pete shouted a warning. Steady Eddie rushed forward. But plunge joyfully, Padre was thinking—the chance taken, the trust maintained, the greater love at last and beyond any question admitted by him. Plunge joyfully!

That was the final thought in his head. After it, avoiding a frantic outward grab for his legs by Steady Eddie, Father Joseph Leo Shanahan moved quickly but calmly to the edge of the parapet, crossed himself there, put up the other hand in a last moment of weakness to cover his eyes—and stepped straight out.

Then the blinker light shone down on a stone ledge empty save for the still corked whiskey bottle, and there were left only the three men, but not the fourth, to gape stupidly and unbelievingly from back in the shadows.

*Paul Theroux is the author of an admirable series of novels, highly praised by critics, which often contain strong elements of crime and suspense—as in his 1976 study of London terrorists,* The Family Arsenal. *His travel book,* The Great Railway Bazaar, *was a popular best seller in 1975. An American living in London, Theroux is often compared to Graham Greene and Somerset Maugham. The Maugham influence was especially noted in his 1977 collection of short stories,* The Consul's File, *about the diverse adventures of the resident American consul in a small Malaysian town. In this story, an MWA Edgar nominee, the consul investigates a pair of seemingly motiveless murders.*

# PAUL THEROUX
# The Johore Murders

The first victim was a British planter, and everyone at the Club said what a shame it was that after fifteen years in the country he was killed just four days before he planned to leave. He had no family, he lived alone; until he was murdered no one knew very much about him. Murder is the grimmest, briefest fame. If the second victim, a month later, had not been an American, I probably would not have given the Johore murders a second thought, and I certainly would not have been involved in the business. But who would have guessed that Ismail Garcia was an American?

The least dignified thing that can happen to a man is to be murdered. If he dies in his sleep he gets a respectful obituary and perhaps a smiling portrait; it is how we all want to be remembered. But murder is the great exposer: Here is the victim in his torn underwear, face down on the floor, unpaid bills on his dresser, a meager shopping list, some loose change, and worst of all, the fact that he is alone. Investigation reveals what he did that day—it all matters—his habits are examined, his behavior scrutinized, his trunks rifled, and a balance sheet is drawn up

From *The Consul's File* by Paul Theroux. Copyright © 1972, 1974, 1975, 1976, 1977 by Paul Theroux. Reprinted by permission of Houghton Mifflin Company. "The Johore Murders" first published in *The Atlantic Monthly*.

at the hospital giving the contents of his stomach. Dying, the last private act we perform, is made public: The murder victim has no secrets.

So, somewhere in Garcia's house, a passport was found, an American one, and that was when the Malaysian police contacted the embassy in Kuala Lumpur. I was asked to go down for the death certificate, personal effects, and anything that might be necessary for the report to his next of kin. I intended it to be a stopover, a day in Johore, a night in Singapore, and then back to Ayer Hitam. Peeraswami had a brother in Johore; Abubaker, my driver, said he wanted to pray at the Johore mosque; we swanned off early one morning, Abubaker at the wheel, Peeraswami playing with the car radio. I was in the back seat going over newspaper clippings of the two murders.

In most ways they were the same. Each victim was a foreigner, unmarried, lived alone in a house outside town, and had been a resident for some years. In neither case was there any sign of a forced entry or a robbery. Both men were poor, both men had been mutilated. They looked to me like acts of Chinese revenge. But on planters? In Malaysia it was the Chinese *towkay* who was robbed, kidnapped, or murdered, not the expatriate planter who lived from month to month on provisioners' credit and chit-signing in bars. There was one difference: Tibbets was British and Ismail Garcia was American. And one other known fact: Tibbets, at the time of his death, was planning to go back to England.

A two-hour drive through rubber estates took us into Johore, and then we were speeding along the shore of the Straits, past the lovely casuarina trees and the high houses on the leafy bluff that overlooks the swampland and the marshes on the north coast of Singapore. I dropped Peeraswami at his brother's house, which was in one of the wilder suburbs of Johore and had a high chain link fence around it to assure even greater seclusion. Abubaker scrambled out at the mosque after giving me directions to police headquarters.

Garcia's effects were in a paper bag from a Chinese shop. I signed for them and took them to a table to examine: a cheap watch, a cheap ring, a copy of the Koran, a birth certificate, the passport.

"We left the clothes behind," said Detective Sergeant Yusof. "We just took the valuables."

Valuables. There wasn't five dollars' worth of stuff in the bag.

"Was there any money?"

"He had no money. We're not treating it as robbery."

"What *are* you treating it as?"

"Homicide, probably by a friend."

"Some friend."

"He knew the murderer; so did Tibbets. You will believe me when you see the houses."

I almost did. Garcia's house was completely surrounded by a high fence, and Yusof said that Tibbets's fence was even higher. It was not unusual; every large house in Malaysian cities had an unclimbable fence or a wall with spikes of glass cemented onto the top.

"The lock wasn't broken, the house wasn't tampered with," said Yusof. "So we are calling it a sex crime."

"I thought you were calling it a homicide."

Yusof smirked at me. "We have a theory. The Englishmen who live here get funny ideas. Especially the ones who live alone. Some of them take Malay mistresses, the other ones go around with Chinese boys."

"No Malay boys?"

Yusof said, "We do not do such things."

"You say Englishmen do, but Garcia was an American."

"He was single," said Yusof.

"I'm single," I said.

"We couldn't find any sign of a mistress."

"I thought you were looking for a murderer."

"That's what I'm trying to say," said Yusof. "These queers are very secretive. They get jealous. They fight with their boyfriends. The body was mutilated—that tells me a Chinese boy is involved."

"So you don't think it had anything to do with money?"

"Do you know what the rubber price is?"

"As a matter of fact, I do."

"And that's not all," said Yusof. "This man Garcia—do you know what he owed his provisioner? Over eight hundred dollars! Tibbets was owing five hundred."

I said, "Maybe the provisioner did it."

"Interesting," said Yusof. "We can work on that."

Over lunch I concentrated on Garcia. There was a little dossier on him from the Alien Registration Office. Born 1922 in the Philippines; fought in World War II; took out American citizenship in Guam; came to Malaysia in 1954; converted to Islam and changed his name. From place to place, complicating his identity, picking up a nationality here, a name there, a religion somewhere else. And why would he convert? A woman, of course. No man changes his religion to live with another man. I didn't believe he was a homosexual, and though there was no evidence to support it, I didn't rule out the possibility of robbery. In all this there were two items that interested me—the birth certificate and the passport. The birth certificate was brown with age, the passport new and unused.

Why would a man who had changed his religion and lived in a country for nearly twenty years have a new passport?

After lunch I rang police headquarters and asked for Yusof.

"We've got the provisioner," he said. "I think you might be right. He was also Tibbets's provisioner—both men owed him money. He is helping us with our inquiries."

"What a pompous phrase for torture," I said, but before Yusof could reply, I added, "About Garcia—I figure he was planning to leave the country."

Yusof cackled into the phone. "Not at all! We talked to his employer—Garcia had a permanent and pensionable contract."

"Then why did he apply for a passport two weeks ago?"

"It is the law. He must be in possession of a valid passport if he is an expatriate."

I said, "I'd like to talk to his employer."

Yusof gave me the name of the man, Tan See Leng, owner of the Tai-Hwa Rubber Estate. I went over that afternoon. At first Tan refused to see me, but when I sent him my card with the consulate address and the American eagle on it, he rushed out of his office and apologized. He was a thin, evasive man with spiky hair, and though he pretended not to be surprised when I said Garcia was an American national, I could tell this was news to him. He said he knew nothing about Garcia, apart from the fact that he'd been a good foreman. He'd never seen him socially. He confirmed that Garcia lived behind an impenetrable fence.

"Who owned the house?"

"He did."

"That's something," I said. "I suppose you knew he was leaving the country."

"He was not leaving. He was wucking."

"It would help if you told me the truth," I said.

Tan's bony face tightened with anger. He said, "Perhaps he intended to leave. I do not know."

"I take it business isn't so good."

"The rubber price is low, some planters are switching to oil palm. But the price will rise if we are patient."

"What did you pay Garcia?"

"Two thousand a month. He was on permanent terms—he signed one of the old contracts. We were very generous in those days with expatriates."

"But he could have broken the contract."

"Some men break."

"Up in Ayer Hitam they have something called a 'golden handshake.' If they want to get rid of a foreigner they offer him a chunk of money as compensation for loss of career."

"That is Ayer Hitam," said Tan. "This is Johore."

"And they always pay cash, because it's against the law to take that much money out of the country. No banks. Just a suitcase full of Straits dollars."

Tan said nothing.

I said, "I don't think Garcia or Tibbets was queer. I think this was robbery, pure and simple."

"The houses were not broken into."

"So the papers say," I said. "It's the only thing I don't understand. Both men were killed at home during the day."

"Mister," said Tan, "you should leave this to the police."

"You swear you didn't give Garcia a golden handshake?"

"That is against the law, as you say."

"It's not as serious as murder, is it?"

In the course of the conversation, Tan had turned to wood. I was sure he was lying, but he stuck to his story. I decided to have nothing more to do with the police or Yusof and instead to go back to the house of Peeraswami's brother, to test a theory of my own.

The house bore many similarities to Garcia's and to what I knew of Tibbets's. It was secluded, out of town, rather characterless, and the high fence was topped with barbed wire. Sathya, Peeraswami's brother, asked me how I liked Johore. I told him that I liked it so much I wanted to spend a few days there, but that I didn't want the embassy to know where I was. I asked him if he would put me up.

"Oh, yes," he said. "You are welcome. But you would be more comfortable in a hotel."

"It's much quieter here."

"It is the country life. We have no car."

"It's just what I'm looking for."

After I was shown to my bedroom I excused myself and went to the offices of the *Johore Mail,* read the classified ads for the previous few weeks, and placed an ad myself. For the next two days I explored Johore, looked over the botanical gardens and the sultan's mosque, and ingratiated myself with Sathya and his family. I had arrived on a Friday. On Monday I said to Sathya, "I'm expecting a phone call today."

Sathya said, "This is your house."

"I feel I ought to do something in return," I said. "I have a driver and a car—I don't need them today. Why don't you use them? Take your wife and children over to Singapore and enjoy yourself."

He hesitated, but finally I persuaded him. Abubaker, on the other hand, showed an obvious distaste for taking an Indian family out for the day.

"Peeraswami," I said, "I'd like you to stay here with me."

"*Tuan,*" he said, agreeing. Sathya and the others left. I locked the gate behind them and sat by the telephone to wait.

There were four phone calls. Three of the callers I discouraged by describing the location, the size of the house, the tiny garden, the work I said had to be done on the roof. And I gave the same story to the last caller, but he was insistent and eager to see it. He said he'd be right over.

Rawlins was the name he gave me. He came in a new car, gave me a hearty greeting, and was not at all put off by the slightly ramshackle appearance of the house. He smoked a cheroot which had stained his teeth and the center swatch of his moustache a sticky yellow, and he walked around with one hand cupped, tapping ashes into his palm.

"You're smart not to use an agent," he said, looking over the house. "These estate agents are bloody thieves."

I showed him the garden, the lounge, the kitchen.

He sniffed and said. "You like curry."

"My cook's an Indian." He went silent, glanced around suspiciously, and I added, "I gave him the day off."

"You lived here long?"

"Ten years. I'm chucking it. I've been worried about selling this place ever since I broke my contract."

"Rubber?" he said, and spat a fragment of the cheroot into his hand.

"Yes," I said. "I was manager of an estate up in Kluang."

He asked me the price and when I told him he said, "I can manage that." He took out a checkbook. "I'll give you a deposit now and the balance when contracts are exchanged. We'll put our lawyers in touch and Bob's your uncle. Got a pen?"

I went to the desk and opened a drawer, but as I rummaged he said, "OK, turn around slow and put your hands up."

I did as I was told and heard the cheroot hitting the floor. Above the kris Rawlins held, his face was fierce and twisted. In such an act a man reverts; his face was pure monkey, threatening teeth and eyes. He said, "Now hand it over."

"What is this?" I said. "What do you want?"

"Your money, all of it, your handshake."

"I don't have any money."

"They alway lie," he said. "They always fight, and then I have to do them in. Just make it easy this time. The money—"

But he said no more, for Peeraswami in his bare feet crept behind him from the broom cupboard where he had been hiding and brought a cast-iron frying pan down so hard on his skull that I thought for a moment I saw a crack show in the man's forehead. We tied Rawlins up with Sathya's neckties and then I rang Yusof.

On the way to police headquarters, where Yusof insisted the corpse be delivered, I said, "This probably would not have happened if you didn't have such strict exchange control regulations."

"So it was robbery," said Yusof. "But how did he know Tibbets and Garcia had had golden handshakes?"

"He guessed. There was no risk involved. He knew they were leaving the country because they'd put their houses up for sale. Expatriates who own houses here have been in the country a long time, which means they're taking a lot of money out in a suitcase. You should read the paper."

"I read the paper," said Yusof. "Malay and English press."

"I mean the classified ads, where it says, 'Expatriate-owned house for immediate sale. Leaving the country. No agents.' Tibbets and Garcia placed that ad, and so did I."

Yusof said, "I should have done that. I could have broken this case."

"I doubt it—he wouldn't have done business with a Malay," I said. "But remember, if a person says he wants to buy your house, you let him in. It's the easiest way for a burglar to enter —through the front door. If he's a white man in this country no one suspects him. We're supposed to trust each other. As soon as I realized it had something to do with the sale of a house, I knew the murderer would be white."

"He didn't know they were alone."

"The wife and kids always fly out first, especially if Daddy's breaking currency regulations."

"You foreigners know all the tricks."

"True," I said. "If he was a Malay or a Chinese I probably wouldn't have been able to catch him." I tapped my head. "I understand the mind of the West."

*Peter Godfrey is a South African writer who now resides in England. During the late forties and early fifties, while also writing a controversial political column in Cape Town, he produced mysteries at such a prolific rate that he required four pseudonyms. Many of those early mysteries showed a preoccupation with time as a necessary plot ingredient. Time also plays its part in this new Godfrey story—one of the most baffling mysteries to come along all year.*

# PETER GODFREY
# To Heal a Murder

It was nearly eight months since Ferris had last opened the front door of his little Richmond flat. At that time he had thought he would be away only two weeks on a package tour to Rumania. Now, after many vicissitudes and constant fears, he was back—and safe. It was an occasion—a triumphant return home.

Only—it wasn't. The floor and furniture in the entrance hall were gray with dust. The pile of letters lay higgledy-piggledy on the floor, just as they had dropped through the letter flap. He felt like a stranger. He remembered with sudden nostalgia his newspaper days when he was always in close touch with friends. Now for the first time in weeks he cursed his new employers, secretive and all-powerful, who demanded his absolute dedication—and gave in return nothing basically human, not even real thanks.

Lost, he picked up the pile of letters and tried to sort them into chronological order by postmark. They were mostly circulars.

But the one that ended on top of the pile had been mailed in Brighton the day he had left on his trip. The handwriting meant nothing to him. He opened the envelope, drew out the notepaper, and glanced at the signature. Rebecca. Of course, the little girl at 63—Rebecca Brink.

"Dear Mr. Joe," said the letter, "I know I should have written before, but really there hasn't been much news. Esther, as you know, has married Mr. Binns, and we're all living together in a big house in Brighton.

"Mr. Joe, I wish you were here right now. You see, I've got a terrible problem to face—something I can't even discuss with Esther. You're the only one I know I could talk to. I wish you were here—but of course I couldn't have the cheek to ask you to come down specially, could I? But I am praying to God that you will have business in Brighton soon. All my love, Rebecca."

There were several lines scrawled below the signature. "P.S. I am really trying to follow your advice—you know, about going out more and meeting people. I've joined a fencing club, where there are lots of other girls and boys. At least ten. I was a bit shy at first, but I'm getting to know them better now. P.P.S. Please try and come."

Somehow the letter prodded Ferris's feeling of unease. He took it next door to Mrs. Venner. "Those girls who used to live at sixty-three," he said, "the Brink sisters. You remember the older one, Esther, left for Brighton to marry a man named Binns. Do you know if she is still living at the same address?"

Mrs. Venner shook her head. "Probably not. I should say that house would have been too full of bitter memories for her."

Ferris said slowly, "Bitter memories?"

"Yes. Oh, of course, you were away at the time. It was a horrible case—particularly to people who knew them."

"What happened, Mrs. Venner?"

"Well, you remember the sister—the girl you were always talking to—Rebecca?"

"Yes?"

"About three weeks after you left she murdered her brother-in-law."

Ferris said, "No, Mrs. Venner, no. Not that little girl."

Early the next day he was at Brighton police headquarters.

"I remember the case well," said Inspector Coombes. "It was a nasty business, but no doubt about the verdict, no doubt at all."

"What actually happened?"

"Well, as you know, this girl Esther Brink married a Brighton estate agent named Charles Binns. Her sister, Rebecca, a girl just turning twelve, came to live with them at their home here.

"As far as we could find out afterward, the household seemed a happy one, although the girl, Rebecca, didn't seem to get on very well with her brother-in-law. Not that there were any quarrels, but she seemed to try and avoid him."

Ferris said, "She was a shy child—it would take her a long time to adjust to a new member of her family."

"Yes. That's what the psychiatrist said—but I'll come to that later. Let's first get the facts straight. The chain of incidents started when Mrs. Binns slipped on the stairs and sprained her ankle badly. She was laid up in bed the following day, a Saturday.

"The housekeeper had been sent on an errand by Mr. Binns. He was home and so was Rebecca, who was keeping Mrs. Binns company. At about two-thirty P.M. Binns called up the stairs and asked if Rebecca would help him for a short while in the study. She seemed unwilling to go. Remember that point, it becomes significant later. Anyway, Mrs. Binns asked her not to be disobliging and eventually she went.

"Mrs. Binns, as I have said, was lying in bed. A short while later she heard Rebecca running rapidly up the stairs, and then the sound of her sobbing on the landing. Thoroughly alarmed, she hobbled out of bed. She found her sister in a hysterical condition. She asked what was the matter and Rebecca answered, 'Oh, Esther, I've killed Charles!'

"Mrs. Binns acted with great presence of mind. She picked up the telephone and dialed the number of her next-door neighbor, Dr. Jack Morgan. Morgan was out, but his wife, who is also an M.D., answered the call. As soon as she had finished speaking, Mrs. Binns tried to hobble down the stairs, but before she had gone more than a few steps, Dr. Betty Morgan arrived and ordered her back to bed.

"In the study, Dr. Moran found the body of Binns. She saw at once that he had been stabbed through the left lung and life was extinct. She immediately telephoned us, and I was at the house within twenty minutes."

Ferris was very still. "Go on," he said.

"As I've stressed, there were no complications. The medical evidence was that the cause of death was a stab wound in the left lung, delivered from below and upwards. The weapon was lying on the carpet near the door. It was a large paper knife which Binns used to keep on his desk. On it were the girl's fingerprints, in a position consistent with her subsequent story that she'd stabbed Binns by thrusting the knife at him in the way she'd learned to thrust a foil in fencing."

Ferris said, unbelieving, "Just like that?"

"Yes. It was an open-and-shut case. The next day she was brought before a special juvenile court, remanded for a week, and then committed for trial to the Crown Court before a High Court judge."

"But why did they say she did it? What was her motive?"

Coombes shrugged. "Let me put it to you this way. You know that at the trial of a juvenile on a serious charge, the judge usually leans over backwards to find extenuating circumstances. Well, Judge Bloxham asked her the same question. At first she wouldn't answer; then she said there had been a quarrel, and she wouldn't give any reason for it. Remember her sister's evidence how unwilling Rebecca had been to do any favor for her brother-in-law? There can't be much doubt about what happened. Binns asked her to do something, she was sullen and refused. Binns got up, perhaps in anger, perhaps to punish, and she grabbed the knife and stabbed."

"Not that way," said Ferris. "Not that little girl."

"No? Even the defense adopted the standpoint that's what must have happened. A psychiatrist gave evidence to help her. He pointed out that Rebecca was a child who had been very much shocked at the death of her own father, that she had been brought up in a very sheltered fashion by her sister, and that unconsciously she would resent her sister's husband as an interloper in her ordered family life. His argument was that although the child was sane, at the time of the murder she was so seriously upset emotionally that any argument with her brother-in-law could have assumed gigantic proportions in her mind."

"And the judge—what did he think of that?"

"He seemed sympathetic, but—well, he questioned the child, you know. There had been no real provocation. She knew what she had done and could assess the consequences of her action. The jury was in no doubt. The verdict and sentence were inevitable."

" 'Detained at Her Majesty's pleasure,' " said Ferris. "But I *know* that child, I tell you. I can't believe that's the whole story."

Coombes hesitated. "Look, Mr. Ferris, apart from the evidence, there's something I heard later, in confidence. I'll tell you what I'll do. You see the girl, her sister, and all the other witnesses. Then if you're still not satisfied, come back to me. I'll tell you then what I know, to add to all the other evidence."

"Why not tell me now?"

"Look, it was a confidence, and I don't want to share it unless it's really necessary. Besides, at this stage you've made up your mind the kid's innocent, and if I tell you now it won't alter your opinion. But if you hear it in addition to what the others tell you—"

"Then I will see the others first. But I'll be back."

All the way to the Borstal, Ferris was thinking of Rebecca as he had known her, as the shy little sprite as much removed from the everyday world as gossamer. And yet she had not been all timorousness; sometimes unexpected facets glinted. Twinkles of elfin humor, and once—what was it he had said to her? Oh, yes, something about Esther taking care of her. And she had answered, with her face puckered seriously and full conviction in her tones, "You know, Mr. Joe, I look after Esther even more than Esther looks after me."

She spoke to him like that, as to a trusted friend.

He had known, of course, that somewhere, sometime, life would bruise that unworldly little personality. In his own way he had tried to cushion the shock in adavnce. He had given her joking, kindly advice—he, sick-joke Ferris, trying to be jocular! Perhaps that was why he felt a pang of shame when he thought of the plea in her letter. If he had only been there to answer her call—

Now, after eight months, facing her in the barred room, he caught his breath in anger and frustration. The butterfly, flitting nervously and fascinatedly from wonder to wonder, had been impaled, and her colors had faded. In her new world her uniform was gray. So were her eyes, her expression, and even—shockingly —her voice.

"Yes, Mr. Joe. I killed him. That's why I'm here."

"Rebecca, you can tell me the truth. If you're lying to protect someone—you can trust me."

"I wouldn't lie to you, Mr. Joe. I did kill him."

"But why? Why? What was your reason?"

"We had a quarrel—but that doesn't excuse me. The judge said so. And you mustn't be sorry for me, Mr. Joe. I'm a murderer. I did a bad thing and I have to be punished for it."

He tried a small joke. "Rebecca, you're my friend. My friends don't kill people merely because of a quarrel."

She said nothing.

"Wasn't there something else? Did he try to do anything or say anything that frightened or disgusted you?"

This time her eyes opened wide, in a kind of curious surprise. "You mean—kiss me? No, Mr. Joe, nothing like that."

"Then what sort of quarrel did you have?"

"I can't tell you, Mr. Joe, not now. It wouldn't do any good."

The "not now" touched a nerve. He said heavily, "That letter you wrote me, Rebecca—I never got it until two days ago. I was abroad. I came as soon as I read it."

Her face was set, a mask.

"Tell me this, at least. Why did you hate him?"

"I didn't mean to listen, Mr. Joe, but I couldn't help hearing. He was talking to a lady about money and business. He was horrible and cruel. She cried. . . . That was when we first came to the house. I thought he was a beast, but Esther loved him. . . . I killed him. That's murder, and there's no excuse. One thing's got nothing to do with the other."

Ferris said, "I must go now, Rebecca. I'll be seeing Esther tomorrow. I'll tell her I visited you."

"Give her my love." The voice was drab, impersonal. "If you press the buzzer, the screw will come and fetch me."

He pressed. The screw came. She started to lead the girl away.

"Good-bye," said Ferris.

"Good-bye." And then pleasantly, politely, "I'm sorry, Mr. Joe. Perhaps if you had got my letter in time—"

The phrase haunted him. If he had got her letter in time—

Esther Binns, sunk into her own personal misery, was no help at all. "I just can't understand it, Mr. Ferris. When Charles came —how can I explain? I didn't even think of Rebecca. Not right then. Charles was—well, not like other men I'd ever met. He was so strong, so direct. He wanted me and I wanted him. To marry him seemed so good, so right for all of us. And now we're scattered. Charles dead, Rebecca. . . ."

She reached out an urgent hand to clutch his sleeve. "Sometimes I think the fault's mine, Mr. Ferris, all mine. After our father went, I was so afraid of losing her that I wrapped her in cotton wool. Maybe I sheltered her too much. Maybe. . . ."

Other witnesses. Basically the same, varying only in the depth of their sympathy. Like pretty, young Dr. Betty Morgan: "I could weep for the child. But what else could I have done, Mr. Ferris? I had to give my evidence."

"Wasn't there something over and above the evidence? After all, you were the family doctor. Isn't there anything you can tell me about Binns or the child that will throw some light on the motive for the murder?"

"Nothing. It's true, I used to be Binns's doctor, but after he married again he asked specifically for my husband to call. I suppose he thought the new Mrs. Binns would not approve of a woman doctor. So you see, I only happened to know Rebecca because we were neighbors. I don't think I'd spoken a dozen words to the child before the murder."

"You said that Binns married again. I didn't know he was a widower."

"He wasn't. He was divorced from his first wife."

"I see. Tell me this, Doctor, what kind of man was he?"

"Respected. Respectable. Selfish—as I suppose most men are. Otherwise, just a neighbor."

And yet the doubt remained. He sought out Inspector Coombes. "You said if I came back unsatisfied—?"

"I remember," said the inspector. He paused. "I must tell you this—the information was brought to me only after the trial. The person concerned did not come forward at the time because she hated Binns and, quite frankly, did not want to assist in condemning anyone who had caused his death."

"I understand. Go on."

"The woman was Mrs. Joan Binns, the former wife of the murdered man. She was an eyewitness. On the day of the crime she wanted to speak to Binns. For purely personal reasons—she didn't want to meet the new Mrs. Binns—she went round the side of the house to the French windows leading to her ex-husband's study, in the hope that he would be there alone. As she reached the window, she saw Binns coming round his desk toward Rebecca. The girl whipped up the paper knife, thrust it in his chest, and as he collapsed, ran hysterically from the room. Mrs. Binns, quite understandably, also made herself scarce."

Coombes furrowed his brow at the unexpected reaction to his statement: Ferris sat upright and there was a gleam in his eye. He said, "Yes. It could be that. Yes"—and he was obviously talking to himself. He looked at Coombes apologetically. "I'm sorry. You see, the only thing that kept me going on this investigation was that I knew the girl. But now there's something else. A chance. Where can I see Mrs. Joan Binns?"

Coombes said, "I'll take you there myself. But I can't see why—"

"I'll explain afterwards," said Ferris.

She lived in a chrome-and-glass hotel, and she was at home. She took them into a private lounge. She leaned forward in her chair, blond and willowy and appealing, and said, "What do you want to know?"

Coombes told her, and when he had finished, she looked at Ferris.

"Only a few questions," he said. "Binns's attitude when he came round the desk—would you say it was threatening?"

She shook her head regretfully. "I'm sorry. I can't say. The whole thing happened so quickly."

"Then let's take the child. How did she react? When she grabbed the knife and thrust, was it in panic?"

"Panic or anger, I don't know which. But there was violent emotion in the action."

"What makes you say that?"

"Well, it's hard to explain. She grabbed the knife and struck, but when the blade was going home, you could see that, only then, she realized what she was doing. She let go her grip on the knife and stepped back. She became obviously hysterical almost before Charles fell to the carpet. As he slumped she was already running out of the room."

Ferris said, "Thank you. Yes, thank you. And now, just one more thing. What sort of man was your ex-husband?"

She looked at him, puzzled. "A man. Like most men, I suppose—but we had differences. That's why I divorced him." She added flippantly, "*De mortuis.*"

"No," said Ferris, and the vehemence of his attitude caught her attention. "I want the truth. It is the living I am thinking of. I can't explain but, believe me, it is vital that I know what Binns was really like. I've heard from others—that he was successful, virile, a normal man. But you know the other side. Please, will you help me?"

"If it's that important," she said, "yes."

"Thank you. Now tell me, why did you divorce him?"

"Well, there were temperamental differences—we hadn't got on well together for a long time. But that wasn't the basic reason for breaking up. It was because he—I find it very difficult to put it in words, Mr. Ferris."

Ferris said seriously, "Tell me any way you like."

"It was something I found out about him. You see, I'm a woman who makes friends easily, and I was very much in love with Charles. So, in the first few months of marriage, I found it natural to tell him everything that was told me. He used to encourage me, Mr. Ferris. He used to say he loved me so much he hated every moment I was away from him, and he wanted to hear everything that I had seen or done or heard. So I told him—all the little chronicles of my day-to-day activities and sandwiched among them, things I should never have told. Secrets confided to me by my friends.

"Oh, it took me a long time to find out what was happening. I couldn't understand why, through the years, I lost friends as quickly as I made them. And one day I asked a woman with whom I had been very close. She told me.

"Charles had been blackmailing her—on something he had learned from me. And then I checked further. I went to see the others, and they told me the same story. So I divorced Charles. Quietly, and on other grounds. But what I've told you was the real reason."

"Poor Rebecca," said Ferris. "She made the same discovery."

"No wonder they talk about blind justice," said Coombes. The medical officer had just left to draft a new report. Coombes's coffee, which had been hot when Ferris started his explanation, was now cold. He picked up the cup abstractedly, then put it down without tasting the coffee. "I will act immediately, of course. I'll send men out, get new statements, apply for a warrant—"

Ferris said, "Rebecca?"

Coombes sat up suddenly. "There may be a way of cutting the red tape. A pardon. Bloxham, the judge who tried the case, lives in Brighton. When he knows all the facts, I'm sure he'll help. If he contacts the Home Secretary—"

"Yes," said Ferris. "But even before him we must see the girl's sister."

After the first convulsive spasm of weeping Easter Binns said, "You're not just telling me this? You're quite sure?"

Ferris said gravely, "We're quite sure."

"Rebecca, my little Rebecca. What can I do to make this up to her? What can I do?"

"Just tell her the truth and help her to understand it."

Mr. Justice Bloxham sipped moodily at his whiskey.

Ferris said, "Ever since I heard the evidence, I was convinced that this girl would not stab a man in a fit of anger, or even because she disliked him intensely. No, there would have to be something much deeper behind it. And then, when I heard the truth about Binns—about what kind of man he really was—I saw the whole situation as it must have occurred.

"You know, Rebecca had a strange idea of herself as the guardian of her sister's happiness. She once said to me, 'I look after Esther even more than Esther looks after me.' Now imagine the situation in the house; Esther deeply in love with Binns; Rebecca at first happy for her sister's sake, and then making the discovery that Binns was a despicable blackmailer. Gentlemen, try and put yourself into that child's mind. She couldn't bring herself to tell Esther, to shatter her happiness. So she taxed Binns that fateful afternoon when he called her down to his study.

"And now consider Binns a moment. There he was, a hardened man of the world, a practiced trader in sordidness. Not only could Rebecca have no chance of influencing such a mind, it probably took Binns only a second to realize that if she was speaking to him direct, then she would never tell Esther. Knowing her, he could guess her motives; and knowing her motives he could turn the situation to his own advantage.

"Instead of displaying the repentance the child hoped for, the man laughed at her. He told her that if Esther knew of the situation she would probably kill herself, and if Rebecca would not assist him actively in his schemes, he would tell Esther himself.

"And at that psychological moment he came around the desk at her, asserting himself, trying to underline what he had said by the menace of proximity. And the child, partly in panic, partly in frustration, but mainly actuated by a deep, primitive urge to defend her sister, to remove this threat to her happiness, grabbed the paper knife and thrust."

Judge Bloxham said musingly, "Yes—a reflex action. You're right, Mr. Ferris, both in your evidence and your inferences. Poor innocent!" He shuddered. "When I think what I have done to that child!"

Inspector Coombes said tactfully, "What else could you have done, sir? After all, the facts were overwhelming. The child confessed. How could anyone have imagined she was actually innocent of murder?"

"Mr. Ferris did. So clearly, Inspector, that he was able to force a confession from the real murderer."

Ferris interposed gently. "Don't forget I know Rebecca well. Look, if even Esther didn't realize, why should you—a stranger, sitting in a courtroom of strangers?"

"Possibly, but . . . I have arranged to see the Home Secretary first thing in the morning. Matters will be rectified as quickly as possible. God help me, I wish I could unscar that child's mind."

Ferris said, "Perhaps there is a way."

"How?"

"Come with me and Mrs. Binns to break the news to Rebecca. She'll recognize you as the man who condemned her. If you can help me to convince her she is not a murderer, then in time—"

"Yes, you're right again. Thank you. Of course I will come."

The same gray room and the same gray child. With three others—a judge, a woman, an old friend.

Ferris said gently, "Rebecca, your sister has something to tell you."

The child listened, grayly, politely.

"Rebecca darling, I know now. I know all about Charles. About—what you didn't want to tell me."

"I'm glad you know, but—"

"If I had only realized at the beginning . . . a man like that . . . Rebecca, I'm glad he's dead."

"No, Esther, you mustn't say that. Murder's the worst crime there is, even worse than. . . . Your knowing doesn't make much difference, really. I killed him. I'm a murderer."

The judge intervened. "Rebecca, you mustn't think that way. If I'd only known at the trial what your motives were. . . . And besides, Rebecca, you didn't murder him."

"I . . . didn't—?"

"No. Please—you explain, Mr. Ferris."

Ferris said, "Listen carefully, Rebecca. I want you to understand, and it's not very easy. First, we know that when you quarreled with Binns, in panic and anger you picked up the knife and thrust exactly as you had been taught to thrust in your fencing class. We know you did it without thinking, and that as soon as you realized you had stabbed him, you let go the handle of the knife and ran out. The last you saw of him he was slumped on the carpet with the knife in his chest."

The gray shivered. "Yes."

"Now you must remember the doctor at the trial said that the knife had gone into the left lung. You will also remember the police said they found the knife on the floor."

"But I stabbed him. He died. So I'm guilty of murder."

"No, you aren't. The truth is, you did not cause his death. Binns was murdered, yes—*but not by you.*"

"I stabbed him—"

"Yes, you did stab him, Rebecca—you stabbed him in the lung. Let me explain this way. A knife wound in the lung doesn't necessarily kill a person. *He can still be healed.* If a doctor comes quickly enough, there is an emergency procedure. The knife is left in the wound to halt unnecessary bleeding. The chest is bound very tightly so that only shallow breathing is possible, and then the patient is operated on to stitch up the wound. So you see, it's possible the thrust of the knife need not have caused death."

The gray trembled. "But—"

"Wait, Rebecca. *You did not cause his death.* He died because the knife was removed, letting the blood flow into his lungs, killing him in a matter of moments."

"But who—"

"Dr. Betty Morgan, Rebecca. He was blackmailing her, and she hated him. We've seen her and she has confessed. She told us how she came into the study, saw him lying there, and realized in one terrible moment how she could murder him and put the blame on you. She put on her surgical gloves so as not to leave her fingerprints over yours. Then she killed him, Rebecca—not by stabbing him, *but by pulling out the knife.*"

Something fluttered in the girl's eyes. She said, "Does that mean I can go home soon?"

Mr. Justice Bloxham delivered his considered verdict: "It means you can go home *now.*"

Rebecca said, "Esther!" and cried like a little girl.

"I think," said Ferris, "that I too can now go home."

*A new novelette introducing a new detective, from the creator of Travis McGee, is indeed a mystery event. Duke Rhoades is a private consultant who, like McGee, specializes in recovering stolen goods. He looks just a bit like John Wayne and he shares McGee's liking for beautiful women. His first adventure, surprisingly enough, appeared as a four-part serial in the Sunday magazine section of the* Chicago Sun-Times. *(Field Newspaper Syndicate supplied it to other papers as well, some of which published it under the title "Ring Your Love with Diamonds.") This is not only its first book publication but its first appearance all in one piece. You can read more about best-selling author John D. MacDonald in the Biography at the back of this book. Now, settle back and meet Duke Rhoades.*

# JOHN D. MacDONALD
# Finding Anne Farley

I am not an expert on diamonds. I am pretty good at recovering stolen goods. I have had a lot of luck. Equity used to loan me out all over hell and gone until I got smart and set myself up as a consultant. A piece of the action is always better.

This time Equity was paying for my services. First time for them. I thought they were going to stay mad forever.

They briefed me and I left with the thirty-two big color prints of the thirty-two missing items. They had them made from the color slides the jeweler took of his merchandise, everything worth over three hundred dollars. For insurance purposes. A neat and orderly man, and a camera buff. Nice pictures, with a scale next to the item, and technical data on a separate sheet.

Equity is at Park and Fifty-fifth. I walked down to Forty-eighth, four doors west of Fifth Avenue, and waited until Wally Marks got through talking to some fat men from Amsterdam.

He is a totally hairless man. No eyebrows, eyelashes, or hair on the knuckles, even. I think it was a disease he had. He told me I looked bigger than he remembered, and I said I was actually smaller because lately I had more chances to work out. The idea of working out pained him.

I sat across the desk as he went through the thirty-two pictures and thirty-two sets of technical information. I tried to read him as he studied them. No way. A man who makes his living buying and selling diamonds is in a poker game every day. If you can read him, he goes broke.

"Flawless stuff," I said.

He shrugged. "No such thing exists. All flawless means, according to FTC regulations, is that you can't see any flaws with a ten-power glass. But at forty diopters you'll see flaws. If I *believe* what it says here about cut and color and mounting, what you have here, Duke, is maybe six hundred thou wholesale."

"You are twenty thousand higher than the insurance payoff."

"Payoff?" He was startled.

"After six months of delays and some threats of legal action, good old Equity paid off."

"Who got ripped?"

"Wescott and Sons. In Atlanta."

He nodded. "Fancy place. Big stock. Hell, Duke, it would have to be a big stock." He stared at his low ceiling for a few moments, fingers laced across his belly. "What somebody did," he said at last, "they winnowed out the top standard items. Blue whites and whites. Your classic standard cuts. The biggest you've got here is four point nineteen carats. Quality, but anonymous quality. Some you could leave right in the settings. This one, for example. What you've got here is an eight-millimeter-round brilliant cut, two and a half carat, blue white; hand-crafted platinum setting with two fair-size baguettes. I could move that tomorrow, as is, for sixteen thousand five, without a fear in the world. But a lot of them would have to come out of the settings. Nobody took this stuff with the idea of selling it back to Equity."

"So they finally decided."

"Somebody has a channel to feed this stuff right back into the industry. Somebody had a lot of time in the vault to select these items and leave the fancy cuts behind. There's no junk here. All these stones are salable, and probably already sold."

"Somebody had a couple months in the vault."

For an instant he looked startled and then said, "One of those, huh? Made substitutions?"

I took out my pocket notebook to make sure of the name.

"Anne Farley. Trusted employee. Apparently she sneaked the photos and descriptions out one at a time and had pretty fair dupes made—good enough to fool the ignorant eye—saved them until the manager was away from the shop, switched the thirty-two items, and took off."

I had one of the substitute items given me by Equity and I put it in front of him. A solitaire. He pushed at it with a thick white finger and said, "Garbage."

"Workmanship?"

He picked it up. "Pretty good. Not bad."

"Can it be traced by the workmanship?"

"Sure. Maybe fifteen thousand guys could do this, in *this* country. Ask them all. Has to be one of them."

"Very funny."

"Duke, *somebody* is laughing. Somebody made off with a half million in diamonds. Nice thing about them is there is hardly any bulk at all. All the great diamonds of the world would fit in one suitcase, and you could walk away with it. But it is an artificial market. Don't invest for investment. Buy for pretty."

"What's wrong with investment?"

"Where they mine them, the countries are unstable. If they decide not to deal with the cartel, they could bust the price down to maybe ten percent of where it is. Fake scarcity keeps the price up."

"Wally, what do I owe you for your time and advice?"

"Owe? Don't talk about owe. Just tell me how you make out. On this one you are going to swing and miss."

"That's what Equity hopes. Then again, maybe they don't. It's their money."

Wescott and Sons was in a new hotel/bank/office building, shopping plaza, and park complex—one of those places that look as if they have been designed for the elegant people of some remote time in the future; but until the future arrives, they will let us barbarians blunder around, hawking and spitting, gawping and exclaiming, spending all our money, and forgetting where we left our car.

The jewelry store had two entrances, one onto an exclusive little mall, the other opening into a corner of the lobby of a luxury hotel. The display windows, both in the lobby and on the mall, were little niches set behind a reflectionless curve of armored glass, where single items of great value rested on velvet, illuminated by the narrow beams from concealed spotlights.

The interior was deeply carpeted in a tufted blue. Ceiling spots shone down on glass cases, on the twinkle of gold watches, bracelets, chains, and charms, on the polished silver of cigarette cases, wedding gifts, and baby presents. There were some customers. The clerks were slender, pretty ladies, all dressed in gray skirts and white shirtwaist blouses, gold cuff links. A young one came to me and murmured shyly of her great wish to help me in any possible way. I said I would like to see the manager, J. Trevor Laneer, and she asked what about, and I said that it concerned Equity Protection and the recent settlement. She went away with my business card and came back in three minutes and begged me to please follow her.

Laneer stood up from his leather furniture and shook my hand. He was fifty trying to look thirty. Mod clothes, bright-blue contact lenses, forty-dollar hairstyling, and a bandito moustache. But the pouches under his eyes, the turkey neck, and the brown spots on the backs of his hands gave him away. His office was like an alcove in a club lounge. No desk. Clever diorama of the English countryside. He waved me down into a deep leather chair, smiled, and said, "Now then! How may I help you, Mr. Rhoades?"

"I'd like to ask you some questions about the robbery last year."

His smile faded but slightly. He shook his head from side to side, almost regretfully. "Oh, I am sorry, Mr. Rhoades, but that is impossible. It really is. Five different people—two of them from Equity Protection—questioned me at great length over a period of many weeks, you know. They extracted every scrap of information from me. Surely all that material is on record, and if you have a legitimate purpose in all this, surely it will be available to you. Frankly, I am sick unto death of it. I was deceived by a person I trusted. It took *far* too long to get the insurance settlement. I feel I was treated badly. I needed money to replace stock. I deal with some very affluent people, and I cannot afford to have a stock so skimpy they get in the habit of going elsewhere. No, Mr. Rhoades. To me it is a closed book. And don't quote the policy to me, the part about reasonable cooperation. I *have* cooperated. All I am going to. It is over. It cost the business twelve thousand dollars in interest on borrowed money to replenish my stock. I had to borrow against the settlement. I do not feel kindly toward Equity. Good day, sir." He stood up and motioned toward the door. I stood up and walked out and he closed it behind me.

I walked out of his office but not out of the store. I shopped the cases, looking at golden goodies, waving away the shirt-waisted ladies until the one who had caught my eye drifted close enough for me to beckon her over.

"Would you take that bracelet out of there for me?"

"Here you are. Lovely, isn't it? Fourteen carat."

"Now let's pretend to be talking about the bracelet."

"Sir?"

"I investigate insurance claims. There was a big one from here, settled in full. Now Laneer won't talk to me."

"The bracelet is four hundred dollars, plus tax."

"You dont look as demure and bloodless as the rest of the sales staff. I hope Laneer isn't one of your favorite people."

"Hey. Hold it down. Why?"

"What's the office gossip, or store gossip, about where Farley is right now?"

"I can't talk here!"

"I'm in the hotel. I saw a little lounge over on that balcony thing. Named after an animal."

"The Blue Raccoon."

"Five-thirty? Six?"

"Like ten past six."

The Raccoon got a good after-work play, and they were jammed up close and deep at the bar. I had a fine little leather corner with the lady. She said her name was Libby Franklin, a married name but she was not working at it lately, and she thought all guys named Rhoades were called Dusty; and I told her that for the first, terrible twenty-five years of my life, I had been called that, and that my real name was Oliver. But in my twenty-sixth year I had begun to look remotely like John Wayne. She tipped her head and squinted at me, pursed her lips and finally said, "Faintly." So I told her I was a sort of sawed-off version of the real Duke, and then did my imitation, which knocked her out. She told me I certainly was no great judge of womankind if I thought the other girls at Wescott and Sons looked demure and bloodless. She said they were about as sweet

and demure as a pool full of barracudas. She said Wescott and
Sons had always hired better-than-average-looking women and
made them dress alike, paid them well, and gave them a com-
mission on sales over a certain figure each week. She had been
there a little over two years, and J. Trevor Laneer was not, repeat, not one of her favorite people.

When I asked her why not she explained that he was a very
autocratic person. "He expects and gets total obedience. The
girls who can't take that, who give him an argument, last about
two weeks. 'Clean the fingerprints off that case, Laura.' 'I don't
like that hairstyle, Wendy. Change back to the way it was before, please.' 'Print the sales slips, everyone. Do not use script.
Is that clear?' 'Bring me my tea at eleven, Miss Farley.' "

"And Anne Farley didn't resent it?"

"*Resent* it? She adored it! She worked for him for twelve years.
Of course, most of that time was at the old store on Piedmont
before he moved the business here."

"He owns it?"

"Well, for all practical purposes. His wife, Betty, is a Wescott,
the last of the clan. Poor old thing is an invalid."

"And Farley had something going with J. Trevor?"

"What a truly gross idea! She was sort of the head vestal virgin.
She thought it was something very special to sell gems to people
who got their name in the papers. Laneer was cruel and mean
to her, and she passed it along to us peasants."

"So why would she steal?"

She looked at me in a measuring way, head atilt, bright blond
hair hanging to her shoulder. "Fido will be howling his poor
head off. Want to eat Chinese?"

She had a townhouse-type apartment in a new development in
an old area north of Candler Park, near Emory University. I
followed her out in my rental. She had an old Volvo that looked
as if it had been stomped flat and then patted back into shape by
a huge, hasty child. She undid three locks and defused the alarm
system. Fido turned out to be a huge gray altered tomcat, very,
very impatient for his supper. As she waited on him she had me
fix drinks. The apartment was clean, but it was certainly clut-
tered, mostly with books, magazines, records, and tapes.

"I don't really have any date-type dates, anything sincere,"
Libby said. "This is my one night of the week without classes.

Communications and media. I should be studying this evening, but the thing is, nobody would listen to conjecture, you know? Just the facts ma'am. Well, hell, that may be the legal way, but after a couple of tries I shut up because I do not like being classified as some kind of gossipy broad."

Fido sat and washed for a while, and then he came over to my chair and studied me for a long time, then lowered his head and started gently butting it against my leg, while making a sound like a distant snare drum. Libby was astonished that he liked me, and I told her I was hurt that she should be so astonished, and how about the gossip nobody would let her mention officially.

To prove, I guess, that she had an orderly and logical mind, Libby ticked off the facts I knew already. It had been known in the shop that J. Trevor Laneer would not be in on the Friday when apparently the theft took place. At night a great deal of the stock was locked in the vault. In the rear portion of the vault, there was a sturdy cabinet that locked with a key. Laneer, Anne Farley, the bookkeeper, and Laura Wheelock, who had been with the company almost as long as Anne Farley, knew the vault combination. Only Anne Farley and Trevor Laneer had keys to the inner cabinet where the best things were kept. Anne Farley's vacation started on the Monday. On the following Wednesday morning Laneer went and got a tray of rings to show an old and valued customer. He took a close look at one of the rings and became very agitated. In an hour he knew thirty-two had been switched. He informed the police and telephoned the news to Equity Protection. It was soon learned that Miss Anne Farley, age thirty-five, had apparently left for good. She had given up the shadowy old paneled apartment in the downtown apartment hotel, which she had shared with her mother until her death a few years ago, and had lived alone in a motel until that weekend before the Friday theft, seven months ago.

"Starting way before she took the diamonds," Libby said, "she sold everything. Furniture, clothes, books, dishes. Even her old pink VW. What she couldn't sell, she gave to Good Will. Shall we order Chinese now? It takes them eighteen minutes on the average from when you hang up to when they ring my doorbell. Fix the last drink, Duke, and I'll phone. I know what they do best."

I let her keep talking. I was waiting for nuances, looking for inflections, hesitations. It followed the reports I'd studied, to the letter. Farley had moved into a motel by the airport a week before she took the diamonds. Registered as Arleen Fay—a typical amateur selection, almost an anagram. Checked out Saturday morning early. One suitcase. No messages. No mail. A check of airline reservations and travel agencies had come up empty. I was on a very cold trail. By the time I get on them, they are always cold.

Libby had changed to ancient jeans and a work shirt. The man had brought fine food. Fido was eating his egg roll. He was very weird for egg rolls, leaving only the small bits of onion.

"Farley is a bright lady?"

"You can bet on it. She saw everything, knew everything. The thing about it, the store was her life. Come early, leave late. Keep track."

"You girls, I mean ladies, you had no clue she was working up to some big change, selling all?"

"Anne wasn't the sort of person you could ever get too close to. I guess we all had the feeling there was something in the wind. She seemed to be hiding some kind of big excitement. It made her a little bit flushed and bright-eyed and absentminded. We wondered if, unlikely as it seems, she was in love."

I went through the office files in my inside pocket and found the picture of Anne Farley. "She doesn't look unlovable," I said to Libby.

"Wow, this is some old kind of picture." She went away, and over the muted sound of her high fidelity system, I heard drawers opening and banging shut. She came out with color photographs and sat and dealt them out on a table, picked two of them, and gave them to me.

OK, in the color flash shots she did not look lovable. She looked more like she would make you into a lampshade: grim mouth, hair pulled back tightly and welded into a knot. They were taken at an exhibit of jewelry designed by a famous actress.

Libby let me have the negatives. And in time I could find no more new items about Anne Farley in her memory banks, so we went on to other subjects.

In the morning I found a custom photography lab, and they let me work with the technician to get what I wanted. I got some four by fives in black-and-white glossies, cropped to show

Anne Farley full face and in left profile. The face was neurotic, vulnerable, and imperious, all at once. In Underground Atlanta I found an artist who could do very good pencil work. Thirty dollars later I had three realistic sketches of Anne Farley in three different blond hairstyles.

I spent four full days and evenings drawing blanks. I worked through the weekend. People do leave marks. The trick is to find those footprints on the trail and see which way they point. Her bank was no help. She had closed out checking and savings two weeks before the day of the theft. I bought ten minutes with her retail credit bureau records. That led me to Belk-London's, and to a merry, round, white-haired little woman who, she said, had sold Anne Farley and her mother their clothes for twenty years.

"Oh, yes!" she said. "She said to me, 'Mattie'—she always calls me Mattie—'I am going to have to buy some resort clothes for very hot weather. Very, very hot weather.' I was pleased for the poor dear. She has always dressed so much older than her years, you know. And she has a pretty figure. A very pretty figure, a bit too lean maybe. I had to have some idea of where she would wear the resort clothes. You wouldn't take the same things to Cannes you'd take to Sea Island, now would you? She told me never to tell anyone and here I am telling you, breaking my promise, but I think the darling girl has come to harm. She said it would be Cancún, at a fancy hotel called the Garza Blanca. I can remember about the hotel because I looked up the words over in the book section. Garza is a heron, and blanca is white."

"She buy a lot?"

"Very little. But practical. Pretty and practical. Wash-and-wear things. She said she couldn't take much with her."

"What makes you think she has come to harm?"

"I don't know. I really don't. I think this business of the police looking for her because they say she stole diamonds is terrible. I've known her since she was a child. She would never steal."

"Even if she got very, very tired of the life she was stuck with?"

"Not Anne Farley," she said firmly.

With Cancún as a guidepost, I went rooting around in the airlines schedules. The best way to go, it appeared, was by Eastern or National to Miami, and by Mexicana from Miami to

Yucatán. Eastern and National run big, busy desks at Atlanta.
I was a nuisance. Me and my pictures and drawings. Seven
months ago? You've got to be kidding, friend. Do you have the
faintest idea just how many thousand people we run down to
Miami every week? Sorry to have troubled you, fella.

I went back to my uniquely architectured hotel, with its Gee
Whiz lobby and my sterile plastic room on floor nine, and went
through the travel agencies again and made a little list of the
ones close by.

I told Libby Franklin how it went. It was Monday night.
Eighteen pounds of gray cat lay curled up and purring on my
stomach, full of egg roll. The soft denim of her jeans, stretched
tight around a long slim thigh made a pillow effect that just fit
the nape of my neck. Everyone had had some egg roll. And
almond gui ding. And shrimp fried rice.

I said, "It was about the third or fourth agency, a little one
in that arcade off the Omni complex. A neat little redheaded lady
with, I swear, rings on every finger and both thumbs, she looked
a long time at the drawing—the one where he gave her blond
bangs to her eyebrows—and then she went and poked around in
her files, biting her lip, frowning, and came up with a card that
said she had sold such a blond person a round-trip ticket, tourist
class, for two people, Atlanta to Cancún, for cash money, a Mr.
and Mrs. Dan Barley. More anagrams. She figured it was an
illicit pair slipping away for fun and games: the woman buys,
cash deal, no reservation on return. So what she did was tell the
blond person that she was going to have to get tourist cards, and
she could fill out the blank there and take one for her husband,
or they could do it at the Mexicana desk in the Miami airport.
They would have to show birth certificates, passports, or something like that. She said it seemed to upset the blond person a
little, but she said they would apply at Miami."

Libby scowled down at me. "Anne Farley? Fun and games?"

"There is always somebody for everybody," I said. "The reservation was made three weeks in advance for the Sunday flight,
with a two-hour layover in Miami before catching the five-thirty
flight to Cancún. Did the Dan Barley couple catch it? Who
knows? Maybe passenger manifests are tucked away into some
computer somewhere, with no awareness or access except in the
microelectrical heart of some other computer."

"So?" she said.

I tried a fixed leer, staring up at her. "Wanna go to Yucatán, sweetie?"

"I can't take off work, and Fido hates kennels and sitters, and I seldom go out of the country without being married first."

"I could go ask that neat redheaded lady."

"With all the rings? Sure. Good thinking. She can probably get you a discount on everything. Bite him, Fido. Sic'um."

Tuesday morning I plodded into Wescott and Sons, right after my hotel coffee shop breakfast, braced for a lot of resistance from J. Trevor Laneer. But he greeted me with rueful smile, waved me into the deep leather once again, and said, "I'm glad you came back, Mr. Rhoades. I'm afraid I was very rude the last time. You're trying to do a job. I appreciate that. It is in the interests of the industry to—make certain no one gets away with gem theft. And a so-called inside job is especially disheartening."

"So-called?"

He paused, obviously choosing his words with care. He was wearing fawn slacks, a bushy white turtleneck, a long gold neck chain with a dangle of coins and gold replicas of animal teeth. "Miss Farley was such a *scrupulous* person. So loyal and reliable and thorough, I can't help feeling that she was exposed to some terrible pressure from outside, somehow, to do what she did, some merciless form of blackmail."

"You've heard about all the preparations she made, selling everything, moving?"

"Of course. We all had no idea she was doing anything like that. Of course, she would have had to disappear once she had stolen those thirty-two pieces."

"With a man?"

He shrugged. "A blackmailer."

"Or the fellow she fell in love with."

"It is hard to see her in that light—throwing everything away for love."

"It's been done. I suppose she would have had access to a lot of people who could have made the substitutes."

"Oh, yes. I've sent her to some of the shows and exhibitions when I couldn't attend because of my wife's illness. And, of course, she often dealt with salesmen who came by the store here, not the ones selling gemstone quality, but the trinkets we must stock. And many of those, of course, have the skill and equipment necessary to duplicate our best diamond items, as well as they *were* duplicated."

"No leads?"

"What? Oh, I would imagine the police checked out every name we could come up with, and I would have been told, I think, if they learned anything."

"And she asked for her vacation *after* she knew you were not going to be in on Friday."

"And we were closed Saturday. Yes, that's right. She was usually less impulsive about taking time off, but I told her it would be all right. She asked the Monday before her vacation began."

"The summary they sent me said that you were in Chicago on business that Friday."

"Yes. At an auction. A large yellow diamond was coming on the market again after being in a private collection for thirty years. A local collector whose name I am not at liberty to mention, sent me up to place his bid and also verify the description of the stone. Very beautiful. Marvelous color. It went for forty thousand over my client's top limit. I flew back Saturday afternoon."

"Did Anne Farley ever say she'd like to go to Mexico?"

His eyebrows shot up. "Mexico! Is that where she went?"

"I don't know. It's possible."

He frowned. "I *do* remember one thing about Mexico. She was fascinated by ancient ruins. Mayan, Aztec, Toltec, that sort of thing. I suppose there is a lot of that there."

"Yucatán has more than its share?"

"Yes. Yucatán." He made a face and shook his head. "But you see, that presupposes that she acted of her own free will out of self-interest, and I can't believe that."

"Maybe it's the Kepone."

"I beg your pardon?"

"Gets in the fatty tissues. Gets into the fat in your brain. Tells you to go steal stuff, or write protest songs, or turn Mayan. I'll send you a card from Yucatán."

After a full hour's delay, half of it waiting in line with the other birds, my Mexicana flight number 308 took off into the flat, silver light of a rainy day in Miami. It was a 727, and the pilot yanked it up quickly, turning takeoff into an irritable and impatient gesture. It was a single-class flight, less than half full in this May off-season.

The flight attendants were slim, tense, and limber ladies, oppressed by their obligation to serve everyone a hot meal during the hour-and-fifteen-minute flight. I wondered how they could possibly manage it during the three months when their flights would be full.

I had gone to Miami almost empty-handed and spent some money in the airport shops acquiring a tourist costume composed of a lightweight, chino leisure suit with twice as many pockets as necessary, a white denim hat with big brass grommets around the ventilation holes, a couple of rainbow-colored rayon shirts, big blue shades, sandals, and a brand-new, shiny, cheap flight bag advertising the Orient Express. And I smiled a lot. This is called professional invisibility. Indians wearing buffalo skins used to be able to sidle right into the herd and select their dinner.

Dusk was beginning to catch up with us when we landed. The concrete apron had stored sun heat all day and radiated it back up at us as we filed into the modern little airport building, into air conditioning from the steaming heat outside. All the tourists were sorted out by hotels, and after the usual confusions of luggage, we were taken off in blue-and-white vans. I was loaded in with a shy, silent woman and a stately old couple, all three dressed in canary yellow. We were the ones going to the Garza Blanca.

Cancún is a contrived resort. The government planners picked an empty area of small keys and Caribbean beaches, then bridged the keys, put in an elegant highway with sodium-vapor lights, and aided the hotel people in finding the money to put up the hotels. The hotels mark out the narrow keys and causeways— Villas Tacul, Dos Playas, Playa Tortugas, El Presidente, Camino Real, Chac Mool, Cancúm Caribe, and the Garza Blanca, the last one of all, except for the formidable isolation of the Club Mediterranee at the far end, Punta Nizuc, fourteen miles from the mainland.

The van had either a broken muffler or no muffler, and the driver played his tape deck at maximum volume to drown out the muffler noise. Conversation would have been impossible even if anyone had felt like it. I smiled a lot.

We went up a very steep curve of cobblestone driveway to the

impressive entrance. No doors. A vast lobby, dimly lit, open at
the far side as well, looking out from a height across the tropic
sea.

The dark girl at the desk took care of me last, and with cold-
eyed indifference said they could let me have a room for seven
hundred pesos a night, not on the beach of course. "It is always
better, of course," she said, "to make a reservation, Meester
Road-ace." The key she gave me was brass, fastened to an oval
hunk of wood six inches long and an inch thick, stained dark.

I followed a small, stocky Yucatecan who carried my shiny
bag across the lobby, down the curved stairs at the far end, past
the pool, empty and wind-riffled, where the day's litter of towels,
empty plates, glasses, and trash had not yet been cleaned up and
the sun chaises had not been realigned. We went between a row
of two-story buildings separated by a cobbled lane. The ones on
my left were built on the bluff facing the sea. My building was
on the right, my room at the top of an exterior staircase. The
fellow turned on low-wattage bulbs, started the grinding roar of
an air-conditioner set into the plaster wall, shrugged as he pocketed his dollar tip, and went on out, sandals slapping the tile
floor.

I stripped to the waist and stood in front of chilled air
until I dried off. I put my other bright shirt on and went out
in search of a cold beer, wondering if Anne Farley had liked
the Garza Blanca, the beach, the tropic sun tnat maybe melted
her rigidities, her scruples, her reserve. Was the wig for here
too? Do blonds have more fun? Or merely seem to be having
more.

The next morning, after my breakfast of huevos rancheros
and papaya, I encountered total frustration at the big front desk.
The manager was away. He would be back maybe next week,
maybe next month. The assistant manager, he has gone to the
bank in the city. In what city? In Merida, señor. There were
three of them behind the desk, a dark, surly girl; a tall dark,
surly fellow; and a round, chubby man full of false cheer. There
are well-run hotels with efficient desks. There are badly run
hotels with infuriating front desk service. And then there is the
Garza Blanca.

"Please listen. Very carefully. OK?"

"I listen. señor."

"I have written a name on this piece of paper. I have printed it. Mr. Dan Barley. Mr. and Mrs. Dan Barley. They made a reservation in November. Last year. Were they here?"

"I was not here, sir."

"Are there no records?"

"Records?"

"Don't you keep track of reservations?"

"Me, señor? I am a clerk. The manager is. . . ."

"There must be a file of. . . ."

"Excuse me, señor. Yes, madam, I may help you?"

Then when he turned back to me, I had to start all over again. Finally I said, "Suppose I walk in and say I have a reservation. What do you do?"

"I give you one card to sign."

"You don't care whether I have a reservation or not?"

"Don't care? Oh, but yes. I look in the book, señor."

"Ah, the reservation book!"

We beamed at each other. "Let me see the book."

"Is not permitted."

Finally, for a negotiated fee it was permitted, but the book he put on the counter went back to January 1 only. He did not know where the old book was. He had no idea. Then he talked to the surly girl. Another fee was negotiated. She went away, behind the scenes, and returned in ten minutes with the book. I carried it off into the small lounge, pretending not to hear the cries of consternation from the three of them.

I did not see how a hotel could be operated on the basis of such terrible records. Six unkempt varieties of handwriting. Blots, erasures, dates, amounts, and room numbers scratched out and changed. I found the reservation for Mr. and Mrs. Barley. A one-hundred-dollar deposit had been received in October. The room number written beside the name and date had been scratched out and not rewritten. I took the book back to the desk. I pointed to the entry and said, "They never arrived, did they?"

They moved away to have a heated conference, full of gestures and interruptions, flashing eyes and gigantic shrugs. Smiley came back to me and said, "Why you are wanting to know?"

"What difference does that make?"

"You are not wanting the hundred dollars back?"

"No."

"You are right, señor. We never heard again from them. That is what this mark is meaning here."

I took a long walk on the white, hot, empty beach, walking south from the hotel, wearing a new pair of swim pants and a straw hat from the hotel shop. The sun scalded my shoulders. There was an almost total lack of seashells. I walked in the wash of the small waves that were nibbling away at the sand, making small cliffs. I avoided the tar balls, big as plums and apples, rolling in the white foam. I walked by a house so elegantly beautiful and so enormous, I knew it had to belong to a politician. Suspicion confirmed when I saw some Mexican army up on the road, two of them standing in the shade, wearing automatic weapons.

Finally I sat on one of the sand cliffs, chair height, comfortable, the sea sucking at the sand under my bare feet. I felt very grouchy. I had expected some kind of confrontation down here, even though the voice of sanity in the back of my mind had said from the beginning: Don't waste the money on the trip, Duke.

OK. Haul it out into the open and look at it. I never get big brilliant flashes of inspiration. Like a dog with a slipper, I have to pull it out from under the bed and gnaw.

A false trail. Which is a very common happening when straight people suddenly go crooked. A man gets in over his head in business deals, and when he knows the whole thing is going to fall in on him, he grabs the loose cash, leaves his folded clothes on the beach, and heads for Belize. Or he squirrels away money over a period of time, then goes on a sedate trip with the little woman, takes a little walk in downtown Algiers, and is never seen again, he hopes. But I found *that* one in downtown San Miguel de Allende, wearing beard and smock, and he wept when I called him by his old name. Pity.

There is one constant factor. The false trail is always clearly marked. You can't miss it. But this trail had been obscure. I'd reaped the reward of a lot of diligence and a lot of luck. Tired feet and a sharp nose, like a wise old hound dog.

A brown pelican hovered and tilted and came crash-diving down into the blue water next to some floating weed, sat for a moment, then gulped something down.

So either the lady and her partner changed their mind and picked a different hideaway. Or somebody had overlooked or

disturbed or thrown away the false clues left behind. Or the
partnership had come to an abrupt and untidy end somewhere
along the line.

Why come here anyway? The sun, the sand, and the sea. And
Mayan ruins? Not the place to unload stolen gems, apparently.
Maybe they had been fenced on the Saturday in November between the theft and the departure. Because they were very good
diamonds, and selected for anonymity of cut and size once separated from the platinum settings, it could have been for three
hundred thousand. If everybody trusted everybody. But do you
tote that kind of cash to a middle-class, contrived resort? Would
you put that amount of cash in the Garza Blanca office vault?

I could not make the pieces fit properly. I could make them
fit, but I didn't like the fit. I recently saw a puzzle advertised.
The ad said that every piece fit every other piece, but they had
to be assembled in the right order or the puzzle could not be
completed. Optimum sadism.

No light bulbs flashed on above my head. Nobody said,"Aha!"
I followed an old rule. If you go somewhere expensive to get
to, make sure you don't have to return. I had not found a lady
alone in the Garza Blanca pages for November under any kind
of anagram name, in fact not many ladies alone at all. I went
back to the room, changed, gathered up my various photographs
and sketches of Miz Anne Farley, rented a VW bug from a sleepy
man in the lobby, and went droning from hotel to hotel, showing my wares, smiling my smile, doing my John Wayne imitation
where necessary. Kid sister of a dear old friend. She was last seen
down here in November. Could be using the name Farley, Arley,
Barley, Fayhee, Fanny France, Harley, Carlee, Parley, Arleen
Fay. She hadn't wanted her big brother to find her. Now the poor
chap was dying, and desperate. And maybe you could look at
the reservations for last November. . . . Please? Or let me run
down the names. Won't take more than a minute.

The Camino Real was the best organized, and the most helpful.
The attitude at the Presidente was one of hostile indifference.
The Cancún Caribe wanted authorization from the police. When
I got tears in my eyes and shook my head slowly in shocked dis-
belief, they relented. Money worked pretty well. Five-hundred-
peso notes. Worth a little over twenty dollars.

Nothing checked out. So the next day I caught the early afternoon flight to Miami. My back was red-brown and tender from

the two beach sessions. I had the Aztec two-step from the Garza Blanca food. My purse was considerably lighter, with a lot of expense that Equity Protection was not going to pick up and would not have authorized had I asked.

I caught Libby Franklin just as she was leaving her place to go learn a little more about communications. There was concern in her voice when I told her I had come up absolutely empty. Concern changed to coolness when I said I wanted a chance to talk to Laura Wheelock, the one who had been an employee of Wescott and Sons almost as long as Anne Farley. She said of course she could fix me up. Would lunch tomorrow be useful?

On the morrow at a few minutes after twelve, she brought Laura over into the hotel lounge to the designated area. I stood up when I saw them approaching, dressed alike like flight attendants on the Junior League Airlines. Libby was very correct. Mission accomplished, she whirled and headed back to the shop. I called to her to wait. She turned and flashed a totally artificial smile and waved and kept going.

Laura Wheelock was as slim as the rest of them. But older. Gloss of black bangs curling to her dark eyebrows, thick weight of shiny black hair straight to her shoulders. Dark brown eyes, dark complexion, high round cheekbones dotted with the acne scars of her adolescence of twenty years ago.

She looked pleased when I suggested the hotel's best restaurant and told her I had made a reservation. We had a corner table behind a low stone wall, looking down over the length of the Gee Whiz lobby from an elevation about sixty feet above it.

When we had our drinks, she said that she was doing this as a favor to Libby, such a dear child, because she had vowed that she would not talk about the Anne Farley incident anymore. She was desperately tired of it. Everyone had assumed that because they had worked together for over ten years, they were friends. It worked the other way actually. One did not want close friendships with someone one worked with all day, every day, did one? Besides, Anne did not have the gift of friendship. She was second-in-command, Mr. Laneer's assistant, and one was wise never to forget that. If one was insubordinate, Anne Farley gave them the worst chores in the store for weeks on end. You know, like in the army. P.K.

"K.P.?"

"Whatever."

"I am interested in just how totally loyal she was to Mr. Laneer."

"There are no words for it, Mr. Rhoades. People have to *give* themselves to someone or something, don't you think? We all have a terrible need to be needed and necessary. I don't mean to imply there was ever anything emotional or sexual about Anne's relationship to Trevor Laneer. She just wanted to be so diligent, so thorough, so knowledgeable that the business could not survive without her. And the more indispensable she became, the more she cherished her job. It was more than a job to her. It was a dedication."

"OK. Suppose Laneer said to her, 'Miss Farley, for the good of the business, I want you to strip, paint yourself blue, and go live in a tree like a Druid. I don't want you to ask me why. Just do it. I am depending on you.' How would she respond?"

"Twenty minutes later, she'd be blue and living in a tree."

"And if he asked her to steal from the business to save the business?"

Her smile disappeared at once. She frowned and bit her thumb knuckle. "I think I see where you're trying to go. Say it."

"Let's say the business doesn't go too well. So J. Trevor starts quietly turning good stuff into junk, selling the good stuff, and putting the money back in. After he has converted thirty-two pieces, he tells her to go away on a long, long trip. He accuses her of robbing him and collects from Equity Protection."

She shook her head slowly. "The business has been doing *very* well. Much better now than in the old location. I know gems. I have a good eye and good training. I would bet my life those good pieces were there a few days before he went to Chicago."

"Try it another way, then. Maybe it was women or gambling. But he dropped a lot, took it out of the business, and had to replace it."

"That won't work either. The person who keeps the books is very competent. And we are audited frequently by the bank. It's a headache, the way we have to take inventory so often."

"Why by the bank?"

"I don't know, really. It has something to do with the Trust Department. The Wescotts are a wealthy family and there were a lot of trusts set up and the store is in one of the trusts, I think."

"How about J. Trevor's bad habits?"

"Mr. Rhoades, Mr. Laneer is absolutely devoted to his poor wife. She had a terrible stroke, you know? She is absolutely unable to communicate in any way. He spends his free time at home with her, in that lovely old house. His only vice, if you could call it that, is working so hard on that big rock garden he built where she can see it from her bedroom window. It is really something. Waterfalls and boulders and exotic plants and trees and fish ponds and all, and even floodlights at night. A couple of times he's given himself a bad back working so hard. I suppose it is because it takes his mind off . . . her helplessness."

"He dresses like a secret swinger."

"I know. But he sells a lot of diamonds to a lot of ladies and gets along with them beautifully, and that is as far as it goes."

"And there is a lot of money?"

She closed her eyes for an instant, expression beatific, then said, "Gross ugly wads of it. Cellars full of it."

OK. So scrap another set of assumptions, Duke. Try again.

I spent a part of Saturday afternoon in the small, walled sun yard behind Libby's townhouse apartment. Fido stalked imaginary monsters. Libby, in string bikini, atop a picnic table, asprawl on a huge towel imprinted to resemble a thousand-dollar bill, worked on her tan and complained about mine. I carried empties into the apartment and brought new beers back out.

After I had walked around and around the table, reciting my doubts, suspicions, and inadequacies, she said in a sun-dazed mumble, "How'n hell'd she plan so far ahead?"

"You mean making the hotel and air reservations in October? Well, everybody says she was a very orderly person and . . . ."

I stopped. "Hm," I said. "How orderly do you have to be to know you are going to be able to heist all those stones on a Friday when you didn't know whether Laneer would be there or not? Damn it, he told her a week or so ahead of time he was going to that auction in Chicago to bid on the yellow diamond. And that's when she asked if she could start her vacation. Vacation in November?"

"He owed her a week, Duke. She took just two weeks last summer. He owed her another week."

"But she had the reservations all made before she asked!"

"She could be pretty sure he'd say OK."

"Do you think she could have managed the switch anyway? I mean, even if Laneer hadn't gone to Chicago?"

"I suppose so. It wouldn't have been easy, though. It would have been more risky."

"So she had the date all picked," I said, "and his going away was just a lucky accident."

"So why didn't she set the date for the other week of her vacation earlier?" Libby asked. "From what they found out about what she'd been doing, she was already moved out of her apartment by the time she asked for that week."

"Maybe she asked for it a lot earlier," I said. "Would the other women have known?"

"No. She didn't talk about things like that to us. She was always—you know—distant. Are you saying Mr. Laneer lied about it?"

"I don't know what I'm saying. The timing is all screwed up. She had to start planning the robbery months and months before it happened. She had to get thirty-two fake pieces made, smuggling out the photographs and specifications and smuggling them back in again. Careful, careful long-term planning. Very smart in the beginning, and very stupid toward the end."

"So how *should* she have done it, Investigator Rhoades?"

"Don't needle me. She's gone and the diamonds are gone, so it had to be a pretty good job. I keep wanting to tie J. Trevor Laneer into it. But facts and instinct say no. I have seen so many people react to so many different things, I can tell when I'm being conned. Laneer's reaction when I first saw him was exactly right. It wasn't overdone or underdone. He had the settlement. He'd told everything he knew so many times he didn't want to talk about it anymore. And the reaction was exactly right the second time too. Remorse, apology—not too much or too little. You know, Lib honey, I *like* the guy. He is OK."

"Duke, I told you the first time we talked that Laneer is one cruel, mean person."

"Come *on!*"

"I really mean it." She rolled up onto her elbow and squinted at me through the hot yellow sunlight. "Lots of people complain about their boss. It isn't *like* that. He's *really* a bastard. He goes out of his way to do mean things. A long time ago, when I was about twelve, my parents took me and my brother to see him in a play, at Halloween time. It was supposed to be for kids. He was an evil wizard and he scared me so bad I had nightmares for a week."

"In a play?" I said wonderingly.

"Oh, yes, he was very big around town in the Peachtree Playhouse Amateur Theatre, but they have a professional director and a big budget, and they do good things. He quit about seven or eight years ago, I think, when his wife had that stroke. He's an actor, Duke. He can *make* people like him. They say that's how he snared Betty Wescott. She was getting some family jewelry repaired—that was after her divorce—and it must have been twenty-five years ago, and he was the one in the Piedmont store, the old store, who was doing the bench work at that time, and she wanted to explain exactly what she wanted done. At least, that's what they say. She's older than he, by ten years I guess. Because he didn't have . . . the breeding or the advantages, they never had much to do with the social stuff before her stroke. Just the little theatre is all."

I sat on the corner of the picnic table glowering over at where Fido was shaking the shrubbery, and marveling at the chronic incompleteness of the investigations and the reports filed. And I marveled at my own gullibility in believing yet another set of misleading, incomplete reports.

She nudged me in the small of the back with her bare heel and said, "Hey! You!"

"He just left," I said.

"Let me know when he gets back."

She was a little bit of a woman, somewhere on the windward side of sixty, living alone in a high-ceilinged apartment full of mahogany, silver, lace, and old portraits. Her cropped hair was dyed fudge brown, and her face was weathered to a red-brown. She wore jeans and an embroidered cotton blouse. She was slim and moved well. She let me in at a little past nine in the evening.

"It's good of you to see me so late, Mrs. Culver."

"Late, hell, Mr. Rhoades. I'm a night person, and you better call me Mim because everybody else in the world does."

"I'm Duke."

"There's ice and water and bourbon over there, if you'd fix us both one, Duke. I spent four hours on the practice range today. I had to stop when I started to get this blister. They won't let women play at the club on Saturday, the chauvinist rats. But I think I found my trouble. I was coming off the ball too soon. On Monday I am going to see just how much of Doris Jane Cupper's money I can take away from her. Thank you, dear. No, sit there, on the side where I hear better. You said on the telephone you had talked to Tammy Rice? Yes, she was right. I was Betty Wescott Boland Laneer's best friend in all the world, all through school and Briarcliffe; but who sent you to Tammy Rice?"

I explained that I had got access to the back file of clippings on the Wescott family at the newspaper and had weeded out some people who might have been lifelong friends and then tried to find them. "I'm a hired snoop," I said.

She studied me pertly. "I would say you are probably brighter than you look, young man. And I am not as rattlebrained as I might seem to some. So I will have to know why you are snooping around."

I smiled my best smile and said, "I am presently representing a company that paid out over half a million dollars to J. Trevor Laneer, and we want to be sure he deserves it. And needs it."

"Oh, Anne Farley! You know, that used to be a *very* good family name in Atlanta. Every bit as good as Culver or Boland. Wescott wasn't *quite* as good a name because, you see, they were in trade, but really they made most of their money in land way out north of town. I knew Roger Farley, her father, quite well. Nearly married him, in fact. Oh dear, all my . . . values mean so little nowadays. Atlanta has turned into a monstrous place, really. We are all swallowed up by this terrible energy of growth. Every time you look around, there is a new bank or a new hotel or a lot of yellow machines tearing up lovely old buildings. Trevor Laneer was what my father would call a counter jumper. My departed husband couldn't stand him. Betty and I used to see each other for lunch often. It makes me feel guilty to think about the poor dear. But I just can't go see her. It's too horribly depressing. And what good does it do? Those blank, dead eyes. And she has to be waited on hand and foot. He talks to her as though she could understand every word. There's something very strange about that, somehow. Does Trevor Laneer need the money? Well, I would hardly *think* so. I have to say that one must credit the man with compassion. I would think it has been a very long eight years for him. But he does seem unwaveringly faithful and constant. I went to see her—would it be six months ago or longer? Longer, God help me. It could be a year. That lovely rock garden. On a slope, you know, below the bedroom window. He turned a downstairs study into her bedroom because it is so much easier that way for the nurses. Her grandfather built that house. Except for the sound of traffic—not very loud because of all the trees—you would think you were in the country. It is very private, really. There must be at least three acres there, and heaven only knows what that land might be worth now."

"I suppose the house and land are in a trust arrangement too."

"Too?"

"The store is."

"Really? I didn't know that. I do know that her affairs are handled by Mid–Georgia Fidelity. And mine and Tammy's. We all have the same trust officer. Tammy's grandfather *founded* that bank. Bunny Gearhart takes care of us old ladies. He's a dear young man. Well, not so young, I guess. Young to me. He must be getting on toward fifty. I could call him if you want to talk to him, but I have to ask you something first."

"Anything. Almost."

"Could this all wind up in such a way people find out that Anne Farley was innocent?"

"It could," I said, and, smiling, she reached for the phone.


Those determined ladies, Mim Culver and Tammy Rice, put so much pressure on Bunny Gearhart I was able to see him at his tennis club on Sunday morning. He was a big, pink, rubbery fellow with all the social graces and a very correct tennis outfit. As a senior trust officer, he felt that he should not disclose any information at all without a court order. After I told him all my reasons he looked slightly ill. But he wouldn't talk until I threatened to call Mim Culver and tell her that her favorite banker was being uncooperative. And then he sighed, shrugged, and talked. I have discovered one thing about the professions. Get a banker, lawyer, doctor, politician away from his familiar office and he is much more likely to tell secrets. One of the interesting things Bunny told me was that the doctors did not believe Betty Laneer could last much longer. Eight years of inactivity had caused a fatty degeneration of the heart muscle structures and decreasing circulation was beginning to affect the other major organs. And, of course, Trevor Laneer knew this.

"The Wescott estate used to be much larger, of course," Trevor Laneer told me.

"I didn't mean to interrupt your Sunday afternoon, Mr. Laneer."

He smiled. We were walking from the iron gates up the gentle slope toward the house. "You said on the phone it was important, Rhoades. I have to hope you've located Anne. If you can recover the diamonds, you won't have to prosecute, will you?"

I admired the rock garden. He took me over for a closer look. It seemed to cover a half-acre slope at least, where probably it had once been lawn. There were paths, raked gravel, river stones, huge boulders, pools, fountains, rivulets of water over stone. The plantings were not overdone. The whole area had a sparse, Japanese flavor. The back of his work shirt was dark with sweat in a pyramidal pattern. His bare arms were sinewy. I could see the place where he had been working with a shovel. He said he was preparing a place for another boulder, a very interesting one he had picked out at the stone yard. They brought them in by flatbed and crane to place them in the prepared spot.

I looked up at the house and saw a pale oval beyond the glass, a motionless face, a motionless woman apparently on a chaise longue or uptilted hospital bed. Two dark circles and a slit for a mouth. A child's drawing of a face.

"It gives her something beautiful to look at," he said.

We talked inside a garden house, an octagonal, screened structure with a Japanese roof. It was in heavy shade and smelled of wood rot. I moved a little way from him so I could face him more directly.

"Preface to my question," I said. "Your wife's father, Prentiss Wescott, reorganized his personal financial affairs a few months before he died, when his daughter was separated from her previous husband, but not divorced. He put everything in trust for her, all the securities, this house, the business, everything. Income during her lifetime, with the income divided between her and any children she might have as they reached twenty-one. Is that your understanding?"

"Yes, of course. The bank manages the estate."

"If she dies without issue, everything goes to Emory University Hospital. Immediately after her death the trust officer must start the liquidation of everything not in cash or securities, close the estate as soon as possible, and turn over the bequest to the hospital trustees. And your wife, I understand, is not expected to last out this year."

He laughed as he held his hand up. It was a very good laugh. "Wait! You are really straining at a gnat, Mr. Rhoades. Are you serious? Is that your script? Store manager conspires with clerk to steal diamonds? Fears unemployment? I think I'd be angry if it weren't so amusing. Whoever buys the business would be a fool not to hire me to operate it my own way. If that didn't work out, I'd start my own shop. My customers would be loyal. I have savings, you know? Quite a lot. The trust department has always paid our living expenses, and I get a salary in line with my position. I suggest you stop inventing fantasies and get on with finding Anne Farley."

On Monday I was very busy. On Tuesday the signs on the doors of Wescott and Sons said "Closed for Inventory." It was a rainy Tuesday afternoon. I didn't want to be out in Libby's enclosed yard with her and Fido anyway, for fear I wouldn't hear the phone.

"*He* made the duplicates, then?" she asked.

I told her he had made them and made the switch himself, and they did not know where he'd done the work yet, but they would probably find out. She told me to stop pacing around and I told her I was too tense to sit down.

"What are you saying is that he talked Anne Farley into laying her own false trail. Why would she do such a dumb thing?"

"She believed whatever he told her. Some plot against him or the business. Some kind of ripoff he was trying to avoid. He told her to paint herself blue and live in a tree, and she did."

"What?"

"Never mind, honey. He thought she'd lay a clumsy trail and it would have been followed to a dead end in Yucatán a long time ago. But nobody found the loose ends except me, the old hound with the sore feet and the great nose."

"That nose has been broken."

"I didn't mean great looking. I mean function."

"Oh."

"The way I read it, he had her all set to leave for someplace else on the Saturday he got back from Chicago. Per instructions, she had checked out of that airport Holiday Inn with her suitcase and her tropical clothes and waited for his plane. His car was at the airport. He took her home and . . . ."

The phone rang. I didn't knock anything over getting to it. A wonder. I didn't have to say much. Grunt and listen. Sigh and listen. Hang up. Plod back to the couch and sit down heavily. Sigh.

I finally responded to her anxious questions. "After locating the right stone yard and talking them into letting me see the records on delivery dates to Laneer, and after talking all those official types into picking him up and getting the warrant, wouldn't I have looked like all kinds of damn fool if I'd been wrong."

"But . . . they found her?"

"Under the boulder they delivered the day before he found, to his horror, all those diamonds were missing. Since then he's been selling them back to the business a few at a time under a dummy name and pocketing the funds. He paid himself almost seven hundred thousand to buy them back, they think."

"Poor Anne," she whispered.

"The weather bureau says it was a nice November afternoon. Warm and sunny. They say it looks as though he clubbed her in the back of the head with the flat of his spade, using a full swing. Then he dug the hole, buried her and her suitcase, and prepared the site for the two-tone boulder he'd preselected. Journey to nowhere."

She shuddered and looked gray. I put my arm around her. "And it's a good guess that woman in the house watched it all through the window. I wonder how much she saw, how much she comprehended. J. Trevor couldn't care less, because she could not tell anyone anyway."

It got to me too, just then. A little more than usual, and I put both arms around the lady, looking for, as much as trying to give, comfort.

Laneer had told me to get on with finding Anne Farley. And, God help me, I had. Cold winds blow through the loveless heart.

*Five years ago Joyce Harrington won an MWA Edgar Award for her first published story, "The Purple Shroud." She produces some of the most tantalizing mood pieces in the suspense field. And often, while weaving her spells, she manages a few deft surprises for the unwary reader. Mrs. Harrington works in public relations in New York City. We are pleased to introduce her to these pages with this story of an unusual animal lover.*

# JOYCE HARRINGTON
# The Old Gray Cat

"I should kill her. I should really kill her."

"Yeah, yeah. But how, how?"

"I could find a way. I bet I could."

"Oh, sure."

"You don't think I could? I could put poison in her cocoa."

"What kind of poison?"

"Ah, you know, arsenic. Something like that."

"Sure. You gonna go down to the store, say, 'Gimme a pound of arsenic, something like that.' Nobody's gonna ask what you want to do with it?"

"I could push her down the stairs. She'd die."

"Maybe not. She could break all her bones and still live. She'd say, 'Ellie pushed me down the stairs.' Then what?"

"She lies. Everybody knows she tells lies."

"Somebody would believe her. A thing like that, why would she lie?"

"Everybody knows she hates me. She steals my things. Remember the time I had that box of chocolate-covered cherries and she took a bite out of every one and put them all back in the box? Even you said she was the one."

"Probably she was. But everybody knows you hate her right back."

"You think I shouldn't kill her? You think I should just let her get away with this?"

"I didn't say that, did I? You want to kill her, go ahead. Only be smart. Don't get caught."

"I don't care if I get caught."

"You'll care. If you have to spend the rest of your life in jail, you'll care all right."

"Is this better than a jail? Listen, if I get caught I'll play crazy. You think I can't play crazy? Watch this."

Ellie crossed her eyes, let her tongue loll out of her mouth, and waggled her head. "Glah-glah-glah," she said.

"Nobody would believe that for a minute. You need some lessons in playing crazy."

"That's funny. You know, you're really funny. Ha, ha. See how I'm laughing? You don't think I'm crazy enough. I suppose you think you're crazier than I am?"

"The whole world is crazy. Just act normal. Then everybody'll think you're crazy."

"Margo, you're my best friend. But you're wrong. Anyway, if I really do kill her, which maybe I won't, but if I do, nobody will know I did it. Not even you."

"Will you tell me?"

"I guess so. Maybe. I could put a deadly snake in her bed. I read that in a book once."

"Where would you get a deadly snake?"

"That's a problem."

A bell rang. The door banged open and Miss Swiss marched into the room.

"Lunchtime, girls," she announced. Her voice was brassy and her hair was the color of tarnished trumpets, stiff and shiny with hair spray. She wore a pink ruffled pinafore over a green nylon dress. The ruffles flapped over her bulging frontage, lending a quivering vitality to the corseted flesh beneath.

"Put your games away," she blared. "Books and magazines back on the shelf. Let's keep this room tidy, girls." Her eyes swept the room like twin beacons, flashing malice.

Ellie picked up a fistful of marbles from the Chinese checkers board that lay on the table between them. She aimed at the back of Miss Swiss's metallic coiffure. Margo grabbed her arm across the table.

"Don't be stupid," she whispered.

Miss Swiss turned. "Fighting again, girls? Margo, I'm surprised at you. Ellie, you've been warned before. I'll have to report you to the director. No dessert for either one of you." She smiled widely, showing gold inlays. "It's apple brown Betty today."

"Damn your apple brown Betty!" Ellie shouted, throwing marbles onto the worn wine-colored carpet. "And damn you, you fat elephant!"

"Shut up, you dummy," Margo whispered more urgently.

"Language, Ellie. Shocking," said Miss Swiss with an even more complacent smile. "The director will be terribly disappointed. Margo, leave the room. Ellie will stay and pick up all those marbles. She will get no lunch at all. She will go to her room and stay there until I tell her she may come out. After lunch there will be a movie. I believe it is a film about Hawaii. Move along, girls."

Margo joined the drift of others toward the door of the recreation room. The smell of overbaked fish and boiled potatoes crept in at the door as the group of twenty or so trickled out. In the doorway Margo turned and mouthed silently at Ellie, "I'll bring you some food later."

Ellie shook her head and blinked back tears. Suddenly she felt hungry. The food was usually tasteless but, now that it was being withheld, she felt a gnawing in her stomach that could only be assuaged by large helpings of hot food.

"I'm hungry," she whined.

"You should have thought of that before," snapped Miss Swiss, no longer smiling. "Pick up those marbles."

Ellie hunkered down on her heels, her thin legs disappearing into the folds of her wrinkled cotton skirt. She dropped her head onto her bony knees and folded her arms over both.

"I'm really going to kill you," she muttered into the flower-printed fabric.

"What was that?" demanded Miss Swiss. And, "What did you say?" when she got no answer. "Look at me!"

Ellie said nothing and did not raise her head. She remained folded into an unresponsive mound on the floor.

Miss Swiss reached down and prodded Ellie's shoulder with a sharp forefinger. Her nails were filed into curving talons and were painted a frosted pink.

"Pick. Up. Those. Marbles." said Miss Swiss, forming each word as if it were a stone falling from her lips onto Ellie's head.

Ellie grunted and toppled over. She lay on the floor, amid the brightly colored marbles, gazing up with hatred at Miss Swiss.

"Where's the cat?" she said.

"What cat?" Miss Swiss stepped back, looking surprised. "You know we don't allow cats in here. Or dogs, for that matter."

"My old gray cat. That's what cat. The one that came to my room." Ellie knew that Miss Swiss was only pretending to be surprised. She knew Miss Swiss was somehow responsible for the nonappearance of the rangy gray tomcat who had the habit of leaping onto Ellie's windowsill and wolfing down whatever tidbit she had left for him there, favoring her with a wicked leer and departing with an arrogant flirt of his crooked tail. All summer long the cat had appeared with the first morning light while Ellie lay sleepless, with no reason to get up and no company but her hatred for Miss Swiss.

"If you've had a cat in your room, you've been breaking the rule. I don't know what we're going to do with you, Ellie. You're a very disruptive influence on the other girls. Do you think I like to be always punishing you? Wouldn't you like to be friends?"

"What did you do to him? Did you poison him? Or did you send him to the A.S.P.C.A.? They put cats in gas chambers there. Did you know that? I'd like to put you in a gas chamber."

Ellie felt tears rising again and rolled over to hide her face from Miss Swiss's inquisitory stare. She felt a marble under her hip and concentrated on that small pain to keep the tears in check.

"Ellie, Ellie," said Miss Swiss, her voice wheedling now, placatory. "That's a terrible thing to say. But I won't hold it against you. I won't even report it to the director. But you've really got to get up now and pick up those marbles. I'll help you. And then later on, when I take my break, you can come and have cocoa in my room and we'll talk about this cat."

Ellie sat up. So, she thought, she does know about the cat. She can't fool me. She's trying to get around me so I won't kill her. Fat chance, the fat slob. Ellie picked up a red marble and then a yellow one. Miss Swiss was on her hands and knees, her green rump in the air, gathering marbles.

"Maybe I can even save you some apple brown Betty," she said.

"With whipped cream," said Ellie. "I like whipped cream."

"We'll see," said Miss Swiss.

Ellie made a rude gesture toward Miss Swiss's backside. . . .

Ellie waited in her room for Miss Swiss's summons. It wasn't much of a room, but as Miss Swiss often reminded her, it was one of the best in the house. It had a window that looked out over the little park across the street. The leaves were falling now from the spindly trees that dotted the shriveled grass, and a gusty wind blew the leaves in erratic spirals between the benches.

Ellie lay on her bed and let her mind drift. Her pillow smelled musty, and the smell evoked a memory, not of an event, but of a life lived in a house where a dark closet under a staircase smelled just that way, and fetching galoshes on a rainy day was an occasion for terror. But the tall woman with the soft brown hair and the long, strong hands was there to dispel morbid fancies with raisin cookies, a song, and the certainty of love.

"Ma. Oh, Ma," Ellie sighed.

Ellie had no memory of the death of her mother; she had been too young. There was only the unbearable absence, the loss of love, the vacancy that could never be filled no matter how hard she tried. And she had tried.

The cat had been her latest attempt. Too well she realized that the cat's attachment to her had been cupboard love. His first visit had coincided with half a tuna sandwich smuggled into her room from the regular Sunday evening cold supper. She had wrapped it in a paper napkin and placed it on the windowsill to eat later before she went to bed. But a quarrel over the television set had brought a scolding from Miss Swiss, and Ellie had gone to bed spurting wrathful tears. The tuna sandwich had been forgotten.

A rustling had awakened her to a gray dawn and a gray shape on the windowsill. The cat, sensing her movement, had looked up from his feast and hissed a warning at her. Then he had resumed his marauding, ignoring her as the sandwich disappeared and the napkin fell, limp and shredded, from his claws.

From her bed, Ellie had watched the cat's thin sides heave in and out as he chomped voraciously. She'd heard a sound, not quite a purr, yet not a growl, as the cat broadcast his ownership of the food. As the light gradually increased, she saw his tattered ear, his patchy fur, a scab, a clouded eye. He's like me, she thought. Alone and hungry. He left abruptly, not stopping to preen as house cats do after eating.

After that she always left something on the windowsill. And always the cat came in the still hour of dawn. After a few visits he permitted Ellie to approach the window, each time a little closer until, by midsummer, he presented his scruffy head to be scratched. Ellie scratched diligently. She fondled his torn ear and passed her fingers gently over the milky eye. The first time she did that, the cat moved swiftly, clamping her hand between sharp yellow teeth.

Ellie was startled, but she didn't flinch. The cat held on for a minute. Two minutes. Ellie stood very still, sweating in her thin nightgown. Then the cat released her hand and nuzzled it with his damp, scarred nose. It was as close as they ever became to each other. The cat would not permit himself to be picked up. Ellie never thought of a name for him. He was just "the old gray cat."

Ellie told no one about the cat. No one but Margo. After her transistor radio disappeared, Ellie had to talk to someone.

"Bet I know who took it," said Margo.

"You think she did? Ooh, I could kill her!"

"She took my Snoopy dog away, didn't she? Said I was too old for baby toys. I bet she has a closet full of stuff she's taken away from people here. She's bad news."

"Well," said Ellie proudly, "I've got something she can't take away from me." And she told Margo about the visits of the cat in the early morning. "Of course," she added, "he's ugly as sin, and probably dirty and diseased. Nobody would want him but me, and she couldn't keep *him* in any closet. He'd scratch her eyes out." Ellie giggled. "Serve her right," she said.

"Be careful," Margo had warned her. "Don't let her find out. She'll figure out some way to spoil it for you. She's a genius that way."

Ellie had been careful. But somehow Miss Swiss had found out. The cat had been absent for over a week now. Almost ten days. At first she told herself that a tomcat might have got into a fight and gone away to heal himself. She waited and watched every morning, wishing he might feel safe enough with her to come

and have his injuries tended. Then she thought he might have
been hit by a car. She envisioned him lying stiff and bedraggled
in a filthy gutter somewhere in the city. But that didn't feel right
to her. The cat was too wary, too wise, to be the vicim of an
accident.

No, she decided, the cat had been intercepted on one of his
morning visits. The cat had been on his way to her and had
been trapped because of his faithfulness. Trapped and killed,
and who would have been mean enough, ruthless enough, cruel
enough to do such a thing? Only Miss Swiss.

Ellie rummaged in her bureau drawer, and failing to find her
embroidery scissors, remembered she had loaned them to Margo.
She crept out of her room and down the hall to Margo's room.
Everyone was at the movie. Hawaii! All hula dancers and pine-
apples and surfing. As if any of them could ever hope to go there.

Margo's room was dark, even in the middle of the day, and it
smelled bad. Margo wasn't very clean. And her window looked
out on an alley where the garbage cans were kept. She found
her scissors lying on the floor where Margo had been cutting up
magazine pictures for a decoupage project. The floor was littered
with scraps of paper and there were dollops of dried glue on the
rug. Ellie hurried back to her own room, the embroidery scissors
safe in her pocket.

Back in her room, she cast about for some other weapon
against Miss Swiss. The embroidery scissors were sharply pointed,
but short-bladed. Miss Swiss was thickly clothed in fat. The
short blades might not be equal to the task. But search as she
might, there was no other possibility in her room; no pills,
potions, or powders. Certainly not a knife, and Ellie had never
seen a real gun. She considered wrenching one of the iron rail-
ings from the foot of her bedstead, but knew without trying
that she lacked the strength. Maybe there would be something
lying about Miss Swiss's room, some innocuous object that she
could use if the right moment came.

If the moment came. But it probably would not come. Ellie
would drink cocoa in Miss Swiss's room and listen to the lecture
that would accompany it. She would nod and smile and promise
to be good, all the while thinking deadly thoughts at the pink
and falsely smiling Miss Swiss. But thoughts, however deadly,

couldn't kill. Ellie's hand groped in the folds of her skirt, pressing the hard, sharp outline of the small scissors against her thigh.

There was no knock at the door. Miss Swiss never knocked. The doorknob turned and the door opened just wide enough to admit the stiff curls and the painted smirk.

"Come along now, Ellie. The cocoa's ready and that movie's good for another half hour. At least we'll have some privacy for our chat."

"Coming, Miss Swiss."

With her hand still pressing the scissors against her thigh, Ellie followed the fluttering pink pinafore down the hall. Miss Swiss had, undoubtedly, the best room in the house, if you discounted the director's office on the second floor, which was paneled in glowing rosewood and draped in burgundy velvet. But the director didn't live on the premises and Miss Swiss did.

Miss Swiss opened the massive door and ushered Ellie into her sanctum.

"Take the rocking chair, Ellie, dear. Pull it right up to the table. I'll pour the cocoa. There's the dessert I saved for you. *And* a bowl of whipped cream. We can have some in our cocoa, too. Although I really shouldn't, should I? Not with my weight problem."

While Miss Swiss babbled on, Ellie glanced around the room appraisingly. There were china animals everywhere. Quaint mice were pursued by cunning cats who were chased in turn by winsome dogs across the top of a bookcase. A pyramid of owls perched wisely in a whatnot by the window. Beasts of prey were restricted to a bureau where lions, leopards, and bears indiscriminately stalked each other across a long lace doily. A barnyard group browsed placidly atop a console television set. Ellie sneered inwardly at Miss Swiss's execrable taste, while envying both her freedom and her privacy to indulge her whims.

"I see you're admiring my menagerie. I've been collecting them for years. I just love animals, don't you?"

"No," said Ellie, and shifted her gaze to the fireplace. More animals paraded across the mantel: elephants, deer, and a particularly ugly version of a camel complete with howdah.

"No? But I thought that was why we're here. Something about a cat. Help yourself to cream, dear."

Ellie did, and spooned dessert in her mouth before answering. "One cat," she said, while taking careful note of the brass andirons and the iron poker that stood beside the firescreen.

"Well? What about this cat? You know we can't allow you girls to keep animals."

"I wasn't keeping him. Nobody could keep him. He came to visit. He was my friend, and now you've gone and done something to him." Ellie continued spooning up cream and chunks of apple.

Miss Swiss sipped cocoa and licked chocolate foam from her plump pink lips. "But I never saw this cat, Ellie, dear. If I had, I could not have allowed you to continue having him in your room. I would have spoken to you about it. Fair is fair."

"Fair is fair," mocked Ellie. "You killed him, didn't you?" She finished her dessert and stuck her finger into the remaining cream in the bowl.

"Ellie," chided Miss Swiss, "don't eat with your fingers. Use a spoon. I most certainly did not kill your cat. I love animals. I understand how you feel. Suppose I give you one of these?"

She set down her cocoa mug and walked across to the bookcase.

"Now, which one shall it be? A Siamese? Or would you like to have this dear little fluffy white kitten? I can't give you the tabby. She's my absolute out-and-out favorite, given to me by a girl who left us seven years ago. But any of the others. You may take your pick."

While Miss Swiss stood fondling each china cat in turn, Ellie took a final swipe at the bowl of cream and noiselessly left the rocking chair. She felt that the moment had come. If she didn't do it now, she never would. And after all her talk to Margo, she felt obliged to carry out her intentions. She sidled closer to the fireplace. And closer.

Miss Swiss continued to hover lovingly over the glossy representations of cat antics. "Now here's a cutie. I call him my Manx cat because his tail broke off, but he looks so lifelike playing with his tiny ball of yarn."

Ellie picked up the poker. It dragged at her arm and she wondered if she would have the strength to raise it. Her heart pounded and her head felt as if it would float off her shoulders with excitement. She felt an odd drawing together in her stomach almost as though all her vital organs were gathering themselves for one enormous effort. With both hands she raised the poker over her head. Her feet started traveling across the braided rug.

Miss Swiss looked over her shoulder and screamed. The poker flew from Ellie's hands. Miss Swiss stepped to one side, quickly for a woman of her size and weight. The ruffles on her pinafore fluttered wildly and her normally pink face turned the color of used chewing gum. The poker smashed into the bookcase and devastated the prim line of smirking cats.

Ellie's hand fumbled in the folds of her skirt, but before she could find her pocket her knees buckled and she fell to the floor with a thump. She fought for breath and fought the pain that scuttled like a trapped animal through her body. She gritted her teeth and closed her eyes. Her hand found its way into her pocket and she clutched the cold steel scissors.

"My cat," she gasped. "I'll kill you for that."

And she died. Ellie died.

Miss Swiss had seen death before. She recognized its awful presence on Ellie's face, bluish now and set forever in a snarl. But never had she come so close to death herself. If she hadn't moved quickly, she might have been lying on the rug beside Ellie with her head smashed in. Shakily she tiptoed around the pitiful corpse and opened the heavy door.

In the hall wondering eyes stared at her.

"We heard a noise," said Margo. "Anyway, the movie's over. It wasn't any good."

"Ellie has suffered a collapse," said Miss Swiss in answer to their unspoken question. "I shall have to call the doctor and the director. And that son of hers."

"Is she dead?" asked Margo.

"She is," said Miss Swiss softly, and then resuming her trumpet-like tone, "Go to your rooms, girls. This is no time to be wandering about."

Gray and white heads nodded and carpet-slippered feet shuffled away. There were a few disheartened whispers, but for the most part there was silence as each old woman reflected on the nearness of her own inescapable end.

Only Margo remained.

"Miss Swiss," she said. "May I have Ellie's room? I know this may not be the right time to ask, but it is a much nicer room than mine, and if I wait someone else might get it. So may I, please?"

"Yes, yes," said Miss Swiss. "Margo, you were her friend. Do you know why . . . ? No, never mind. Go along now."

Margo lurched down the hall, scarcely needing to lean on the cane that was never out of her hand these days. In her room she began hauling things out of her bureau drawers and piling them on her bed in preparation for moving into Ellie's room: flannel nightgowns, warm winter underwear, a transistor radio. Too bad about Ellie, she thought, but if she hadn't died she would have got herself tossed out one of these days.

When she came to the closet, she paused. The smell was getting rather bad. She groped on the floor of the closet and came up with a plastic bag. The bag sagged heavily and Margo handled it gingerly, holding it away from her body with stiff fingertips.

It had been so easy to lure the cat onto her own windowsill. All it took was a morsel of greasy hamburger. So easy to pretend insomnia and get a sleeping capsule from Miss Swiss. One capsule taken apart and its contents mixed with the meat. The cat, disarmed by Ellie's kindness, had allowed Margo to come close. One swift blow with her cane, and then pop into the plastic bag. Margo never knew whether the cat had died from the capsule or from a crushed skull. Or whether he had suffocated inside the plastic bag. Maybe all three.

But now she had no further use for him. Ellie was dead, too. If Ellie hadn't died this afternoon or at least provoked Miss Swiss into having her removed, Margo had one final scheme in mind. Early tomorrow morning she would have placed the dead cat on Ellie's windowsill. That would surely have done the trick. Ellie would have gone on a rampage and they would have had to get rid of her. But none of that was necessary now.

Margo carried the reeking plastic bag to the open window and dropped it into a lidless garbage can below. Then she cheerfully set about removing her clothes from the closet.

It had been worth it. The best room in the house was now hers. Next to Miss Swiss's, of course.

*Brian Garfield was a professional musician playing in a jazz band before he turned to a writing career. Many of his early stories and novels—perhaps inspired by his early years in the West where he attended the University of Arizona—were westerns, and he is a former president of the Western Writers of America. Today he is best known as a writer of thrillers like* Death Wish *and spy novels like the MWA Edgar winner* Hopscotch. *But some of his best short fiction still combines modern suspense with a western setting. In the Edgar nominee that follows, his almost cinematic pacing seems to create true movies of the mind. We welcome his first appearance in this annual.*

# BRIAN GARFIELD
## Jode's Last Hunt

The night watchman thought he saw a flicker in the woods. He stepped off the platform and looked away and then looked again, but there was nothing.

Could be a squirrel. Sunday dawn was always jumpy. Any other morning the mill would be working—shifts moving in and out—but Sunday was silent because that was the Keenmeier management: pious about the Sabbath. On Sunday the only face he'd see would be the day watchman's at eight o'clock and that was still three hours away.

Red shafts of light slanted through the lodgepoles. He looked at his watch. Another half hour he'd do another round of inspection.

He walked to his car and got in. The coffee was still hot, but there was only half a cup left. He thought about saving it, but it would only get cool. He drank it down.

His eyes drifted along the length of the paper mill out of habit. It looked new and raw—they hadn't bothered with much paint. Smoke had discolored the buildings in patches. The big metal chutes were coated with ugly splashes. Along the parking lot the pines had been stained by the mill's outpourings.

He could hear the river. It birled over rocks just below the mill. Those rocks were colored by the guck that poured out of the mill's spouts through the spillway. Once in a while he walked over there and just looked at the colors on the rocks. Weird and very pretty—metallic colors, hard and brilliant.

Something flickered again in the corner of his vision and he looked that way into the woods.

He was reaching for the door handle to get out of the car when the mill blew up.

Sheriff Ben Jode in his Grant County Sheriff car made the turn off a paved road into the graded ranch drive. It lifted him to a rise where he put the brakes on and stopped at the crest to reconnoiter the situation.

Over across the valley was a mountain with a top shaped just like a biscuit, even to the corrugated cliffs that ran around its sides. That mesa dominated the valley. It was the highest point in the range; the other mountains swept gracefully away from it to either side, tier by tier. There were still white spots on the peaks—the remains of winter snow.

The valley was undulant, high-country terrain—yellow grass slopes dotted with piñon and juniper and scrub oak. He counted more than forty horses on the near pasture.

The road slumped into the valley. The main house was set up on a hilltop with a commanding view of its surroundings; below it the outbuildings and work headquarters were some distance away—corrals, two windmills, tack sheds, crew quarters, barn, silo. The house was isolated on its hilltop.

Several police cars of various persuasions stood parked askew a hundred yards or so below the house. Jode started driving down toward them. He made out a local cop car from Aravaipa town, two Highway Patrol cruisers, a white Rincon County Sheriff car, and even a station wagon with a dome light on top of it—Fort Defiance Indian Reservation Apache Police. This was twenty miles outside the Reservation. It made Jode grin.

He went down the drive slowly and parked a distance behind the other cars. Cops in various uniforms were hunkered behind the cars. They were clutching rifles and riot guns and a variety of such artillery. The Rincon sheriff, as tall as Jode and sixty pounds heavier, had a bullhorn in his hand.

Someone inside the house was shooting deliberately, without hurry, with a rifle. The reports were thin in the high air; the house was downwind and the shots almost seemed distant rumors, but Jode could see the pinpoint flashes from the windows.

Jode crouched low and made his way over to the Rincon sheriff.

"Out of your bailiwick, but I'm glad to have you, Ben."

Jode said, "I picked up the radio call. Looks like everybody did. Who's the guy in mufti?"

"FBI. Name of Vickers."

"FBI?"

"He's out of his bailiwick too."

The rifle kept popping at intervals. Not shooting at the cops, Jode noticed. Shooting at tires. The bullets were flattening nearly every tire on the various police cars. Jode looked back over his shoulder. He'd left his car far enough back; that rifle would have to be uncannily accurate to reach it from the house. At the moment the rifle wasn't even trying for it—there were plenty of easy targets right here up front.

"You're going to have quite a bill for tires."

The Rincon sheriff grunted.

Jode said, "Who've you got forted up in the house?"

"Maria Skelton."

Jode felt the shock. It grenaded into him. "You're putting me on."

"No, sir."

"All alone?"

"All alone except she's got that rifle, and she knows just exactly how to use it."

Jode laughed out loud.

"Yeah, well, it's very humorous," the Rincon sheriff said. "You notice she's got all the shutters closed. We can't get tear gas in there. I been yelling at her for an hour on the bullhorn. Didn't do no good, except about five minutes ago she took a notion to start target practice on our radial tires. Seems to have plenty ammunition up there." He looked down the row of cars at the fellow in the gray business suit. "Vickers wants to burn her out."

"Does he now?"

"I'll tell you, Ben, twenty cops against one woman and we had to resort to burning down a sixty-thousand-dollar house to get her out? How you figure that's going to look in the news-papers tomorrow morning?"

"Not too good, Roy."

"Yeah. Well, there you are then. I figure the only thing to do is wait her out. Sooner or later she'll get tired or she'll get bored."

"That could take quite a while."

"You got any other ideas? I'd appreciate a suggestion if you got one, Ben."

"My county line's seven miles way. It's your jurisdiction, not mine."

"I don't mind deferring to you," the Rincon sheriff said. "You been at this longer than I have. And besides—"

The Rincon sheriff didn't finish it, but the meaning was clear enough. Jode might be a little past his prime, but he was a leader. They all knew him in this corner of the Southwest. The combat medals from Korea. The reform ticket on which he'd come into the sheriff's office. The fact that Grant County used to be the most corrupt county in Arizona until Jode took the job; now it was one of the cleanest counties. The fact that the mob types who'd tried to establish a real-estate foothold had been run out ignominiously. And the spectacular solution Jode had provided to the string of psycho murders of teen-age girls back in sixty-eight. When he'd brought the Breucher kid in that after-noon, there'd been TV news cameras all over the courthouse lawn. The news films had been picked up by the networks and Jode had been in the limelight, a national celebrity for two days.

Jode had 16mm prints of those news films at home.

But since that episode it had been downhill for years. Things were quiet. Nobody messed around in Jode's jurisdiction. It was a big deal if his deputies had to arrest a routine gas station holdup team. Most of the time it was a matter of keeping drunks quiet in the roadside taverns and taking care of traffic duty.

Jode was still revered by people like the Rincon sheriff and rural folk who thought of him as a cross between John Wayne and Buford Pusser. He knew it and he enjoyed it. But it was glory in the past and now they treated him as if he'd already retired. At times he felt things slipping away from him.

He kept remembering the Hollywood producers who'd talked to him back in 1968 when he was hot news. They'd wanted to make a movie about him, but finally they backed away. It would take something new and fresh—a new triumph to rekindle the legend of Ben Jode, get his name back in the headlines, and bring the TV vans pouring back into Grant County.

The woman forted up in the shuttered house—now there was a headline maker!

Jode knew quite a bit about her. Everybody did. He'd never met her, but he knew the stories.

Maria Skelton had been a champion rodeo rider. She wasn't Indian, but she'd grown up on the Fort Defiance Reservation. Her parents were missionaries. She knew horses and she knew the wild country—it was said she used to hang out with an Indian family that ran white lightning out of a still back up in the Biscuit peaks, and Maria ran pack trains of the stuff along the back trails, or at least that was the rumor. She had a wild reputation as a kid. Then she took to winning horse-show ribbons and rodeos.

And along about 1961 she'd appeared in some western movies. She didn't last too long as a movie star, but she'd invested her movie money and rodeo winnings; she bought this ranch in 1963. She'd settled down to develop the place into an important horse-breeding outfit and to enjoy life with her bridegroom who was a fun-loving stunt man she'd met when she was working in Hollywood. Between them they worked on the Appaloosa breeding strain that they hoped would make the ranch world famous.

Maria had a reputation for being in and out of trouble constantly. They said she had a hearty tendency to get drunk and lay about her with chairs and handbags. For a slim small woman she managed to create quite a ruckus. She'd busted up some of the classier bars in California and Arizona. On one occasion it took four Hollywood cops to subdue her.

Then apparently as she'd got into her thirties she'd begun to grow up—laying off the firewater, staying closer to home, taking the horse-ranching job seriously.

Her bridegroom began to get bored. Or that was the story.

Then the Keenmeier lumber outfit alongside the ranch had decided to go into the paper business. It had built the enormous paper mill right on the bank of the river that separated the two properties.

The smoke and stink from the mill had begun to foul the air

on the whole plateau. The effluents from the paper mill did unspeakable things to the river.

It had been common knowledge all through the high country: Maria was upset. She'd been yelling at the state's environmental protection people. But the Board numbered some people who were not to be believed. She'd got nowhere with them. She'd had to quit using the river to water her stock; she'd had to drill wells.

About that time her stunt-man husband evidently had got tired of the bucolic sameness of life on the isolated ranch with a wife who'd suddenly turned soberside. So he'd taken off for Los Angeles where rumor had it he was living with a TV starlet and doing movie stunt work and refusing to answer his wife's phone calls.

They said there were community property legal problems involved in the settlement that had made Maria even more miserable.

About ten days ago somebody had tried to set fire to the baled paper on the mill's loading platform. But heavily compressed paper does not burn readily. The matches had done minimal damage. It was common knowledge Maria was the culprit, but there was no proof.

"She went and did it this time," the Rincon sheriff told him. "Dynamite."

"The paper mill?"

"Sure enough. Good thing she's not an explosives expert. She didn't use enough dynamite. Didn't set the charges in the right places. All she did was knock off a corner of the building."

"Anybody hurt?"

"No. I guess that's why she picked Sunday morning—nobody around to get hurt. The night watchman spotted her running away this morning right after the blast. Called my office. We headed out here and you can see the rest of the story for yourself."

"What's she trying to prove, Roy?"

"God knows what goes on inside the head of a crazy woman." The Rincon sheriff looked up at the house with jaundiced resignation.

A cop made a run from one car to another. Maria's rifle spoke.

Kicked up some dust, sending the cop leaping to cover. The Rincon sheriff said, "She's just having herself some sport. If she'd wanted to hit him she'd have hit him."

"I'll tell you," Jode said, "I've got an idea."

In the night he took three of the deputies and moved in on the house; circling wide while the Rincon sheriff tried to divert Maria by firing at the front of the house, Jode eased up on the back.

Jode pried a shutter open with a tire iron. He stood aside then. Two deputies threw tear-gas canisters inside.

They gave the gas a little time to spread. Then they fitted on their gas masks and climbed into the dark house.

They spread through the house. Open a door, throw a gas canister through it, wait. Then go in. You'd know if she was in there—you'd hear the coughing.

They split up, going into various rooms peering through their gas masks, hunting for Maria.

They didn't find her.

Jode searched every room, but there was no sign of Maria. He went outside and waved the Rincon sheriff up the hill. The posse approached hesitantly, wary of Maria's rifle. Two deputies came out of the house behind Jode, stripping off their gas masks; they stood there coughing, clearing their lungs.

As the Rincon sheriff approached the house one deputy walked away from the house past Jode. The deputy was still wearing his gas mask and that puzzled Jode a bit. Some suspicion stirred in him, but then the Rincon sheriff met him and they both turned to go inside—to conduct a more thorough search this time.

Jode went inside in his gas mask, throwing windows open to clear the place out. Peering into crannies. He glanced into the utility closet where the furnace and water heater were. He was about to turn away when something caught his eye—a boot. He went around behind the furnace and found that the boot was attached to a body.

Not a dead body. A live deputy, neatly tied up and gagged, wearing only his drawers and shirt sleeves. Shorty, the smallest of the deputies.

"Oh, no," Jode said.

By the time he reached the front door he heard the mesh of the car's starter. The car drove away fast.

"My car," he said to the Rincon sheriff. "She's got my damn car."

"That deputy in the gas mask leaving the house—"

"That was her."

The Rincon sheriff threw his hat violently to the floor. Jode went outside and watched the dust diminish in the moonlit distance, silver on the hills.

The two men looked at each other. The Rincon sheriff's mouth began to twitch. Then they both started to laugh.

Jode was half-asleep in the swivel chair behind his desk. It was getting dark and the deputies went around the room turning on the lamps. After all these weeks they were still gossiping about Maria Skelton. A legend had started up.

"Maybe she's dead. Out there in the hills someplace."

"Me, I heard she's down in Mexico getting up an army of mercenaries to come back and wipe out the Keenmeier mill."

"Naw. I heard she went back to Hollywood. Getting her face fixed up by one of them plastic surgeons so nobody'll ever recognize her. Wants to get a job in the movies."

Jode said, "All of you shut up. I've heard all I care to hear about the woman."

And then Maria walked into his office.

She didn't come in voluntarily. She was handcuffed to Vickers, the FBI agent. Vickers was yawning with great apparent fatigue. "I want her locked up for the night so I can get some sleep before I have to drive her the rest of the way down to Phoenix."

They put her in a cell. Jode said, "What about the handcuffs?"

"She keeps the handcuffs on. Damn slippery eel!" The FBI man glared at Maria and returned with Jode to the front office. Jode noticed the fingernail scratches on Vickers's face.

Vickers said, "I spotted her out in bare-eye daylight over in Albuquerque of all places. She was coming out of a bar drunk as a coot. She crossed state lines getting to Albuquerque, and they found your car down in Socorro, so that makes it a federal case. My case." Vickers challenged Jode to dispute it. Jode didn't say anything.

Without asking permission, Vickers used the phone to call his district office in Phoenix. Listening to him talk, Jode knew what the FBI man was thinking: It was only a three-hour drive to Phoenix on the Interstate and Vickers couldn't be *that* tired, but he obviously wanted to trundle into Phoenix in the morning instead of the middle of the night because he wanted plenty of sunlight for the cameras. He wanted the news media to have plenty of time to set up for the triumphant arrival.

Jode had no love for the FBI man.

"You can sack out in the side room there. The night-duty cot."

Vickers didn't thank him, just went into the side room and shut the door, yawning ostentatiously.

Jode went back into the cells and shooed the wide-eyed deputies out. Maria was glaring at them like a caged cougar. When they left she glared at Jode the same way.

He said, "You may as well get some sleep."

"I don't need any sleep." She was still half-drunk, he saw.

"That was pretty dumb, blowing up the paper mill."

"No. What was dumb was two things. I didn't blow up enough of it. And I got spotted by the watchman. Those things were dumb. Blowing up the mill wasn't dumb. That stinking paper mill. Listen, if I get another chance at it I'll finish the job."

Jode said, "What's it like being a movie star?"

"That puking paper mill," she said. "Ruining the earth. Poisoning the planet."

"Is it kind of fun out there in Hollywood? Wild parties like they say?"

"You let me get another load of dynamite out there and we'll see about that paper mill."

The office was a hubbub, all the deputies excitedly talking. Jode said, "I'm fed up. That FBI man's trying to sleep. Now you can all get in your cars and go home or go out and patrol the county highways. Doesn't make any nevermind to me, but just get yourselves out of here."

When he was alone in the office he looked in on Vickers. The FBI man was pretending to be asleep on the cot. After a few moments he began to snore. Jode made a face and shut the door, closing out the offending sound. He went back to the desk but didn't sit down. A thought had exploded into his mind. He went back into the cells.

She glared at him. He stood at the door and spoke. "Funny about Hollywood. I mean the way celebrities sometimes get to be movies stars. Athletes, they do it all the time—Jim Brown, Joe Namath. You got in the movies because you were a rodeo star, right? All it takes is some kind of famousness, don't matter what kind. You can get into the movies, right? A cop like Eddie Egan, for example—he's in that TV series now."

"It helps if you can act."

"What?"

"That was my problem, the reason I didn't last in pictures. I had the looks and I could ride a horse. Period."

All this time Jode was thinking very fast. Abruptly he left the cellblock.

He set things up swiftly. He took a rifle and a box of cartridges outdoors and put them in his jeep. He detached the glass face of the fuel gauge, which read nearly empty because he'd been meaning to fill it on his way home for supper but had forgotten. He broke off a piece of a paper match and used it to wedge the fuel needle over against the FULL mark. Then he replaced the glass. He drove the jeep around to the front and parked it in the No Parking zone and went back into the office, leaving the keys dangling in the ignition.

Vickers was genuinely asleep by now. Carefully Jode relieved him of the keys to the handcuffs.

In the cells he motioned Maria to come to the barred door. She hung back.

"I just want to take those things off your hands."

"What for?"

"You don't need them inside a cell, for Pete's sake."

"What about Vickers?"

"The hell with Vickers."

"You can say that again."

He unlocked the handcuffs and took them off her wrists. She watched him dubiously.

Then he unlocked the cell door. He didn't open it, but she knew it was unlocked. He went away, back to the office.

He crept into the side room, then silently and carefully placed the handcuffs, the handcuff keys, and the cell-door keys on the blanket beside the sleeping Vickers.

When he withdrew from the room he closed the door on Vickers and went back to his desk and sat.

After a while Maria came suspiciously into the room.

"Just one thing," Jode said. "Anybody asks, that FBI guy went soft on you, turned you loose."

She didn't answer.

"It doesn't matter what you say, lady, they'll take my word over yours. I'm just telling you what to say to make it easier on yourself."

"Why?"

"Maybe I just don't like the FBI."

"Nuts."

Jode smiled. "Don't try the main roads. I'll have to set up roadblocks. You head back in the hill country. You got a few hours while I make noise around here."

"Jode, you're crazy or what?"

"You're pretty good back in the hills. Raised on the Reservation, right? But I'm just a little better. I'm going to catch you."

Now she smiled. She didn't speak. Her smile was as much as *That'll be the day, Jode. Old man.*

Fifty-one? Old?

She tossed her head and strode out.

In a moment Jode heard the sound of the jeep rolling away. He smiled.


He gave her twenty minutes to get clear of town, then he got on the radio and had the roadblocks set up. A couple of deputies came in for instructions. Vickers was waking up; Jode opened the door and the deputies looked in at Vickers as he sat up, looking in bafflement at the keys and handcuffs on the bed.

Jode said, "I step out for fifteen minutes and look what happens. She must've seduced him or something."

The deputies restrained Vickers when he tried to get to Jode.


When the undersheriff arrived, rubbing sleep from his eyes, Jode told him to hold the fort. "I got an idea where she might be. You keep tabs on my roadblocks. I'll be in touch—may take a day or two. Keep hunting, right?"

Jode got in his sheriff car and drove toward the mountains. He went up some back roads, found nothing, tried other back roads. She hadn't had much gas.

Probably she'd head for the Reservation, he reasoned. And finally he found the jeep up in the foothills near the Reservation fence where Maria had run out of gas. He looked inside and saw the fuel gauge still jammed over on the FULL mark. He lifted the faceplate off and removed the piece of match. The needle fell over to EMPTY.

Jode took the rotor out of his own car, disabling it so that Maria couldn't double back and steal it. You couldn't count on her not knowing how to hot-wire a car; she was a pretty astute lady. Then he looked up at the towering mountains ahead. There was a whole range of them between here and the Biscuit.

He went back to the car, got out a backpack, strapped it on, and slung the rifle over his shoulder.

And started tracking. On foot.

Her spoor took him high, back into the mountain passes. Once he found a place where she had stopped and thought about setting up an ambush. He looked back down the slopes from this point—he could see for miles, all the way out onto the plain to the town. So she'd seen him coming after her. She knew he was back there. But she'd decided against waiting for him.

She had something else on her mind.

The paper mill, he reckoned.

He kept climbing. He was going to have to catch her fast because he'd given her this chance, and she'd meant it when she'd said she'd take care of that paper mill. It put an urgency in him, because he knew if he didn't nail her fast there wouldn't be much in the way of headlines for him.

So he put on an added burst of speed.

And walked right into her trap.

It was just on sundown. She disarmed him efficiently. At gunpoint she forced him to build a fire; then she told him to take off his belt and make a loop, and when she had him the way she wanted him she sat down on his rear and pulled the belt up tight, fastening his hands together behind his back. She used a rifle sling on his feet and when he was trussed up properly she retreated to the fire.

She said, "I didn't see the point in the both of us freezing to death in the dark. This way I can keep an eye on you and at the same time we can have a nice cozy fire. Besides, you didn't put any food in the jeep."

"Sorry. I forgot."

She raided his pack for food. Jode said, "How about me?"

"Suffer. I'm not untying your hands. And I'm damned if I'll spoon-feed you."

So he went hungry.

After a while he said, "You could just kill me, I suppose."

"What for?"

"I'm going to make trouble for you otherwise."

"Well, I don't kill people. What do you think I am?"

"You don't mind blowing up buildings."

"This is Friday night, Jode. Sunday's my day for blowing up buildings. With nobody in them to get hurt."

"You got the dynamite right handy, have you?"

"Right where I left it. Not two hundred yards upstream from the mill. Cached it in a beaver hole by the riverbank."

"Well, then you've got the whole thing figured out, haven't you?"

"Sure have."

"Except one thing."

She said, "What thing?"

"Me. I don't aim to let you do it."

"You don't have a whole lot of choice, Jode."

He considered that. "Well, look, you may blow up the building all right, but sooner or later I'm going to catch you."

"Somebody will. I doubt it'll be you. You're not fast enough."

She washed the last of her meal down with coffee, glanced at him, made a face, and brought the coffee over to him. He tipped his head back and she gave him all he wanted to drink. Close up to him that way she seemed small and fragile; he marveled at her physical stamina. She was a good-looking woman, he couldn't deny it. How old did she have to be? Well, somewhere short of forty, he reckoned. But not far short of it. She could have passed for a lot less, though.

"If you know you're going to get nailed anyway, why do it?"

"Because it's got to be done. The damn paper mills of the world are destroying everything anybody ever had that was worth living for. I'll tell you, that paper mill is everything that's wrong with the world. They run it with a big computer that just doesn't listen. The computers run the industrialists and the polluters—they just think they're human beings. The computers run the government too. Government just sits by while the paper mill ruins my marriage and my ranch and the whole damn world."

"You going to rail against everything that's happened since the year eighteen and twelve?"

"I'm talking about paper mills and everything they stand for. Among other things, of course, they stand for paper. The world is strangling to death, Jode, in a big old bureaucratic snarl of paper. How many forms and reports you got to fill out every time you go and arrest somebody for denting his neighbor's car or letting his dog loose on private property?"

"Well, you do have a point there."

"Somebody has got to stand up and make a very loud statement right here and now about the damn paper mills in the world, Jode. Because if we just let them go on and on the way they're going now, the whole world is going to drown in a sea of paper and get poisoned to death by the junk that comes out of those flumes in the river and those smokestacks on the top. And I'm just the person to make a very loud statement about all that. I've had plenty of practice being loud and obstreperous and obnoxious. I've been a pain in the neck to everybody ever knew me. It's my chance to do my penance, and I'm taking it. Man I wish I had a drink. You haven't got any puma sweat in that pack, by any chance?"

"No. I had a couple beers, but I drank them on the way up."

"Inconsiderate of you."

"Yeah, well if I'd known we were going to have a picnic together I'd have saved them."

"That paper mill's ruining the whole valley under the Biscuit."

"You already said that."

"Maybe this time you're listening."

"Lady, what if I agree with you? It still doesn't matter. I still got the laws to enforce."

"Why? That law is wrong, Jode, and you know it. Any law

that lets a computer poison the earth for the people is wrong."

"The Keenmeier brothers aren't computers. They're real. I've met them."

"The Keenmeier brothers are pencil-pushing accountants. All they know is numbers. You call that a human being?"

"Well—"

"You think I'm some kind of ecology freak?"

"I don't know, Maria. All I know is I'm the sheriff and you're the bad guy and I've got to arrest you and take you in."

"Well, you didn't do a very good job of that, did you?"

"We're still a long way from the finish line," he said. And then he realized what was happening. How distracting she was being. Trying to get his guard down, trying to make sure he was too occupied seeing her side of it and sympathizing about her plight to worry about escaping.

He thought about all those TV cameras again. Hollywood. It brought him back to reality. He started burning his brain to figure out a way to get loose and get the drop on Maria. There had to be a way.

But he was still trussed up at dawn when Maria said, "So long," and walked away into the mountains, heading down-slope toward the pass by the Biscuit and the valley below—toward the ranch, the river, and the Keenmeier paper mill.

Feverishly Jode tried to get loose. He started shredding the flesh off his wrists, but the belts were tight.

It took him nearly two hours of rubbing the belt against the blade of a quartz outcrop before the leather parted. He unstrapped his feet and stood up, a bit wobbly and cramped. He stamped around to quicken the circulation.

Then he started down the mountain.

He kept imagining the headlines. His future when Hollywood filmed "The Ben Jode Story" with Jode himself playing the title role. He ran pell-mell down the canyons.

"Now quit this," he told himself, "don't be so stupid. You twist your ankle you'll never catch up." So he forced himself to slow down and move with reasonable care through the rocks.

He still had the rifle sling. He'd left the near-empty pack up on the mountain because it would only have slowed him down;

he'd eaten and drunk what he could and now he was traveling light. He had a use for the rifle sling; everything else had been superfluous.

It took him the rest of the day to get down onto the slope of the Biscuit with the cliffs looming high above him. The valley was still ten miles away, but he kept going in the night—it was a quarter moon, enough to see by, and he knew damn well *she* wouldn't stop. She had that Sunday morning appointment at the paper mill. And anyhow there was no need for light to follow her tracks. He didn't need to follow tracks. He knew where she was going.

It must have been three in the morning when he finally came down off the foothills and into the valley. So footsore he could hardly keep moving, but he did.

From a hillside he surveyed the night. Dark spots on yonder hills might be scrubs and might be grazing horses; he kept looking until one of the scrubs moved and he knew it was a horse. Maybe half a mile down. He went that way.

This hour of the night a horse was bound to be skittish and he worked his way carefully, staying downwind, making a loop in the rifle sling. An ambush wasn't going to work; he came around a piñon slowly into the horse's eyeline and started speaking with soft persuasion.

"Ho boy, take it easy now, ho."

He kept talking while the Appaloosa eyed him suspiciously. It snorted a couple of times and pawed the earth. A gelding, about fourteen hands. Handsome spotted coat. Bright-eyed, a young one. He kept talking amiably.

"Gentle down now, ho boy, ho."

The gelding whickered and then he had the loop around its muzzle. He patted the horse's neck and talked to it for a while before he swung up bareback, clinging to the end of the rifle sling that he kept wrapped around his knuckles.

The horse pitched him off, but he made it a point to keep his grip on the end of the sling. He climbed on again and got bucked off again, but after the third try the horse was resigned to the idea and only did a few token scampers before settling down.

Jode eased his bruised hip to one side and rode awkwardly, sitting on one buttock mostly, walking the horse for the first half-mile or so. Then he knew that wasn't going to do. He wasn't the only one out here with a reason to snag a horse—and these were Maria's horses. She'd have snagged one a lot faster than Jode did. So she still had a good jump on him and he had to move as fast as the horse could take him.

He came over the last hill and got off the horse, turned it loose, and threw the rifle sling around his waist, cinching it up in case there'd be a later use for it. He ran down into the trees, guided by the sound of the river somewhere in the pines.

He came in through the woods and found Maria skulking near the mill—moving crouched over, backing up—paying out wire.

Jode searched the trees swiftly and found the plunger about forty yards behind her. She was still backing toward it, uncoiling the wire. It meant she'd already set the charges under the mill and she was ready to hook up the wires and blow the detonators. He was just in time.

He crept up behind the plunger and waited behind a tree until she backed right up to him and then he grabbed her.

She struggled so much that she put him in mind of a wolverine he'd cornered once. But he got the rifle sling around her and pinioned her arms with it. Neither of them cried out; it was a silent struggle, and he had the advantage of weight. He used her belt to bind her wrists and then he sat her down to tie her ankles. She glared her rage at him.

Jode grinned. "Guess I knew one more shortcut than you did. Did I tell you my daddy used to take me hunting up along the Biscuit all the time?"

"Well, I guess you got your movie deal."

"Bet your bottom."

She sat there staring through her frustrated tears at the paper mill over there through the trees. The night watchman sat in his car drinking coffee. Water frothed over the rocks and Jode saw the fantastic colors.

"Beautiful, aren't they?" she said.

"What?"

"Another five years every tree on that bank will be dead. That stuff gets into the roots."

The water swirled over the fancy colors in the rocks. Jode looked at the ugly stains on the pines, at the smoke stains on the stacks of the mill. He smelled the pervasive stink.

He heard the car before he saw it. He looked that way, saw it flickering through the pines, recognized it, and therefore wasn't surprised when it pulled in beside the watchman's car and Jode saw the man in the gray business suit at the wheel.

Vickers glared around with hard, angry eyes.

So the FBI man wasn't as dumb as he seemed. He'd figured this out for himself.

"Well, hell," Jode said. He fixed the wires onto the plunger.

"What the hell you doing, Jode?" She was excited.

Jode pushed the plunger and the blast threw him back flat on the earth.

Pieces of paper mill hurtled through the forest. A wave of sudden heat swept over him, curling the pine needles around them.

He kept his arms over his face until the debris settled. When he sat up he saw the two cars half-buried under debris. A door opened, shoving stuff aside. Vickers came out and stood on top of the junkpile. The watchman came struggling out.

Jode pushed her down—slowly because it was movement, not presences, that Vickers would see if he looked. On the ground he worked the leather bindings loose and freed her. Then they crept, belly-flat and worm-slow, until they were far back in the shadowed woods.

When he looked back he could see the two men climbing through the rubble. Nothing left of the mill above its foundation. A tall, heavy pine had toppled across the site. He said, "You used enough dynamite this time for sure."

"Jode, what on earth did you do that for?"

He considered the wreckage; he took her hand and walked her away through the pines, and after a little while he began unaccountably to laugh. "Beats hell out of me, honey."

*Each of Bill Pronzini's fine stories is quite different from the others. He can write chilling suspense (especially in his frequent collaborations with Barry Malzberg) or nostalgic mood pieces or straight detection. In the story that follows he's managed to combine nostalgia with detection to produce one of his best stories to date.*

# BILL PRONZINI
## Smuggler's Island

The first I heard that somebody had bought Smuggler's Island was late on a cold, foggy morning in May. Handy Manners and Davey and I had just brought the *Jennie Too* into the Camaroon Bay wharf, loaded with the day's limit in salmon—silvers mostly, with a few big kings—and Handy had gone inside the processing shed at Bay Fisheries to call for the tally clerk and the portable scales. I was helping Davey hoist up the hatch covers, and I was thinking that he handled himself fine on the boat and what a shame it'd be if he decided eventually that he didn't want to go into commercial fishing as his livelihood. A man likes to see his only son take up his chosen profession. But Davey was always talking about traveling around Europe, seeing some of the world, maybe finding a career he liked better than fishing. Well, he was only nineteen. Decisions don't come quick or easy at that age.

Anyhow, we were working on the hatch covers when I heard somebody call my name. I glanced up, and Pa and Abner Frawley were coming toward us from down-wharf, where the café was. I was a little surprised to see Pa out on a day like this; he usually stayed home with Jennie when it was overcast and windy because the fog and cold air aggravated his lumbago.

The two of them came up and stopped, Pa puffing on one of his home-carved meerschaum pipes. They were both seventy-two and long-retired—Abner from a manager's job at the cannery a mile up the coast, Pa from running the general store in the village—and they'd been cronies for at least half their lives. But that was

Copyright © 1977 by Bill Pronzini. Reprinted by permission of the author. First published in *Alfred Hitchcock's Mystery Magazine*.

where all resemblance between them ended. Abner was short and round and white-haired, and always had a smile and a joke for everybody. Pa, on the other hand, was tall and thin and dour; if he'd smiled any more than four times in the forty-seven years since I was born I can't remember it. Abner had come up from San Francisco during the Depression, but Pa was a second-generation native of Camaroon Bay, his father having emigrated from Ireland during the short-lived potato boom in the early 1900s. He was a good man and a decent father, which was why I'd given him a room in our house when Ma died six years ago, but I'd never felt close to him.

He said to me, "Looks like a good catch, Verne."

"Pretty good," I said. "How come you're out in this weather?"

"Abner's idea. He dragged me out of the house."

I looked at Abner. His eyes were bright, the way they always got when he had a choice bit of news or gossip to tell. He said, "Fella from Los Angeles went and bought Smuggler's Island. Can you beat that?"

"Bought it?" I said. "You mean outright?"

"Yep. Paid the county a hundred thousand cash."

"How'd you hear about it?"

"Jack Kewin, over to the real-estate office."

"Who's the fellow who bought it?"

"Name's Roger Vauclain," Abner said. "Jack don't know any more about him. Did the buying through an agent."

Davey said, "Wonder what he wants with it?"

"Maybe he's got ideas of hunting treasure," Abner said and winked at him. "Maybe he heard about what's hidden in those caves."

Pa gave him a look. "Old fool," he said.

Davey grinned, and I smiled a little and turned to look to where Smuggler's Island sat wreathed in fog half a mile straight out across the choppy harbor. It wasn't much to look at, from a distance or up close. Just one big oblong chunk of eroded rock about an acre and a half in size, surrounded by a lot of little islets. It had a few stunted trees and shrubs, and a long headland where gulls built their nests, and a sheltered cove on the lee shore where you could put in a small boat. That was about all there was to it—except for those caves Abner had spoken of.

They were located near the lee cove and you could only get into them at low tide. Some said caves honeycombed the whole underbelly of the island, but those of us who'd ignored warnings from our parents as kids and gone exploring in them knew that this wasn't so. There were three caves and two of them had branches that led deep into the rock, but all of the tunnels were dead ends.

This business of treasure being hidden in one of those caves was just so much nonsense, of course—sort of a local legend that nobody took seriously. What the treasure was supposed to be was two million dollars in greenbacks that had been hidden by a rackets courier during Prohibition, when he'd been chased to the island by a team of Revenue agents. There was also supposed to be fifty cases of high-grade moonshine secreted there.

The bootlegging part of it had a good deal of truth though. This section of the northern California coast was a hotbed of illegal liquor traffic in the days of the Volstead Act, and the scene of several confrontations between smugglers and Revenue agents; half a dozen men on both sides had been killed, or had turned up missing and presumed dead. The way the bootleggers worked was to bring ships down from Canada outfitted as distilleries— big stills in their holds, bottling equipment, labels for a dozen different kinds of Canadian whiskey—and anchor them twenty-five miles offshore. Then local fishermen and imported hirelings would go out in their boats and carry the liquor to places along the shore, where trucks would be waiting to pick it up and transport it down to San Francisco or east into Nevada. Smuggler's Island was supposed to have been a short-term storage point for whiskey that couldn't be trucked out right away, which may or may not have been a true fact. At any rate, that was how the island got its name.

Just as I turned back to Pa and Abner, Handy came out of the processing shed with the tally clerk and the scales. He was a big, thick-necked man, Handy, with red hair and a temper to match; he was also one of the best mates around and knew as much about salmon trolling and diesel engines as anybody in Camaroon Bay. He'd been working for me eight years, but he wouldn't be much longer. He was saving up to buy a boat of his own and only needed another thousand or so to swing the down payment.

Abner told him right away about this Roger Vauclain buying Smuggler's Island. Handy grunted and said, "Anybody that'd want those rocks out there has to have rocks in his head."

"Who do you imagine he is?" Davey asked.

"One of those damn-fool rich people probably," Pa said. "Buy something for no good reason except that it's there and they want it."

"But why Smuggler's Island in particular?"

"Got a fancy name, that's why. Now he can say to his friends, why look here, I own a place up north called Smuggler's Island, supposed to have treasure hidden on it."

I said, "Well, whoever he is and whyever he bought it, we'll find out eventually. Right now we've got a catch to unload."

"Sure is a puzzler though, ain't it, Verne?" Abner said.

"It is that," I admitted. "It's a puzzler, all right."

If you live in a small town or village, you know how it is when something happens that has no immediate explanation. Rumors start flying, based on few or no facts, and every time one of them is retold to somebody else it gets exaggerated. Nothing much goes on in a place like Camaroon Bay anyhow—conversation is pretty much limited to the weather and the actions of tourists and how the salmon are running or how the crabs seem to be thinning out a little more every year. So this Roger Vauclain buying Smuggler's Island got a lot more lip service paid to it than it would have someplace else.

Jack Kewin didn't find out much about Vauclain, just that he was some kind of wealthy resident of southern California. But that was enough for the speculations and the rumors to build on. During the next week I heard from different people that Vauclain was a real-estate speculator who was going to construct a small private club on the island; that he was a retired bootlegger who'd worked the coast during Prohibition and had bought the island for nostalgic reasons; that he was a front man for a movie company that was going to film a big spectacular in Camaroon Bay and blow up the island in the final scene. None of these rumors made much sense, but that didn't stop people from spreading them and half-believing in them.

Then, one night while we were eating supper Abner came knocking at the front door of our house on the hill above the village. Davey went and let him in, and he sat down at the table next to Pa. One look at him was enough to tell us that he'd come with news.

"Just been talking to Lloyd Simms," he said as Jennie poured him a cup of coffee. "Who do you reckon just made a reservation at the Camaroon Inn?"

"Who?" I asked.

"Roger Vauclain himself. Lloyd talked to him on the phone less than an hour ago, says he sounded pretty hard-nosed. Booked a single room for a week, be here on Thursday."

"Only a single room?" Jennie said. "Why, I'm disappointed, Abner. I expected he'd be traveling with an entourage." She's a practical woman and when it comes to things she considers nonsense, like all the hoopla over Vauclain and Smuggler's Island, her sense of humor sharpens into sarcasm.

"Might be others coming up later," Abner said seriously.

Davey said, "Week's a long time for a rich man to spend in a place like Camaroon Bay. I wonder what he figures to do all that time?"

"Tend to his island, probably," I said.

"Tend to it?" Pa said. "Tend to what? You can walk over the whole thing in two hours."

"Well, there's always the caves, Pa."

He snorted. "Grown man'd have to be a fool to go wandering in those caves. Tide comes in while he's inside, he'll drown for sure."

"What time's he due in on Thursday?" Davey asked Abner.

"Around noon, Lloyd says. Reckon we'll find out then what he's planning to do with the island."

"Not planning to do anything with it, I tell you," Pa said. "Just wants to *own* it."

"We'll see," Abner said. "We'll see."

Thursday was clear and warm, and it should have been a good day for salmon; but maybe the run had started to peter out, because it took us until almost noon to make the limit. It was after two o'clock before we got the catch unloaded and weighed in at Bay Fisheries. Davey had some errands to run and Handy had logged enough extra time, so I took the *Jennie Too* over to the commercial slips myself and stayed aboard her to hose down the decks. When I was through with that I set about replacing the port outrigger line because it had started to weaken and we'd been having trouble with it.

I was doing that when a tall man came down the ramp from the quay and stood just off the bow, watching me. I didn't pay much attention to him; tourists stop by to rubberneck now and then, and if you encourage them they sometimes hang around so you can't get any work done. But then this fellow slapped a hand against his leg, as if he were annoyed, and called out in a loud voice, "Hey, you there. Fisherman."

I looked at him then, frowning. I'd heard that tone before: sharp, full of self-granted authority. Some city people are like that; to them, anybody who lives in a rural village is a low-class hick. I didn't like it and I let him see that in my face. "You talking to me?"

"Who else would I be talking to?"

I didn't say anything. He was in his forties, smooth-looking, and dressed in white ducks and a crisp blue windbreaker. If nothing else, his eyes were enough to make you dislike him immediately; they were hard and unfriendly and said that he was used to getting his own way.

He said, "Where can I rent a boat?"

"What kind of boat? To go sport fishing?"

"No, not to go sport fishing. A small cruiser."

"There ain't any cruisers for rent here."

He made a disgusted sound, as if he'd expected that. "A big outboard then," he said. "Something seaworthy."

"It's not a good idea to take a small boat out of the harbor," I said. "The ocean along here is pretty rough—"

"I don't want advice," he said. "I want a boat big enough to get me out to Smuggler's Island and back. Now who do I see about it?"

"Smuggler's Island?" I looked at him more closely. "Your name happen to be Roger Vauclain, by any chance?"

"That's right. You heard about me buying the island, I suppose. Along with everybody else in this place."

"News gets around," I said mildly.

"About that boat," he said.

"Talk to Ed Hawkins at Bay Marine on the wharf. He'll find something for you."

Vauclain gave me a curt nod and started to turn away.

I said, "Mind if I ask *you* a question now?"

He turned back. "What is it?"

"People don't go buying islands very often," I said, "particularly one like Smuggler's. I'd be interested to know your plans for it."

"You and every other damned person in Camaroon Bay."

I held my temper. "I was just asking. You don't have to give me an answer."

He was silent for a moment. Then he said, "What the hell, it's no secret. I've always wanted to live on an island, and that one out there is the only one around I can afford."

I stared at him. "You mean you're going to *build* on it?"

"That surprises you, does it?"

"It does," I said. "There's nothing on Smuggler's Island but rocks and a few trees and a couple of thousand nesting gulls. It's fogbound most of the time, and even when it's not the wind blows at thirty knots or better."

"I like fog and wind and ocean," Vauclain said. "I like isolation. I don't like people much. That satisfy you?"

I shrugged. "To each his own."

"Exactly," he said, and went away up the ramp.

I worked on the *Jennie Too* another hour, then I went over to the Wharf Café for a cup of coffee and a piece of pie. When I came inside I saw Pa, Abner, and Handy sitting at one of the copper-topped tables. I walked over to them.

They already knew that Vauclain had arrived in Camaroon Bay. Handy was saying, "Hell, he's about as friendly as a shark. I was over to Ed Hawkins's place shooting the breeze when he came in and demanded Ed get him a boat. Threw his weight around for fifteen minutes until Ed agreed to rent him his own Chris-Craft. Then he paid for the rental in cash, slammed two fifties on Ed's desk like they were singles and Ed was a beggar."

I sat down. "He's an eccentric, all right," I said. "I talked to him for a few minutes myself about an hour ago."

"Eccentric?" Abner said, and snorted. "That's just a name they give to people who never learned manners or good sense."

Pa said to me, "He tell you what he's fixing to do with Smuggler's Island, Verne?"

"He did, yep."

"Told Abner too, over to the Inn." Pa shook his head, glowering, and lighted a pipe. "Craziest damned thing I ever heard. Build a house on that mess of rock, live out there. Crazy, that's all."

"That's a fact," Handy said. "I'd give him more credit if he was planning to hunt for that bootlegger's treasure."

"Well, I'm sure not going to relish having him for a neighbor," Abner said. "Don't guess anybody else will either."

None of us disagreed with that. A man likes to be able to get along with his neighbors, rich or poor. Getting along with Vauclain, it seemed, was going to be a chore for everybody.

In the next couple of days Vauclain didn't do much to improve his standing with the residents of Camaroon Bay. He snapped at merchants and waitresses, ignored anybody who tried to strike up a conversation with him, and complained twice to Lloyd Simms about the service at the Inn. The only good thing about him, most people were saying, was that he spent the better part of his days on Smuggler's Island—doing what, nobody knew exactly—and his nights locked in his room. Might have been he was drawing up plans there for the house he intended to build on the island.

Rumor now had it that Vauclain was an architect, one of those independents who'd built up a reputation, like Frank Lloyd Wright in the old days, and who only worked for private individuals and companies. This was probably true since it originated with Jack Kewin; he'd spent a little time with Vauclain and wasn't one to spread unfounded gossip. According to Jack, Vauclain had learned that the island was for sale more than six months ago and had been up twice before by helicopter from San Francisco to get an aerial view of it.

That was the way things stood on Sunday morning when Jennie and I left for church at 10:00. Afterward we had lunch at a place up the coast, and then, because the weather was cool but still clear, we went for a drive through the redwood country. It was almost 5:00 when we got back home.

Pa was in bed—his lumbago was bothering him, he said—and Davey was gone somewhere. I went into our bedroom to change out of my suit. While I was in there the telephone rang, and Jennie called out that it was for me.

When I picked up the receiver Lloyd Simms's voice said, "Sorry to bother you, Verne, but if you're not busy I need a favor."

"I'm not busy, Lloyd. What is it?"

"Well, it's Roger Vauclain. He went out to the island this morning like usual, and he was supposed to be back at three to take a telephone call. Told me to make sure I was around then, the call was important—you know the way he talks. The call came in right on schedule, but Vauclain didn't. He's still not back, and the party calling him has been ringing me up every half hour, demanding I get hold of him. Something about a bid that has to be delivered first thing tomorrow morning."

"You want me to go out to the island, Lloyd?"

"If you wouldn't mind," he said. "I don't much care about Vauclain, the way he's been acting, but this caller is driving me up a wall. And it could be something's the matter with Vauclain's boat; can't get it started or something. Seems kind of funny he didn't come back when he said he would."

I hesitated. I didn't much want to take the time to go out to Smuggler's Island; but then if there was a chance Vauclain was in trouble I couldn't very well refuse to help.

"All right," I said. "I'll see what I can do."

We rang off, and I explained to Jennie where I was going and why. Then I drove down to the basin where the pleasure-boat slips were and took the tarp off Davey's sixteen-foot Sportliner inboard. I'd bought it for him on his sixteenth birthday, when I figured he was old enough to handle a small boat of his own, but I used it as much as he did. We're not so well off that we can afford to keep more than one pleasure craft.

The engine started right up for a change—usually you have to choke it several times on cool days—and I took her out of the slips and into the harbor. The sun was hidden by overcast now and the wind was up, building small whitecaps, running fog-banks in from the ocean but shredding them before they reached the shore. I followed the south jetty out past the breakwater and into open sea. The water was choppier there, the color of gunmetal, and the wind was pretty cold; I pulled the collar of my jacket up and put on my gloves to keep my hands from numbing on the wheel.

When I neared the island I swung around to the north shore

and into the lee cove. Ed Hawkins's Chris-Craft was tied up there, all right, bow and stern lines made fast to outcroppings on a long, natural stone dock. I took the Sportliner in behind it, climbed out onto the bare rock, and made her fast. On my right, waves broke over and into the mouths of the three caves, hissing long fans of spray. Gulls wheeled screeching above the headland; farther in, scrub oak and cypress danced like line bobbers in the wind. It all made you feel as though you were standing on the edge of the world.

There was no sign of Vauclain anywhere at the cove, so I went up through a tangle of artichoke plants toward the center of the island. The area there was rocky but mostly flat, dotted with undergrowth and patches of sandy earth. I stopped beside a gnarled cypress and scanned from left to right. Nothing but emptiness. Then I walked out toward the headland, hunched over against the pull of the wind. But I didn't find him there either.

A sudden thought came to me as I started back and the hairs prickled on my neck. What if he'd gone into the caves and been trapped there when the tide began to flood? If that was what had happened, it was too late for me to do anything—but I started to run anyway, my eyes on the ground so I wouldn't trip over a bush or a rock.

I was almost back to the cove, coming at a different angle than before, when I saw him.

It was so unexpected that I pulled up short and almost lost my footing on loose rock. The pit of my stomach went hollow. He was lying on his back in a bed of artichokes, one arm flung out and the other wrapped across his chest. There was blood under his arm, and blood spread across the front of his windbreaker. One long look was all I needed to tell me he'd been shot and that he was dead.

Shock and an eerie sense of unreality kept me standing there another few seconds. My thoughts were jumbled; you don't think too clearly when you stumble on a dead man, a murdered man. And it *was* murder, I knew that well enough. There was no gun anywhere near the body, and no way it could have been an accident.

Then I turned, shivering, and ran down to the cove and took

the Sportliner away from there at full throttle to call for the county sheriff.

Vauclain's death was the biggest event that had happened in Camaroon Bay in forty years, and Sunday night and Monday nobody talked about anything else. As soon as word got around that I was the one who'd discovered the body, the doorbell and the telephone didn't stop ringing—friends and neighbors, newspaper people, investigators. The only place I had any peace was on the *Jennie Too* Monday morning, and not much there because Davey and Handy wouldn't let the subject alone while we fished.

By late that afternoon the authorities had questioned just about everyone in the area. It didn't appear they'd found out anything though. Vauclain had been alone when he'd left for the island early Sunday; Abner had been down at the slips then and swore to the fact. A couple of tourists had rented boats from Ed Hawkins during the day, since the weather was pretty good, and a lot of locals were out in the harbor on pleasure craft. But whoever it was who had gone to Smuggler's Island after Vauclain, he hadn't been noticed.

As to a motive for the shooting, there were all sorts of wild speculations. Vauclain had wronged somebody in Los Angeles and that person had followed him here to take revenge. He'd treated a local citizen badly enough to trigger a murderous rage. He'd got in bad with organized crime and a contract had been put out on him. And the most farfetched theory of all: He'd actually uncovered some sort of treasure on Smuggler's Island and somebody'd learned about it and killed him for it. But the simple truth was, nobody had *any* idea why Vauclain was murdered. If the sheriff's department had found any clues on the island or anywhere else, they weren't talking—but they weren't making any arrests either.

There was a lot of excitement, all right. Only underneath it all people were nervous and a little scared. A killer seemed to be loose in Camaroon Bay, and if he'd murdered once, who was to say he wouldn't do it again? A mystery is all well and good when it's happening someplace else, but when it's right on your doorstep you can't help but feel threatened and apprehensive.

I'd had about all the pestering I could stand by 4 o'clock, so I got into the car and drove up the coast to Shelter Cove. That gave me an hour's worth of freedom. But no sooner did I get back to Camaroon Bay, with the intention of going home and locking myself in my basement workshop, than a sheriff's cruiser pulled up behind me at a stop sign and its horn started honking. I sighed and pulled over to the curb.

It was Harry Swenson, one of the deputies who'd questioned me the day before, after I'd reported finding Vauclain's body. We knew each other well enough to be on a first-name basis. He said, "Verne, the sheriff asked me to talk to you again, see if there's anything you might have overlooked yesterday. You mind?"

"No, I don't mind," I said tiredly.

We went into the Inn and took a table at the back of the dining room. A couple of people stared at us, and I could see Lloyd Simms hovering around out by the front desk. I wondered how long it would be before I'd stop being the center of attention every time I went someplace in the village.

Over coffee, I repeated everything that had happened Sunday afternoon. Harry checked what I said with the notes he'd taken; then he shook his head and closed the notebook.

"Didn't really expect you to remember anything else," he said, "but we had to make sure. Truth is, Verne, we're up against it on this thing. Damnedest case I ever saw."

"Guess that means you haven't found out anything positive."

"Not much. If we could figure a motive, we might be able to get a handle on it from that. But we just can't find one."

I decided to give voice to one of my own theories. "What about robbery, Harry?" I asked. "Seems I heard Vauclain was carrying a lot of cash with him and throwing it around pretty freely."

"We thought of that first thing," he said. "No good, though. His wallet was on the body, and there was three hundred dollars in it and a couple of blank checks."

I frowned down at my coffee. "I don't like to say this, but you don't suppose it could be one of these thrill killings we're always reading about?"

"Man, I hope not. That's the worst kind of homicide there is."

We were silent for a minute or so. Then I said, "You find anything at all on the island? Any clues?"

He hesitated. "Well," he said finally, "I probably shouldn't discuss it—but then, you're not the sort to break a confidence. We did find one thing near the body. Might not mean anything, but it's not the kind of item you'd expect to come across out there."

"What is it?"

"A cake of white beeswax," he said.

"Beeswax?"

"Right. Small cake of it. Suggest anything to you?"

"No," I said. "No, nothing."

"Not to us either. Aside from that, we haven't got a thing. Like I said, we're up against it. Unless we get a break in the next couple of days, I'm afraid the whole business will end up in the Unsolved file.—That's unofficial, now."

"Sure," I said.

Harry finished his coffee. "I'd better get moving," he said. "Thanks for your time, Verne."

I nodded, and he stood up and walked out across the dining room. As soon as he was gone, Lloyd came over and wanted to know what we'd been talking about. But I'd begun to feel oddly nervous all of a sudden, and there was something tickling at the edge of my mind. I cut him off short, saying, "Let me be, will you, Lloyd? Just let me be for a minute."

When he drifted off, looking hurt, I sat there and rotated my cup on the table. Beeswax, I thought. I'd told Harry that it didn't suggest anything to me, and yet it did, vaguely. Beeswax. White beeswax. . . .

It came to me then—and along with it a couple of other things, little things, like missing figures in an arithmetic problem. I went cold all over, as if somebody had opened a window and let the wind inside the room. I told myself I was wrong, that it couldn't be. But I wasn't wrong. It made me sick inside, but I wasn't wrong.

I knew who had murdered Roger Vauclain.

When I came into the house I saw him sitting out on the sun deck, just sitting there motionless with his hands flat on his knees, staring out to sea. Or out to where Smuggler's Island sat, shining hard and ugly in the glare of the dying sun.

I didn't go out there right away. First I went into the other rooms to see if anybody else was home, but nobody was. Then, when I couldn't put it off any longer, I got myself ready to face it and walked onto the deck.

He glanced at me as I leaned back against the railing. I hadn't seen much of him since finding the body, or paid much attention to him when I had; but now I saw that his eyes looked different. They didn't blink. They looked at me, they looked past me, but they didn't blink.

"Why'd you do it, Pa?" I said. "Why'd you kill Vauclain?"

I don't know what I expected his reaction to be. But there wasn't any reaction. He wasn't startled, he wasn't frightened, he wasn't anything. He just looked away from me again and sat there like a man who has expected to hear the words for a long time.

I kept waiting for him to say something, to move, to blink his eyes. For one full minute and half of another, he did nothing. Then he sighed, soft and tired, and he said, "I knew somebody'd find out this time." His voice was steady, calm. "I'm sorry it had to be you, Verne."

"So am I."

"How'd you know?"

"You left a cake of white beeswax out there," I said. "Fell out of your pocket when you pulled the gun, I guess. You're just the only person around here who'd be likely to have white beeswax in his pocket, Pa, because you're the only person who hand-carves his own meerschaum pipes. Took me a time to remember that you use wax like that to seal the bowls and give them a luster finish."

He didn't say anything.

"Couple of other things too," I said. "You were in bed yester-day when Jennie and I got home. It was a clear day, no early fog, nothing to aggravate your lumbago. Unless you'd been out someplace where you weren't protected from the wind—some-place like in a boat on open water. Then there was Davey's Sportliner starting right up for me. Almost never does that on cool days unless it's been run recently, and the only person be-sides Davey and me who has a key is you."

He nodded. "It's usually the little things," he said. "I always figured it'd be some little thing that'd finally do it."

"Pa," I said, "why'd you kill him?'

"He had to go and buy the island. Then he had to decide to build a house on it. It couldn't let him do that. I went out there to talk to him, try to get him to change his mind. Took my revolver along, but only just in case; wasn't intending to use it. Only he wouldn't listen to me. Called me an old fool and worse, and then he give me a shove. He was dead before I knew it, seems like."

"What'd him building a house have to do with you?"

"He'd have brought men and equipment out there, wouldn't he? They'd have dug up everything, wouldn't they? They'd have sure dug up the Revenue man."

I thought he was rambling. "Pa. . . ."

"You got a right to know about that too," he said. He blinked then, four times fast. "In 1929 a fella named Frank Eberle and me went to work for the bootleggers. Hauling whiskey. We'd go out maybe once a month in Frank's boat, me acting as shotgun, and we'd bring in a load of 'shine—mostly to Shelter Cove, but sometimes we'd be told to drop it off on Smuggler's for a day or two. It was easy money, and your ma and me needed it, what with you happening along; and what the hell, Frank always said, we were only helping to give the people what they wanted.

"But then one night in 1932 it all went bust. We brought a shipment to the island and just after we started unloading it this man run out of the trees waving a gun and yelling that we were under arrest. A Revenue agent, been lying up there in ambush. Lying alone because he didn't figure to have much trouble, I reckon—and I found out later the government people had bigger fish to fry up to Shelter Cove that night.

"Soon as the agent showed himself, Frank panicked and started to run. Agent put a shot over his head, and before I could think on it I cut loose with the rifle I always carried. I killed him, Verne, I shot that man dead."

He paused, his face twisting with memory. I wanted to say something—but what was there to say?

Pa said, "Frank and me buried him on the island, under a couple of rocks on the center flat. Then we got out of there. I quit the bootleggers right away, but Frank, he kept on with it and got himself killed in a big shoot-out up by Eureka just before Repeal. I knew they were going to get me too someday. Only time kept passing and somehow it never happened, and I almost had myself believing it never would. Then this Vauclain came along. You see now why I couldn't let him build his house?"

"Pa," I said thickly, "it's been forty-five years since all that happened. All anybody'd have dug up was bones. Maybe there's something there to identify the Revenue agent, but there couldn't be anything that'd point to you."

"Yes, there could," he said. "Just like there was something this time—the beeswax and all. There'd have been something, all right, and they'd have come for me."

He stopped talking then, abruptly, like a machine that had been turned off, and swiveled his head away and just sat staring again. There in the sun, I still felt cold. He believed what he'd just said; he honestly believed it.

I knew now why he'd been so dour and moody for most of my life, why he almost never smiled, why he'd never let me get close to him. And I knew something else too: I wasn't going to tell the sheriff any of this. He was my father and he was seventy-two years old; and I'd see to it that he didn't hurt anybody else. But the main reason was, if I let it happen that they really did come for him he wouldn't last a month. In an awful kind of way the only thing that'd been holding him together all these years was his certainty they *would* come someday.

Besides, it didn't matter anyway. He hadn't actually got away with anything. He hadn't committed one unpunished murder, or now two unpunished murders, because there is no such thing. There's just no such thing as the perfect crime.

I walked over and took the chair beside him, and together we sat quiet and looked out at Smuggler's Island. Only I didn't see it very well because my eyes were full of tears.

*Lawrence Block is already well known for his paperback mysteries and is increasingly recognized for his hardbound novels and a dazzling array of novelettes and short stories. This story is not about one of his series detectives like Matt Scudder or Evan Tanner. Rather it's about . . . . Well, read it and you'll see.*

# LAWRENCE BLOCK
## Gentlemen's Agreement

The burglar, a slender and clean-cut chap just past thirty, was rifling a drawer in the bedside table when Archer Trebizond slipped into the bedroom. Trebizond's approach was as catfooted as if he himself were the burglar, a situation which was manifestly not the case. The burglar never did hear Trebizond, absorbed as he was in his perusal of the drawer's contents, and at length he sensed the other man's presence as a jungle beast senses the presence of a predator.

The analogy, let it be said, is scarcely accidental.

When the burglar turned his eyes on Archer Trebizond his heart fluttered and fluttered again, first at the mere fact of discovery, then at his own discovery of the gleaming revolver in Trebizond's hand. The revolver was pointed in his direction, and this the burglar found upsetting.

"Darn it all," said the burglar, approximately, "I could have sworn there was nobody home. I phoned, I rang the bell—"

"I just got here," Trebizond said.

"Just my luck. The whole week's been like that. I dented a fender on Tuesday afternoon, overturned my fish tank the night before last. An unbelievable mess all over the carpet, and I lost a mated pair of African mouthbreeders so rare they don't have a Latin name yet. I'd hate to tell you what I paid for them."

"Hard luck," Trebizond said.

"And just yesterday I was putting away a plate of fettucini and I bit the inside of my mouth. You ever done that? It's murder, and the worst part is you feel so stupid about it. And then you keep biting it over and over again because it sticks out while it's healing. At least I do." The burglar gulped a breath and ran a moist hand over a moister forehead. "And now this," he said.

"This could turn out to be worse than fenders and fish tanks," Trebizond said.

"Don't I know it. You know what I should have done? I should have spent the entire week in bed. I happen to know a safecracker who consults an astrologer before each and every job he pulls. If Jupiter's in the wrong place or Mars is squared with Uranus or something, he won't go in. It sounds ridiculous, doesn't it? And yet it's eight years now since anybody put a handcuff on that man. Now who do you know who's gone eight years without getting arrested?"

"I've never been arrested," Trebizond said.

"Well, you're not a crook."

"I'm a businessman."

The burglar thought of something but let it pass. "I'm going to get the name of his astrologer," he said. "That's just what I'm going to do. Just as soon as I get out of here."

"If you get out of here," Trebizond said. "Alive," Trebizond said.

The burglar's jaw trembled just the slightest bit. Trebizond smiled, and from the burglar's point of view Trebizond's smile seemed to enlarge the black hole in the muzzle of the revolver.

"I wish you'd point that thing somewhere else," he said nervously.

"There's nothing else I want to shoot."

"You don't want to shoot me."

"Oh?"

"You don't even want to call the cops," the burglar went on. "It's really not necessary. I'm sure we can work things out between us, two civilized men coming to a civilized agreement. I've some money on me. I'm an openhanded sort and would be pleased to make a small contribution to your favorite charity, whatever it might be. We don't need policemen to intrude into the private affairs of gentlemen."

The burglar studied Trebizond carefully. This little speech had always gone over rather well in the past, especially with men of substance. It was hard to tell how it was going over now, or if it was going over at all. "In any event," he ended somewhat lamely, "you certainly don't want to shoot me."

"Why not?"

"Oh, blood on the carpet, for a starter. Messy, wouldn't you say? Your wife would be upset. Just ask her and she'll tell you shooting me would be a ghastly idea."

"She's not at home. She'll be out for the next hour or so."

"All the same, you might consider her point of view. And shooting me would be illegal, you know? Not to mention immoral."

"Not illegal," Trebizond remarked.

"I beg your pardon?"

"You're a burglar," Trebizond reminded him. "An unlawful intruder on my property. You have broken and entered. You have invaded the sanctity of my home. I can shoot you where you stand and not get so much as a parking ticket for my trouble."

"Of course you can shoot me in self-defense—"

"Are we on *Candid Camera?*"

"No, but—"

"Is Allen Funt lurking in the shadows?"

"No, but I—"

"In your back pocket. That metal thing. What is it?"

"Just a pry bar."

"Take it out," Trebizond said. "Hand it over. Indeed. A weapon if I ever saw one. I'd state that you attacked me with it and I fired in self-defense. It would be my word against yours, and yours would remain unvoiced since you would be dead. Whom do you suppose the police would believe?"

The burglar said nothing. Trebizond smiled a satisfied smile and put the pry bar in his own pocket. It was a piece of nicely shaped steel and it had a nice heft to it. Trebizond rather liked it.

"Why would you want to kill me?"

"Perhaps I've never killed anyone. Perhaps I'd like to satisfy my curiosity. Or perhaps I got to enjoy killing in the war and have been yearning for another crack at it. There are endless possibilities."

"But—"

"The point is," said Trebizond, "you might be useful to me in that manner. As it is, you're not useful to me at all. And stop hinting about my favorite charity or other euphemisms. I don't want your money. Look about you. I've ample money of my own—that should be obvious. If I were a poor man you wouldn't have breached my threshold. How much money are you talking about, anyway? A couple of hundred dollars?"

"Five hundred," the burglar said.

"A pittance."

"I suppose. There's more at home, but you'd just call that a pittance too, wouldn't you?"

"Undoubtedly." Trebizond shifted the gun to his other hand. "I told you I was a businessman," he said. "Now if there were any way in which you could be more useful to me alive than dead—"

"You're a businessman and I'm a burglar," the burglar said, brightening.

"Indeed."

"So I could steal something for you. A painting? A competitor's trade secrets? I'm really very good at what I do, as a matter of fact, although you wouldn't guess it by my performance tonight. I'm not saying I could whisk the *Mona Lisa* out of the Louvre, but I'm pretty good at your basic hole-and-corner job of everyday burglary. Just give me an assignment and let me show my stuff."

"Hmmmm," said Archer Trebizond.

"Name it and I'll swipe it."

"Hmmmm."

"A car, a mink coat, a diamond bracelet, a Persian carpet, a first edition, bearer bonds, incriminating evidence, eighteen and a half minutes of tape—"

"What was that last?"

"Just my little joke" said the burglar. "A coin collection, a stamp collection, psychiatric records, phonograph records, police records—"

"I get the point."

"I tend to prattle when I'm nervous."

"I've noticed."

"If you could point that thing elsewhere—"

Trebizond looked down at the gun in his hand. The gun continued to point at the burglar.

"No," Trebizond said, with evident sadness. "No, I'm afraid it won't work."

"Why not?"

"In the first place, there's nothing I really need or want. Could you steal me a woman's heart? Hardly. And more to the point, how could I trust you?"

"You could trust me," the burglar said. "You have my word on that."

"My point exactly. I'd have to take your word that your word is good, and where does that lead us? Up the proverbial garden path, I'm afraid. No, once I let you out from under my roof I've lost my advantage. Even if I have a gun trained on you, once you're in the open I can't shoot you with impunity. So I'm afraid—"

"No!"

Trebizond shrugged. "Well, really," he said. "What use are you? What are you good for besides being killed? Can you do anything besides steal, sir?"

"I can make license plates."

"Hardly a valuable talent."

"I know," said the burglar sadly. "I've often wondered why the state bothered to teach me such a pointless trade. There's not even much call for counterfeit license plates, and they've got a monopoly on making the legitimate ones. What else can I do? I must be able to do something. I could shine your shoes, I could polish your car—"

"What do you do when you're not stealing?"

"Hang around," said the burglar. "Go out with ladies. Feed my fish, when they're not all over my rug. Drive my car when I'm not mangling its fenders. Play a few games of chess, drink a can or two of beer, make myself a sandwich—"

"Are you any good?"

"At making sandwiches?"

"At chess."

"I'm not bad."

"I'm serious about this."

"I believe you are," the burglar said. "I'm not your average wood-pusher, if that's what you want to know. I know the openings and I have a good sense of space. I don't have the patience for tournament play, but at the chess club downtown I win more games than I lose."

"You play at the club downtown?"

"Of course. I can't burgle seven nights a week, you know. Who could stand the pressure?"

"Then you *can* be of use to me," Trebizond said.

"You want to learn the game?"

"I know the game. I want you to play chess with me for an hour until my wife gets home. I'm bored, there's nothing in the house to read, I've never cared much for television, and it's hard for me to find an interesting opponent at the chess table."

"So you'll spare my life in order to play chess with me."

"That's right."

"Let me get this straight," the burglar said. "There's no catch to this, is there? I don't get shot if I lose the game or anything tricky like that, I hope."

"Certainly not. Chess is a game that ought to be above gimmickry."

"I couldn't agree more," said the burglar. He sighed a long sigh. "If I didn't play chess," he said, "you wouldn't have shot me, would you?"

"It's a question that occupies the mind, isn't it?"

"It is," said the burglar.


They played in the front room. The burglar drew the white pieces in the first game, opened king's pawn, and played what turned out to be a reasonably imaginative version of the Ruy Lopez. At the sixteenth move Trebizond forced the exchange of knight for rook, and not too long afterward the burglar resigned.

In the second game the burglar played the black pieces and offered the Sicilian Defense. He played a variation that Trebizond wasn't familiar with. The game stayed remarkably even until in the end game the burglar succeeded in developing a passed pawn. When it was clear that he would be able to queen it, Trebizoned tipped over his king, resigning.

"Nice game," the burglar offered.

"You play well."

"Thank you."

"Seem's a pity that . . . ."

His voice trailed off. The burglar shot him an inquiring look. "That I'm wasting myself as a common criminal? Is that what you were going to say?"

"Let it go," Trebizond said. "It doesn't matter."

They began setting up the pieces for the third game when a key slipped into a lock. The lock turned, the door opened, and Melissa Trebizond stepped into the foyer and through it to the living room.

Both men got to their feet. Mrs. Trebizond advanced, a vacant smile on her pretty face. "You found a new friend to play chess with. I'm happy for you."

Trebizond set his jaw. From his back pocket he drew the burglar's pry bar. It had an even nicer heft than he had thought. "Melissa," he said, "I've no need to waste time with a recital of your sins. No doubt you know precisely why you deserve this."

She stared at him, obviously not having understood a word he had said to her, whereupon Archer Trebizond brought the pry bar down on the top of her skull. The first blow sent her to her knees. Quickly he struck her three more times, wielding the metal bar with all his strength, then turned to look into the wide eyes of the burglar.

"You've killed her," the burglar said.

"Nonsense," said Trebizond, taking the bright revolver from his pocket once again.

"Isn't she dead?"

"I hope and pray she is," Trebiozond said, "but I haven't killed her. *You've* killed her."

"I don't understand."

"The police will understand," Trebizond said, and shot the burglar in the shoulder. Then he fired again, more satisfactorily this time, and the burglar sank to the floor with a hole in his heart.

Trebizond scooped the chess pieces into their box, swept up the board, and set about the business of arranging things. He suppressed an urge to whistle. He was, he decided, quite pleased with himself. Nothing was ever entirely useless, not to a man of resources. If fate sent you a lemon you made lemonade.

*Barbara Callahan's stories, often dealing with commonplace things, are fine examples of the everyday gone wrong, as someone once wrote about Cornell Woolrich's work. Here she examines the world of the television soap opera and one of its faithful viewers.*

# BARBARA CALLAHAN
# To Be Continued

I wept when Jason Carruthers told Amanda Armstrong the real reason he couldn't marry her. It was the most moving scene I had ever watched on the daytime TV serial, *To Live and to Love.*

He put his arms around her and said that his love for her almost consumed him. Then he revealed that years ago he had fathered a child, a baby girl. He and the baby's mother had been forbidden by their parents to marry. The baby had been given out for adoption.

There were tears in Jason's eyes as he explained to Amanda that he must find his child before he could marry her and burden her with his great sorrow. His first wife had divorced him because of his anguish over his unknown child. She felt that Jason loved the child more than he did her. But then Cecily, Jason's first wife, was irrational. I disliked her for the entire two years she was on the show.

When Jason asked Amanda to wait for him until he had found his daughter, she sobbed and nodded yes. I knew Amanda would wait. She has character.

After I turned off the TV set, I went to the sofa and sat there thinking quietly for a long time. The only sounds that penetrated my reverie were the beating of my heart and the jubilant howling of the March winds outside my window.

"You've found your father, you've found your father," the winds sang.

I opened the window to admit the winds to the living room. They tumbled in like exuberant children, upsetting the vase on the coffee table and knocking over the picture of Mother, Father, and me. The glass covering the picture shattered, but I didn't care. The part of my life represented in that photograph had ended. Those two people were my adoptive parents. For years I had wondered who my real parents were. After watching *To Live and to Love*, one-half of the deepest mystery of my life was solved.

I knew now who my father was. Jason Carruthers was my father. That's why the winds sang "You've found your father" to me. The winds always understood how much I yearned to know him. I could never talk to anyone about my feelings for my real parents. My adoptive parents became sad whenever I talked about my real father and mother. They thought I didn't love them. I did, but the love I felt did not eliminate my need to know who I belonged to. When I sat on the hill behind our house, I had to confide in the winds.

Dear friends, I told them, as they whirled around the living room, tell Jason Carruthers that I am coming to him. Tell him that the words he spoke to Amanda about his daughter apply to me. Jason said his daughter was born nineteen years ago in New Jersey. She was cared for by a religious social agency until she was three months old. Then she was adopted.

I was born in New Jersey nineteen years ago. I was cared for by a religious social agency for three months before being adopted. That's all I was ever told.

The star of *To Live and to Love* had to be my father. Not only did his daughter's background match mine, but his appearance was similar to mine. He was tall and thin the way I am. He had dark brown eyes and dark brown hair the way I have.

It was imperative that I go to New York immediately. I must reach Jason before he set off on his quest for his daughter. When I found him, we would search for my mother together. It would be easy to find her because Jason had a picture of her in his wallet. He showed it to Amanda Armstrong.

My adoptive parents were at work. I considered leaving a note for them, but I decided not to. If I told them that I had found my real father on *To Live and to Love*, they would send the police after me. They were always telling me that I took daytime serials too seriously. They were upset with me when

I spent twenty-five dollars to send flowers to Melissa Oliver, one of the stars of *The Dawning of Day*, after she had her baby. They didn't understand that it was important for me to send flowers to Melissa because she had decided to keep her baby and not put her up for adoption.

After I packed my bag, I suddenly became frightened. I prodded my mind for the reason and remembered what my adoptive father had said about New York. Muggers, he had said, the city was full of muggers. I went to his bureau drawer and took the gun he kept there. The gun would protect me.

I slid the gun into my pocketbook. I shooed the winds out of the living room and closed the window behind them. They had had a real frolic in there. Picking up the picture of my adoptive parents, I noticed a copy of *Daytime TV* on the floor. After I swept up the glass I put the magazine in my handbag. There was a picture of Jason in it and I wanted him with me.

As I closed the door behind me, I felt a sense of loss. I quickly shook it off because I knew Jason would always let me visit my adoptive parents. They had been good to me.

My business at the bank went smoothly. I withdrew all my savings, which amounted to three hundred dollars. I told the teller I was taking a trip. Then I took a cab to the bus station.

On the bus I had plenty of time to make my plans. I decided to check into a YWCA to conserve money. Then I planned to make the rounds of private detective agencies. I was sure Jason would have hired one to search for his daughter, for me.

During the last few miles of the ride I settled back against the headrest and closed my eyes. The image of Jason and me embracing in the swanky office of a private detective agency filled my heart with joy.

It was so wonderful to be able to put a face into the warm scene of the father-daughter meeting I had dreamed of so many times. I always pictured my father as tall and dark-haired, but his face was always blurry. The scene had become such a part of my life that because of it I lost my job as a file clerk in an insurance company. My boss told me that she could do without an employee who stared into space so much of the time.

During my first week in New York City I learned two things— that three hundred dollars did not last long, and that there were many, many private detective agencies.

The usual reply to my question about their being hired by Jason Carruthers was a frosty: "We do not give out the names of our clients." Only once did a receptionist say something different.

"Jason Carruthers," she said, "that name is sure familiar. Isn't there a guy by that name on *To Live and to Love*? I watch it on my lunch hour. If you're looking for him, honey, you'd better go tripping down the yellow brick road."

She laughed at the joke she thought she had made. When Jason would have me appear with him on *To Live and to Love*, she would regret her poor attempt at humor.

When my rounds of detective agencies proved fruitless, there was only one thing left for me to do. I remembered that the restaurant where Jason was photographed for the magazine was called Sardi's. For three days in a row I went there for lunch, hoping that he would stop there for a rest from his efforts in finding me. On the fourth day I was rewarded.

He came into the restaurant with a man. I scarcely breathed as they took seats not far from me. I ordered dessert so that I could stay longer and watch them, but I was too excited to eat it. I could only stare at his handsome face. But Jason looked tired and somewhat older than he did on TV. The strain of searching for me must be affecting him.

After they had finished their lunch, I followed them outside, standing only a few feet away when Jason said good-bye to his friend. As Jason walked to the curb, I hurried up behind him. I touched his arm when he raised it to flag a cab. He spun around and looked angrily at me. Smiling, I savored the irony of the moment I had long awaited. We would laugh afterward about his initial reaction to me. The brown eyes that Amanda Armstrong had found so irresistible flashed at me.

"I lost that cab because of you," he complained.

"You lost that cab, but you found something more important," I answered.

"Yes," he sighed, "I guess I did. I found a fan. I find them everywhere."

He put his hand into his overcoat pocket and pulled out a piece of paper. He wrote something on it and handed it to me.

It said: "Best wishes, Avery Wilson."

He started back to the curb. I dropped the autograph with

the strange name on it into my pocketbook. My hand brushed against the gun I had brought to New York to protect me from muggers. I took it out. Jason was leaning over to open the back door of a cab when I put the gun against his back. I hated to do that, but it was the only thing I could think of to keep him from riding away from me.

His body jerked forward as if it had been stabbed. Turning halfway around, his eyes focused on the gun in my hand. This time his brown eyes showed terror instead of anger. I motioned him into the cab. Unresisting, he slid onto the seat. Gently I pushed him over toward the farther door as I climbed in beside him. I covered the gun with my pocketbook.

"Where to, mister?" asked the cabbie.

Jason said nothing.

"Central Park," I told the driver.

I felt sorry for Jason. His hands were clasped so tightly together on his lap that I could see a tiny white arc on each knuckle. There were beads of perspiration on his forehead. He seemed to be swallowing a lot.

But it was impossible for me to tell him who I was in the cab. I didn't want the driver to intrude on our meeting. The scene I had so lovingly imagined to myself all those years did not include an onlooker.

Once, when we stopped for a traffic light, Jason unclasped his hands and put one on the door handle. I lifted the pocketbook off my gun. He locked his hands together again.

When we reached the park, Jason paid the driver before I could get my wallet out. He gave him a ten-dollar bill. The driver beamed when Jason told him to keep the change. Jason kept staring at the driver. I read the message his eyes were trying to send to the man. His eyes were signaling: *Help me.* The cabbie was too busy stuffing the bill into his pocket to notice his fare's silent pleading.

I had to nudge Jason with the gun to get him to open the door to the sidewalk. I was beginning to feel bad. Nothing was happening like the scene I had pictured over the drawers of the filing cabinet.

Walking into the park, I felt a little better. The ugly charade I had had to play would soon be over. A park was the perfect setting for a father-daughter introduction. My steps became springy, but Jason's were slow and shuffly. Once he stopped to stare hard at a forsythia bush that swayed and bobbed under the pounding of the winds. It was good to see the winds at work. They had followed me, their friend, to rejoice at my happiness. They were trying so hard to help me that they toyed with Jason's hair. Their teasing did not soften the set lines of his face, so they shifted their jabbings to his eyes. Those winds actually made his eyes water.

Jason continued staring at the bush as if it were the loveliest thing on earth. I had to poke him again with the gun to make him move. As we walked I looked up at him. He suddenly seemed very old. The wrinkles around his eyes had become furrows moistened by the tears the March winds had coaxed from his eyes. Walking seemed to be an exertion for him, so I glanced around and saw a bench sheltered from the winds, only a few feet away. Nobody was sitting there. I poked Jason again and he quickened his steps to keep up with me. I pointed to the bench. When he sat down, he didn't look at me.

In the father-daughter scene in my mind I had always been standing, so I remained that way. Sometimes in my scene my father was running toward me. I backed up a little so that Jason could spring joyously to me when I told him who I was.

"I'm sorry it has to be this way," I began, but I couldn't continue because Jason choked out something that sounded like "Oh, God." Then he covered his face with his hands. I realized that he must have thought my words were a prologue to using the gun.

"What I meant to say was that I'm sorry I had to use a gun to get you to talk to me. You were going to leave me and I had to stop you. Jason, I am not just a fan. I am your daughter, the one you told Amanda Armstrong about. I am the child you have been longing for."

Jason dropped his hands into his lap and stared at me. He was too overcome by emotion to speak.

"Well, aren't you going to say something?" I asked.

He cleared his throat. "If you'll put that gun over there by that tree, I'll talk to you."

"Of course," I answered.

As I walked to the tree, I turned around to look at Jason. He hadn't moved. I was so happy that I almost skipped back to the bench.

"Sit down," he said.

"Yes, Father," I replied.

He looked at me as intently as he had at Amanda Armstrong. "Listen carefully to what I am going to say. I am not your father. In fact, I am not Jason Carruthers. My name is Avery Wilson and I'm an actor who portrays a character on a television serial. The story of Jason's search for his daughter is only a story. Do you understand?"

I laughed. "I know what you're doing," I told him. "You're testing me. You want to be sure that I'm the right person. I'll show you my voter registration card with my age and address on it. You'll see that I'm nineteen and that I live in New Jersey. I'm the same age and I live in the same area as your daughter. I *am* your daughter."

He sighed. "You've evidently been under a great strain. Come with me and I'll take you to a doctor."

I jumped off the bench. "I'm tired of people saying that I need a doctor, Jason. So tired of it. Give me your wallet."

He reached into his pocket. "If it's money you want, I'll be glad to give it to you."

When I grabbed the wallet from him, my fingernail scratched his hand and drew blood from his pale skin. I wasn't sorry about that. He deserved the scratch for spoiling the scene I had so lovingly tuned into all those years.

"I don't want money, Jason," I want to see the photograph of my mother that you carry in your wallet, the one you showed to Amanda Armstrong. I am tall and slender like you, but my face doesn't resemble yours. I must look like my mother."

Quickly I flipped through all the photographs in his wallet. She wasn't there. I pulled out all the credit cards and money. There was no photograph of my mother wedged in with them. I tore the snapshots out of their windows, thinking her photo might be underneath another photo. She wasn't there.

The photographs in the wallet were all of the same person, the man who had lunched with Jason at Sardi's. There were all sorts of photos of him—on a beach, on a sofa, in a swimming pool. There was even a photograph of him with Jason. They were wearing Mexican hats and standing in front of a fountain. Jason had his arm around the man. They were both smiling.

"What have you done with her picture?" I shouted.

"There was never a photograph of her in my wallet, only in the wallet I use when I play Jason Carruthers on *To Live and to Love*.

"Stop saying that you *play* Jason Carruthers. You *are* Jason Carruthers. You've been looking for your daughter all week. You haven't been on the show."

He shook his head. "I've been making a commercial all week. That's why I've been off the show."

Everything was wrong, all wrong. Not once in the scenes I had pictured did my father ever deny me. Why was Jason doing this? He told Amanda he wanted to find his daughter and there I was sitting on a park bench beside him, sobbing. Why wouldn't he believe me?

"Don't cry," he said gently.

"I'm not crying," I said. "These March winds are tearing at my eyes just as you are tearing at my heart."

He put his hand on my shoulder. "You must understand this. I am nobody's father. The photos you've seen in my wallet are of the man with whom I've shared my life for twenty years. There was never anyone else. Can't you understand that?"

Of course I could understand that. I understood exactly what he was doing. He was making up a story for me just as he had once made up a story to prevent my mother from marrying him. He was a man who couldn't accept responsibility. He had a ready-made excuse to keep from getting involved with someone. My adoptive parents had told me that discovering the truth about my origins might be painful. They were right.

"You can leave now," I told him, thinking that those words must have been the same as those my mother had spoken to him years ago.

I watched him walk away. He started out slowly, but when he reached the forsythia bush he began to run. Run, I thought, run! Run away from me as you did from my mother. Run from the truth. Run as fast as you can to the nearest policeman. Tell him to come back here to the lunatic in the park. Tell the policeman to come back with his gun drawn.

My gun. I had almost forgotten it. I ran to the tree and lifted it from its cradle within the roots that were as interlocked as Jason's hands had been in the cab.

Thinking about Jason's hands made me cry. I ran from the park, from the setting of the father-daughter scene that had been so cruel. I wanted to get as far away from the park as I could. I jumped on a bus and stayed on it for a long time, until I tired of all the stopping and starting. I got off at a corner next to a department store. I wanted to walk and walk, but those treacherous March winds, no longer my friends, were following me, laughing at me, tearing at me. Those winds knew my dream had been shattered. They knew it and they rejoiced over it. I had to get away from them.

I went into the store and walked all over the first floor, and then the second. When I reached the third floor, I saw Jason smiling at me. He was self-assured, with no beads of perspiration on his forehead. He was saying something to me. I had to walk closer to hear what he said. He was telling me what to take for acid indigestion.

The utter insensitivity of that man! He was acting as if the agony he had caused me could be bubbled away by a seltzer tablet. It was not my stomach that ached, it was my heart.

My hand trembled as I pulled out the gun. It steadied when I aimed it directly at his smile. Then glass shattered, a puff of smoke billowed into the air, and people screamed.

"She shot the TV set!" I heard a woman shout.

I dropped the gun and walked to the escalator. I felt so much better than I had when I came into the store, until a man with viselike hands grabbed me.

They call the place where they took me a hospital, but I never before saw a hospital with bars on the windows. The bars don't bother me as much as the sounds in here. They are ugly sounds, sounds of doors banging, keys jangling, footsteps clattering, people moaning. I have difficulty hearing the TV set in the recreation room. I've asked my adoptive parents to send me my own TV for my room, but they won't do it. They say that I'm better off without a TV set. They say that TV was the triggering mechanism for my problem.

The people in group therapy with me say that I am making progress. When I admitted to them last week that I realized

Jason wasn't my real father, they all cheered. One of the shyest in the group patted me on the arm. She hates to touch anyone or have anyone touch her, so I guess my admission helped her with her problem. The nurse who leads our sessions says therapy enables us to help each other.

Helping others is very satisfying. I'm going to continue helping others when I get out of here. I hope I leave soon because I know the ones I must help. When I watch *To Live and to Love* here, after Crafts in the recreation room, I shiver when I hear everyone happily discussing Jason and Amanda's forthcoming marriage. It seems that Jason was unsuccessful in finding his daughter and he's given up trying. He and Amanda are going to be married in a few weeks.

Amanda needs my help. She must be told that Jason does not really love her. As painful as it will be for her, I must insist that she look at the photographs in Jason's wallet, the wallet he doesn't use on the show. I hope I can find her at the TV studio. I hope when I do that she doesn't try to run away before I can speak to her. I hope I won't have to get another gun to make her listen to me.

*What ever happened to the sort of hard-edged story that made* Black Mask *and some of the other pulps so popular during the 1930s? Has it simply vanished from the mystery scene? No indeed—here's a good example from Robert Colby, a California writer who produced some fine paperback originals during the fifties and sixties. It's a story* Black Mask *would have been pleased to publish, no doubt. The protagonist, T. C. Brock, is no private eye, but he knows how to use a gun and make a buck.*

# ROBERT COLBY
# Paint the Town Green

When the plane set down at L.A. International, Brock rented a car and drove to the Beverly Hills Hotel, a rambling cloistered structure in the lush money-green suburbs. By 9 o'clock he was checked into one of the private bungalows on the grounds, and within an hour he was placing an ad in the *Los Angeles Times*:

> LARGE CASH SUMS OFFERED FOR QUICK, SURE PROFITS
> *Out-of-state speculator with heavy capital reserve considering unique, exciting ventures with instant profit potential. No fast-buck deal too adventurous. Calls accepted daily between noon and 2 P.M. only. Ask for Mr. T. C. Brock.*

At the bottom of the ad he wrote the phone number and paid for a one-week run. Then he checked into another hotel, a towering structure in the heart of L.A. He took a splendid room overlooking the city on the floor just below the top of the building, which was occupied by a skyview restaurant. To this room he brought the fine custom suitcase containing his clothing and other belongings, having left a cheap overnighter and an attaché case, both weighted with old magazines, at the bungalow. Long experience had taught him that when trouble developed, as it often did, it was best to conduct business in one place and sleep in another.

The next day at noon Brock was in the bungalow screening calls from the hustlers who had read his ad in the paper. Most of the shell-game propositions to take the rich dude from out of town were obvious frauds. There were offers of ready-to-soar mining stocks—gold, diamond, or uranium, take your choice. Land that was fairly bubbling with oil could be leased for a bargain price. The scoop on a fixed horse race was for sale, and there was a matchless opportunity to back a self-proclaimed card shark in a game of high-stakes poker. A map guaranteed to pinpoint the location of buried treasure on an island in the South Pacific was a steal at fifty grand.

Brock wasted no time on these: They were small-time cons with nothing that suited his purpose. He needed the perfect combination.

In the first three days he took only two calls that were intriguing enough to arouse his interest. The first call was from a man with just a hint of Spanish accent. He spoke softly and with soothing charm, in the formal, nearly stilted manner of one who has learned his English in the old country.

"My name is Carlos," he said. "The last name is difficult and of no importance. The only importance, sir, is the extent of your interest to purchase a quantity of, uh, not so legal items that can be instantly exchanged for a profit ratio in the near vicinity of eight and one-half to one."

"Are you going to tell me what you're talking about, or do you want me to guess?"

"On the phone, Mr. Brock, it is not possible to be so very much definite. But let me say further that the items I will exhibit to you for your approval are green in color and of a size to fit the wallet. They are of a quality not to be believed. In fact, without a tiresome study, they cannot be told from the genuine article. Yes?"

"Yes. I'll take a look and decide for myself. Meet me here at my bungalow on the hotel grounds—number fourteen. If you're not here within the hour, I'll be gone."

"I am not far removed," said Carlos. "Half an hour will be sufficient."

The second offer that seemed worthy of at least a look came just a few minutes later. The woman had a cultured, weary way of speaking, as if she had done it all and had it all long ago. Her name was Mila—they rarely gave last names—and she was forced to part with a fabulous diamond ring worth six hundred thousand for a paltry four hundred grand. The ring had been a gift from her husband and she had told him that she had lost it. Though he was an extremely rich man he refused to give her more than a meager amount of money to spend, and this was her way of getting the cash she needed to cover some pressing personal debts.

The story was probably a fabrication, but diamonds never lie to people who understand them and, telling the lady to stop by with the gem in exactly two hours, he put down the phone and began a regal lunch, delivered complete with a frosty martini, by room service.

A wiry man of medium height, Brock seemed always a bit wide-eyed, his expression slightly startled, as if he were a visitor in an alien land which he found full of curious and entertaining surprises. His manner of dress, though somewhat excessive, was grand. Against the background of a midnight-blue suit, he wore a pearl-gray tie that was fastened with an emerald-studded pin. His gold wristwatch was embellished by a dial of ruby chips, and his outsize diamond ring had the wink of superb quality.

Carlos arrived just as a waiter was removing the debris of Brock's lunch. A small neat man with a small neat moustache, he had jet-dark hair, mild coffee-colored eyes, and an apologetic smile. He was impeccable in a beige gabardine suit with stitched lapels and leather-trimmed pockets. He said he came from Bogotá, and there was about him the quiet, well-mannered air of Latin aristocracy. Chatting easily, in no apparent haste to transact his business, he told Brock he had once been in partnership with his father, an exporter of coffee to the United States and other countries.

"For a long time," said Carlos with one of his apologetic smiles, "my father's business of exporting the coffee was truly magnificent. Then it became very bad, you see. And my father, he began to export in secret a few drugs—the heavy stuff—you know? He was soon caught and sent to prison where, sadly I must tell you, he died."

Carlos smiled in a way that was appropriately sad. "I was not used to poverty, could not abide with it," he continued. "So now I make my living where you find the much greener pastures, on the other side of the fence." With a twinkle he lowered his head in a mock attitude of shame.

Probably, thought Brock, the superfluous charm and small talk concealed as wily a rascal as could be found anywhere. "All right," he said, "let's see what you're selling."

"Pardon?"

"Did you bring it with you—the funny money?"

"Funny money?" Carlos presented a face of round-eyed innocence.

"Carlos, don't waste my time with games."

"Very well. But how do I know you are not the police?"

"Counterfeiting comes under the jurisdiction of the Secret Service. And the boys of the SS don't usually advertise to catch criminals."

Carlos nodded. "Yes, I suppose not. In any case, I have brought nothing with me to sell, only samples."

He removed three bills from an envelope he took from his pocket and handed them over. There was a twenty, a fifty, and a hundred. The texture of the paper was excellent. It was aged just enough to give it the authentic feel of usage. More, the color of the ink was exact, and with the naked eye Brock could not find the least imperfection in the engraving of the bills. Only after he examined them minutely with a pocket magnifying glass under a strong light did he spot the single flaw—the absence of red and blue fibers in the paper.

"Well, what do you think?" said Carlos. "Are they not beautiful?"

"They appear to be quite good," Brock said carefully, though he had never seen better and doubtless they would be accepted by anyone but an expert who had been forewarned. "Where did you get them?"

Carlos shrugged. "The details, no. But I will tell you this much: The bills were shipped from my country where we have some of the world's finest papers and inks—and a retired engraver who fashioned plates for the U.S. government before he entered our service."

"A former U.S. engraver, huh?" Brock snorted. "And how much can you deliver?"

"At once, three hundred thousand. More in a week or two."

"Mmm. And what is your price?"

"Fifteen percent of face value. Forty-five thousand for the three hundred grand."

It was a good price. Fakes of that quality were so rare that Carlos could ask and get twenty percent. But to test him, Brock shook his head. "Too much. Ten percent—thirty thousand for three hundred of the bogus."

Carlos looked wounded. "But surely, Mr. Brock, you will not haggle with me over bills of such perfection. They will pass anywhere, even in the banks. No, fifteen percent is entirely fair and I will stand firm."

"You're right," said Brock. "I shouldn't haggle with you, and I won't."

Carlos beamed.

"So I'll just say once more—thirty thousand. That's my final offer." He stood and fastened Carlos with the unblinking gaze of relentless decision.

Carlos went through the motions. He groaned, sighed, pursed his lips, and made a pretense of calculation with his fingers. Then, clucking, his face agonized, he slowly nodded and said, "You are a hard man, sir. You leave me just the small margin of profit. But yes, because I have many obligations at this time, I will deal with you on your terms. Thirty thousand it is."

Brock shook his hand and said, "Bring the phonies here tonight at nine. If they're identical to these samples, we'll make the exchange."

"What you ask is impossible, sir," Carlos said, plucking the samples from Brock's fingers, and tucking them into his pocket. "Even when we are most sure, as with a man of your distinction, we never take chances. No, you will come to us, and if we are certain you are entirely alone the transaction will be completed."

"Well, I have little time for such nonsense, but the bills seem good enough to warrant some inconvenience."

Carlos handed him a typewritten slip of paper. "At nine tonight, then."

Brock glanced at the address and nodded. "At nine."

"And the thirty thousand in U.S. legal? You will have it with you?"

"Naturally."

With a fine show of teeth Carlos stepped to the door, flipped a salute, and went out.

Brock ordered another martini from room service. Sipping it as he waited for "Mila," the lady with the diamond, he reflected on his dialogue with Carlos. Since the bills were incredibly good imitations, he would never let them go for ten percent of face value. Therefore, he must be working some sort of flimflam. Well, each to his own game. And his own reward.

Mila was on time. Her knock had the sound of delicate intrigue. A slender young woman with a dainty kind of elegance, she had tawny hair parted in the middle and gathered to one side. Her sleepy eyes and dreamy smile made him wonder if she might be flying on something with narcotic wings. She wore an expensively tailored gray suit that seemed incongruously severe.

"Are you Mr. Brock? My name is Mila." Her speech was over-polished, as if by years of exposure to people of quality and education.

"Come in," he said, and she entered a bit wearily, or timidly —she wasn't an easy person to read. She floated across the room to a chair, her delicate shoulders curved in a languid slouch.

"Would you like something—a cocktail?"

"No, thank you, I don't drink."

"Well, for some people that's wise, I think." He sat facing her.

She toyed with the clasp of her gunmetal leather purse. "I don't usually anwer ads of any sort, Mr. Brock. But yours was irresistible. And quite providential under the circumstances."

"I imagine."

Her drowsy eyes wandered over him. "What sort of business are you in?"

"Various investments, speculations."

"I gathered that from your ad. Would you care to be more specific?"

"No."

"I see. Well, I mean, if you're serious about buying the—"

"Mila—if I wanted seriously to buy a costly ring at Tiffany's, what would they require of me?"

She smiled. "Maybe they would extend credit."

"Will you?"

She shook her head. "Naturally, I must have cash."

"Then it's that simple. You want to sell and I have the cash."

Nodding, she opened her purse and handed him a black velvet box. He lifted the lid and removed the ring, a large pear-shaped stone of fiery brilliance and exquisite cut. Fingering it, finding it cool to the touch, he carried it to the window and drew it across the pane, leaving a sharp clear line where the stone cut the glass. As he studied the impression the diamond had left, he caught sight of two young men who were standing together in front of the opposite bungalow. Dressed in sportcoats and slacks, they seemed merely guests making idle conversation. But Brock's nearly infallible instinct told him they were stationed there as guards to be sure he didn't try to grab the ring, and that likely they were carrying weapons.

Now, with his own diamond, Brock tried to scratch Mila's stone. It was impossible. Inserting a piece of white notepaper beneath the gem, he peered into its center with a magnifying glass, checking color and purity. Then, as he held the ring in the palm of his hand feeling the weight of it and discounting the setting, he decided that the stone was probably worth the four hundred thousand she was asking, and a good deal more. Certainly it was the most beautiful diamond he had ever examined at close range, and there had been many.

"Of course, I don't have enough magnification to be certain," he said as he sank back into his chair and gazed appreciatively at the ring, "but it seems a nearly flawless blue brilliant. Very nice."

"My husband bought it in Europe," she said. "It should be worth more in this country. It weighs nearly fifty carats."

"Well, I don't have the instruments to check it, so I would have to get it appraised."

She looked dismayed.

"Really, you wouldn't expect me to invest that kind of money without an appraisal," he said.

She nodded. "But I can't possibly let the ring out of my sight."

"No, that would be foolish." He considered. "There's a jeweler right here in the hotel. Why don't we take a little walk and see if he can give us an evaluation."

She thought about it, anxious-eyed, biting her lip. "Well, all right—yes, we could do that."

He stood and gave her the ring. "Shall we go then?"

They left the bungalow. The two young men in sportjackets, lean-bodied, hard-faced, were now head to head, studying what seemed a racing form. As they gestured and made comments, one of them darted a glance at him. He wondered if they were hired guards or accomplices. In any case, they were sure to follow.

Mila walked beside him in silence, her tension almost palpable. They entered the hotel. He sensed the watchdogs behind him but did not turn. They went down a flight of stairs to the arcade, following it past assorted shops to the jewelry store.

Mila spoke to the clerk and handed over the ring. For a few seconds he gave it a cursory examination through his loupe. When he removed the eyepiece, his expression was one of contained awe. He flicked a calculating glance at Mila as if trying to match the royal quality of the diamond with the woman who owned it. But then his face became bland and he said, "I'm not prepared to give you a formal appraisal, just an estimate."

Mila looked at Brock, who nodded and said, "For now that would do."

The jeweler removed the stone from its setting and inspected it at length under intense light. He measured it with calipers and weighed it on a scale, jotting figures on a scrap of paper. After pondering over his notations, he returned the gem to its setting and came back with the ring.

"It's a beauty," he said with an approving shake of his head. "I'd say somewhere between six and seven hundred thousand. Call it six-fifty, roughly."

As she carefully tucked the ring back into the velvet box, Mila looked at Brock with an I-told-you-so expression.

Back outside, he spotted her protectors. Not far removed, they stood gazing into a shop window, faking an enthusiastic discussion of the items on display.

"You've got a deal," Brock said. "It's only a matter of price."

"You don't like the price!" She looked indignant. "Mr. Brock, didn't you hear the man say—"

"I heard him, yes."

"Well, then—isn't it an absolute *steal* at four hundred thousand?"

"A steal, yes. No doubt. Then why do you come to me? Why don't you sell it to a commercial buyer of diamonds at four hundred, or even better?"

Her face sagged. "You know very well that I can't. They ask

questions. For a ring worth more than half a million, they want proof of ownership. And only my husband could give them that."

"Exactly."

"So you're ready to take advantage."

"I'm in business to take advantage."

She sighed. "How much, then?"

"Let me think about it. Phone me here at nine in the morning. That will give me time to make arrangements with the bank."

Her lips tightened. "Well, I won't come down much, I'll tell you that. And it must be cash, no checks of any kind."

"Cash, of course."

"Very well, I'll phone you at nine sharp."

"If you don't mind, I won't see you out. I want to stop off at the barbershop."

"Good-bye, Mr. Brock."

Her dreamy expression gone a bit sour, she turned and walked off, clipping past the bodyguards. As Brock went into the barbershop and sneaked a look, they lost interest in the window display and sauntered after her.

He lingered a minute and followed, heading for the lobby. It was a lucky guess. They were there, the three of them huddled in a corner, conversing. Anticipating their departure, he ducked out a side door, found his car in the parking area, and drove it up near the exit. Folded down behind the wheel, two cars in front screening him, he saw them come out, separately—Mila first, her boys behind. The boys went off in a white Ford sedan, she left in a taxi.

He tailed the cab cautiously to the estates of Bel-Air and hung well back as it climbed a road embowered by huge old trees hemming the houses of the rich and the mansions of the very rich. He could see Mila through the back window of the cab. She didn't turn once to look back, though probably in the unfamiliar car and wearing his sunglasses she wouldn't have recognized him.

Soon the taxi wheeled left into a private driveway, and he braked to wait. When the cab returned, he drove on, taking a look at the house as he passed. It was a great library of a place, barely visible from the road. High and square and formal, it sat atop a knoll, neatly combed grounds spilling green around it.

Just beyond, he maneuvered about and parked. As he sat thinking what to do next, a gardening truck slid out of the drive that had swallowed the cab and came toward him. He got out and flagged it down. The driver was an old guy with a craggy, pleasant face. Brock asked him if he worked for the people in the library-type mansion. He said yes, but only once a week. He was an itinerant gardener with other customers in the neighborhood. He had a crew and a couple of his men were on a job down the road. He was on his way to pick them up. Yes, he knew all about the people up there on the knoll, but he was in a hurry. Brock asked him if twenty bucks would buy about ten minutes. He grinned and cut the motor, then motioned for Brock to sit on the seat beside him.

The lady who owned the place was a Mrs. Alberta Wilmont. Before he died, her husband ran a shipping company—freighters. He left her millions. No, the young woman who just arrived in a taxi was not Mrs. Wilmont, she was Marian Ainsworth, a kind of secretary-companion who was distantly related to Alberta Wilmont.

"Did Mrs. Wilmont ever own a diamond ring that was stolen?"

"You bet she did! The ring was worth a fortune. About a month ago, while everyone was away from the house, burglars broke in. How they did it without tripping the alarm system nobody can figure. The thieves drilled the safe, swiped the ring and some less valuable jewelry, and a few hundred in cash. It was front-page stuff in the paper."

Brock asked a few more questions, gave the gardener the twenty, and twenty more to keep his mouth shut. Then he hustled away to the newspaper office and combed back issues until he found the account of the burglary. This done, he made a number of calls and finally hit what could be the jackpot.

Shortly before 9:00 that evening, with just a few magazines locked in his attaché case, he drove toward the address Carlos had given him. It was an apartment house in an old section of Hollywood on a narrow street above Franklin. The building was large and might once have been magnificent, but now its crusty facade cried neglect and despair, most of the windows dark, the entrance bleakly lighted.

He found an alley that led to a subterranean garage below

the apartment house and drove down the ramp. He was in a gloomy dungeon of pillared space, empty but for a pair of junk-yard heaps in a corner, squatting beside a late-model black Cadillac. Parking next to the Cadillac he climbed out cautiously with the attaché case. Clutching the grip of a holstered .38 revolver, one of several weapons he had collected from a long string of bad boys, he stood motionless, listening. The silence was so dense within the cavernous garage he could hear a distant murmur of traffic, the bleating of a horn.

Peering inside the Cadillac he circled quietly to the front and reached under it to test the radiator. It was warm, almost hot. Someone had arrived not long before.

On rubber-soled shoes he crossed the garage and came to the mouth of a dim corridor. Pausing again to listen, he moved on —past the doorways of a shadowy boiler room and a gutted laundry to an elevator. The car was somewhere above, but there was no indicator to show its location.

He pressed the button and heard the creak and whine of the elevator's descent. In the wan light the scabby, cement walls displayed a nearly endless scrawl of graffiti. Cobwebs nestled in corners, a light fixture dangled, the rank odor of urine invaded the torpid air.

When the approaching mutter of the car told him it was near, he stepped aside, out of range. But when it opened, the elevator was empty. Brock thumbed the 7 button, though Carlos's slip of paper designated apartment 8E.

The elevator rattled slowly up to the seventh floor and stopped. He was greeted by a dark, fetid corridor of doors flung wide open upon vacant apartments. Gaping in wonder, he crossed the threadbare remnant of a carpet, found the stair-way, and mounted soundlessly to the eighth. Here he cracked the door and peeked out.

Under the subdued light from overhead fixtures, the eighth and top floor seemed clean and tidy enough, the carpet in good repair, the brown doors to the apartments sealed. Puzzling it, Brock concluded that the rest of the building was probably abandoned. As he stopped to consider his strategy, he saw Carlos hurry around a bend in the corridor and come to stand, head inclined, at the elevator.

He looked so foolishly ineffectual and unfrightening that

Brock wanted to laugh out loud. Instead he moved quietly up behind him and dropped a heavy hand on his shoulder.

Carlos snapped around, wild-eyed, his jaw dropping in terror.

"Looking for me Carlos?" Brock grinned.

Carlos groaned. "What the hell you doing, man! I thought you were—"

"An undercover agent of the SS. Right, Carlos?"

He nodded. "Yeah, something like that. I am looking to see why you don't show," he said.

"I couldn't find 8E," Brock said. "I must've been going the wrong way."

"Ah, well—no problem," Carlos answered. "Come—" He had been staring with fascination at Brock's case and as they moved down the hallway he asked nervously, "You have brought the money?"

Brock gave the case an affectionate pat. "Thirty big ones. And you have the queers?"

"The queers?" His expression flickered, brightened. "The phonies, ah yes, of course!" He gave a dental exhibition. "They are in the apartment, where we shall make the exchange."

He led Brock to the rear of the building and turned into a narrow passage. It terminated at the point where the doors to apartments 8E and 8F faced each other across a faded strip of carpet. The hall, lit by a single naked bulb, was dim. The air had a musty smell, tainted with something indefinable, like molding garbage.

They were at the door to 8E, Carlos bringing out a set of keys, Brock telling himself that he would not go into the apartment unless he entered with an arm locked about Carlos's neck, the .38 visibly pressing his head, when he sensed a movement and turned swiftly. Behind him, the door to 8F had been opened and an enormous Latin towered above him, grimacing fiercely as he hoisted a baseball bat and slammed it down.

Brock had begun to duck out of range or the blow would have crushed his skull. Instead, it glanced thunderously off the back of his head, dropping him to the floor.

Vaguely focused, his eyes opened upon a hazy scene. He was floating above a shimmering landscape. There was a blur of twinkling buildings and streets while below, dim and far away, a pool of white circled and tilted. It appeared to grow toward him, then recede, as if seen through binoculars that would not adjust. And he could feel the hard thrust of something against his chest.

In the background voices drifted to him, as from a radio badly tuned. Carlos was pleading with someone called Mario, saying it wasn't necessary to kill the man, just take his money and run. But Mario said no, it was too risky. "No, Carlos, this mama is gonna commit suicide. He's gonna fly down from that window and—squash!—you got a bird who sings no songs!"

Brock got the message. And fear jabbing him to life, he brought it all into focus. He was draped over a windowsill, gazing down a perpendicular wall to a moon-washed court eight stories below. The tilting, spinning face of the court, composed of unrelenting cement, winked at him.

But even as this understanding jolted and sickened him, Mario reached down and scooped him up with ridiculous ease. Poising himself, aiming Brock at the open mouth of the window, he did not notice that while one of Brock's hands dangled limply the other was under his jacket, bending the barrel of the .38 toward the great mass of his chest.

Brock squeezed the trigger—once, twice, and again, knowing that while the big ones may fall harder, they do not always fall faster. No doubt the first bullet was an incredible surprise, for Mario simply stood rooted, as if considering the impossibility of it, his eyes dilating with astonishment. The second shot caused him to stumble backward, and the third buckled him slowly to the floor. Only then, with a mortal sigh, did he liberate Brock from the clutch of his arms.

Carlos tried to run, but Brock caught him at the door and ordered him at gun point to empty Mario's pockets and bring him the contents. The dead man was carrying $6,700 in hundred-dollar bills that proved, after close examination, to be genuine U.S. green. Carlos, on the other hand, was in possession of only ninety dollars.

"Carlos," Brock said sternly as he pocketed the bills, "I've been thinking seriously of killing you, and this doesn't help your cause."

Seated on the floor, hands laced behind his neck, Carlos had been watching with resignation, as one who hopes for nothing but to survive. His face flashing alarm, he said tremulously, "I have little money because in the organization of the counterfeiting I am only a passer of the bills. Mario was in charge of the passers and the money in his wallet was to pay us our humble percentage."

Brock made a clucking sound. "How sad." Gingerly, he felt the lump on the back of his head. "You may lower your hands now, Carlos, and you may smoke. A condemned man is always entitled to a last cigarette."

Carlos gave him a look of such gaping horror that Brock decided to ease off a bit. "However," he added, "if you can find some way to repay me for this night of treachery, I might be persuaded to change my mind."

"Anything—anything at all that you wish," Carlos said feverishly.

"What did you do with my case, Carlos?"

He pointed. "Over there in the closet. It is locked and we could not open it."

"And where is the three hundred thousand in bogus?"

Carlos hesitated and Brock leveled the .38. "Hurry, Carlos, I'm aching to kill you!"

"No, no! The bills are down in the trunk of Mario's Cadillac. He was supposed to distribute them to the passers later tonight."

Brock reached for a set of keys resting on the floor with the assorted items Carlos had taken from Mario. "You'd better not be lying," he warned. "Let's go and see."

Toting his attaché case, he descended with Carlos to the garage. One of Mario's keys opened the trunk of the Cadillac, and when the lid was raised there was indeed a carton holding three hundred grand in bogus bills. Brock ordered Carlos to transfer the carton to the trunk of his rented sedan. When this was done he locked the attaché case in with the counterfeits and gave Carlos the keys to the Cadillac.

"Because you tried to prevent Mario from killing me," he told Carlos, "I'll make you a present of his car. You're a pussycat in a jungle and I'd advise you to get out of this racket and into plumbing, or something equally suited to your talents. At heart, Carlos, you're not a bad little fellow, and in fact I've become rather fond of you."

"You are fond of me? Truly?"

"Truly." Brock nodded solemnly. He opened the door of his rental, climbed in, and wound the motor.

"You are a strange man," said Carlos. "Most remarkable. But really, who are you, sir?"

"There's a tax on evil, and I'm the devil's own collector," Brock answered with a wisp of a smile. He backed and drove off.

Marian Ainsworth, alias Mila, phoned him the next morning on the dot of nine. "Three hundred thousand," he said.

"No."

"In cash."

"Well—"

"It'll take time for the bank to get that much money together. Be here at four this afternoon."

"I can't make it until eight this evening."

"At eight sharp, then." He cut the connection.

She was a few minutes early. When he opened the door and she stepped in, he spied her accomplices lingering in the shadows. A hundred to one they were the burglars who stole the ring— with her blueprint of the alarm system, and at a time when she told them the mansion would be empty.

She was wearing a black lace cocktail dress. She looked stunning. Was there to be a little party to celebrate the split of a hundred grand apiece?

She stood fidgeting at the center of the room, her eyes screaming her haste.

Enjoying it, he said, "A little drink? To toast our transaction?"

"I told you, I don't drink!" she snapped.

"Ah, that's right. Too bad."

"Have you got the cash?"

"Have you got the ring?"

She dipped into her black-beaded evening bag and passed him the velvet box. It was the same diamond, he determined that immediately, but pretending to suspect otherwise he tested and inspected it with even more care than he had the first time.

"The money is in that overnighter," he told her finally, pointing to the chair where he had left it. "You may keep the bag— I'll toss it in as a bonus."

Counting the cash, she was intensely concentrated, her face

taking on a feral quality. Before she began, she selected several bills from random stacks and examined them closely. But, apparently satisfied, she went on to count the bills with furious speed, then nodded and said with a hectic smile, "Well, it seems to be all here!"

She picked up the bag and all but bolted for the door, where she turned and said, "Now you own a diamond valued at more than half a million dollars, Mr. Brock. All you have to do is find someone to buy it. Mmm?"

She went out.

She was right, of course. It would be difficult to find anyone who would buy the ring at full price, no questions asked. But then, he had never intended to sell it. He hunted his rental in the parking area, found it, backed, and turned to drive away.

Just then Marian Ainsworth's accomplices loomed up out of the darkness. One at each side of the car, they aimed pistols at him. "OK, buddy, let's have the ring!" barked the one at his window.

"Don't get nervous, boys," he soothed. "I've got it right here in my pocket."

It was suicide to reach for his gun, so he brought the box out and started to hand it over. But then, with a trembling hand, he faked dropping the box to the floor. Bending to recover it, he rammed the pedal and gunned off blindly. They both fired at him, almost together. But they were too late.

He sat up just in time. The car was veering off toward a tree as it raced down the drive to the street. He straightened the wheel, braked a bit, and glanced into the rearview mirror. They were jockeying the white Ford out of a parking slot, coming after him. He cut north into a cloistered residential section of fine old houses, squealing around a series of corners.

It was no use. They were trailing him through every turn, hardly a block behind. He thought of braking suddenly and leaping out with his gun to fire at them, but changed his mind when, losing them for a moment as he wheeled around a tight curve, he spotted the tip of a driveway that vanished between a gateway of tall hedges. He swung into it at reckless speed, yawing dangerously, correcting, erasing his lights, slowing as he climbed and swept around to the house, a pillared old colonial.

There was a garage with its door open and a vacant space inside. He slid into it, cut the motor, and listened. Nothing. He had lost them. But now, from a window somewhere above, came the shrill voice of a woman calling, "Is that you, Walter?"

He was seated at a partitioned booth in a secluded corner of the restaurant atop the hotel where he had his getaway room. He had told the hostess that a Mr. Arnold Bevis would be looking for him shortly, and now he was sipping a Manhattan, winding down, feeling good.

He had just ordered another when a plump little man with a Vandyke beard bustled over at the heels of the hostess. "I'm Arnold Bevis," he said and flashed a smile. They shook hands and Bevis squeezed in across the table, seting a briefcase on the cushion beside him. The waitress delivered Brock's second Manhattan and he asked, "Will you have one with me, Mr. Bevis?"

Bevis shook his head. "No, thanks. I have an appointment with Alberta Wilmont and there isn't time."

The waitress departed and Brock said, "You told Mrs. Wilmont you've recovered the ring?"

"I told her we *thought* we had recovered it. And now, if you will, Mr. Brock, let's see if we have."

Brock produced the velvet box, opened it, and slid it across to Bevis, who brought implements from his briefcase and, after testing to be sure the diamond was genuine, removed it from its setting, weighed, and measured it. "Did you know, Mr. Brock," he said, "that like fingerprints no two diamonds are alike? When we insure a diamond, we chart all of its individual characteristics. That way, there can be no mistake about its identity."

He wrote figures in a notebook, fixed a loupe to his eye, and, studying the diamond in the light from the table lamp, continued to make notes. Finally, he took an insurance appraisal form from his case and compared it with his notations.

Nodding, he said, "Yes, this is our baby all right." He returned the stone to its setting, put his tools away, and stared curiously at Brock. "I looked up your ad in the *Times* and I can see how it would attract those two who stole the ring. But how did you get it away from them without giving them the money?"

"That's a trade secret, Mr. Bevis. But I'll say this much—I had to do some fast shuffling to escape them. And if I didn't have the devil's own luck, I wouldn't be sitting here waiting for you to bless me with the reward."

Bevis took a check from his case and passed it to Brock with a release form. "Fifty thousand is a very large sum. We seldom pay rewards in excess of five percent and I had a tough time getting approval from my company—especially since you were in a hurry."

Brock looked at the check and signed the release. "I'm always in a hurry, Mr. Bevis. The coals are hot and I have to jump fast."

"And so do I. I'm running late." Sealing the ring and the release in his briefcase, Bevis eased himself from the booth. "You know, I never will understand how the burglars were able to silence a complex alarm system and break in at the precise time when everyone was out. It makes me wonder if somebody was feeding them information."

"That's possible," said Brock.

"You'll give a description of those hoods to the police, won't you?"

"Of course," Brock lied.

Bevis shook his hand and disappeared.

Brock sipped his Manhattan and gazed out through the wall of glass at the gaudy splash of the night city. Let the cops uncover Marian Ainsworth if they could. She was a crook and her choice of playmates was atrocious. But she was a beauty with plenty of style. Under other circumstances . . . .

He shook his head. In the morning he would fly to Alaska. As the foreman of a welding crew working the pipeline, he would be on leave in Fairbanks with great wads of accumulated pay to spend. The hustlers of that amoral outpost in the wilderness would be lurking there, just waiting for a sucker like him. And his rewards would be extravagant.

*One of O. Henry's most popular stories was "The Cop and the Anthem." Using basically the same situation, James McKimmey here gives us an updated, fleshed-out version. McKimmey, author of several novels, has appeared in four previous volumes of this series. It's a pleasure to welcome him back.*

# JAMES McKIMMEY
# The Crimes of Harry Waters

The ancient hotel, on the brink of being demolished for the general good of the city, stood just to the side of a freeway ramp. Harry Waters, on this late autumn afternoon, sat in a chair of his seventh-floor room and listened to the steady whir of traffic. His ball-point pen was poised over the back of an advertising brochure clamped to an old clipboard—he'd got himself on as many mailing lists as was possible in order to collect paper for his poetry.

He wrote, *Good luck is the result of one's attitude, oh, Bird of Knowledge. Oh, Bird, one's luck can change with the creation of shifting attitude. Oh, Bird, there must come a time—*

He shook his head, unable to continue, because he didn't believe it. Though he had yet to sell more than a handful of poems, he would not compromise himself. Truth was truth. No respectable poet could allow himself to attempt to diminish that fact.

He leaned back, surveying the small room. A bed. A bureau, on which an inexpensive hot plate rested. A cracked mirror. And, despite the low cost of the room, a small adjoining bath which Harry used to keep himself scrupulously clean.

He tossed the clipboard to the bed and got up to examine himself in that mirror. He was twenty-five, slightly built, and reasonably handsome. Dressed cheaply but presentably enough, just the same. So why was he jobless?

He turned from his image, knowing full well why. He did not *want* another job. He wished only to write his poetry. But, on the other hand, he did not wish to be put on the street to starve either, which was what was going to happen shortly if he did not acquire more funds than the five dollars remaining in his wallet.

Ah, but what to do? He had checked with the Welfare Department. As a single individual he would at least be eligible for food stamps and medical assistance if he should need it—but only if he registered with the Employment Department to prove that he was available for hire—and God knew what *they* might come up with that he didn't want. Moreover, he found it a distressing idea to present food stamps to Mr. Canaveslo, whose market he frequented.

So—nothing. Unless he decided to turn to crime. And *could* he do that as the singular alternative? The thought sickened him, because he was, in his own mind, an honest man who had stolen nothing and cheated no one in his life. He simply could not compromise that aspect of himself either.

Even if he should be able to adjust to such a compromise, he would be no good at it. He would undoubtedly fumble the attempt and be caught and . . . .

His eyes widened ever so slightly. Jail? he thought. Was *that* where it lay? A cell, in a jail, with a bed undoubtedly as comfortable as the one he was on right now? Where he could continue to write without financial worry? Was there not a certain honor, even, in finding one's self in jail to continue a decent pursuit?

He lay there, continuing to consider the idea. Then, finally, he made up his mind.

Mr. Canaveslo's small grocery was two blocks from Harry's hotel. He had got to know Mr. Canaveslo, a trim man with thinning gray hair, very well indeed. He knew that Mr. Canaveslo had lost his first wife and had remarried less than a year ago.

He knew that Mr. Canaveslo was less than happy with his second marriage, that his new wife was no helpmate in the business, that the nineteen-year-old stepson who had come along with the union was entirely lazy and leeched off Mr. Canaveslo.

Harry also knew that Mr. Canaveslo closed his store promptly at 9 P.M., if he had no customers inside.

So, with the toy pistol he had purchased at a nearby variety store in a pocket of his old woolen jacket, Harry waited at one side of Mr. Canaveslo's place of business until Mr. Canaveslo came forward, locked the door, and pulled the shade, signaling that he was now alone in the shop.

Harry stepped to the door and rapped on the glass sharply.

"Closed," Mr. Canaveslo called.

"It's Harry Waters."

"I'm *closed*, Harry."

"I have nothing to eat in my room."

"That's pathetic, Harry. Find a restaurant."

"I can't afford a restaurant. I just want a can of lima beans. For the hot plate."

"For the hot plate," Mr. Canaveslo said, opening the door. "You know I close at nine. But you couldn't get here before that. Writers are disorganized."

Mr. Canaveslo was dressed as usual in a white shirt, black tie, and black trousers. He knew that Harry wrote poems, and he'd asked Harry to write a number of special-occasion rhymes for his daughter, a product of his first marriage who was now married and lived in another city. He hadn't paid Harry any money in return, but he'd given him several cans of the beans Harry favored, as well as jars of marinated herring, which Harry also relished.

Mr. Canaveslo removed a can from a shelf and got behind the counter beside the cash register. Harry removed the toy pistol from his pocket and said, "Stick 'em up, Mr. Canaveslo."

Mr. Canaveslo's eyes instantly showed shock. "Put that darned thing away, Harry! Are you nuts?"

"I want the money in the cash register, Mr. Canaveslo."

"Don't josh me that way, Harry."

"I'm not joshing."

"I can't believe this!"

"I want the money."

"Things *can't* be that bad."

"Worse."

"But this is stupid, Harry! Why me? It's a big city! Why not some place they don't know you!"

"I just want the money, please."

Mr. Canaveslo shook his head. "You know how to write jingles. But you don't know how to be a crook. Give it up, Harry! Let's forget all about this!"

"I'm not leaving until I get the money."

"Take the beans and go! No charge."

"The money."

Mr. Canaveslo shook his head again and punched open the register. "I'm ashamed of you, Harry."

"I'm ashamed of myself, but I need the money."

"Take it then! You want all the change, too?"

"Keep the change, Mr. Canaveslo." Harry put the bills in a pocket, said, "I'm sorry."

"Not as much as I am!"

Harry backed to the door, opened it, and stepped outside. He closed the door behind him and moved down the street a little way, then leaned back against the building to wait.

In a short time, a police car stopped in front of Mr. Canaveslo's store and two officers got out.

Harry continued to lean against the building after the officers had gone inside, trying to estimate how long he should take before going back in to tell them he'd reconsidered and was giving up, after which they would stick him in prison.

He had waited almost ten minutes and was preparing to make his entrance when the two officers came out of the door with a handcuffed, frightened-looking fat youth between them. They wrestled Mr. Canaveslo's stepson, Arthur, across the sidewalk and into the police car. Before Harry could call to them, the car was racing off.

Feeling bewildered, Harry went to the door of the grocery, hesitated, then rapped sharply on the glass again.

"*Closed!*" Mr. Canaveslo called.

"It's me—Harry Waters."

"*Harry!*" Almost immediately the door was opened, and a beaming Mr. Canaveslo said, "Step in, my boy!"

Inside, Harry said, "What happened?" He could hear shrieking from the living quarters above.

"*Listen* to her!" Mr. Canaveslo said, smiling happily.

"I don't understand."

"It came to me, while I was dialing for the cops. I realized I didn't want to blow the whistle on you, because I decided you'd do what you just did—come back and then apologize. You're no crook, Harry. But I thought maybe I could get some good out of it anyway. And it came to me—Arthur. I've hated him from the time I married her." He jerked a finger in the direction of the living quarters where the shrieking continued.

"I told them he cleaned me out at gunpoint, then hid the gun and money and acted like he didn't do it. They bought it, hook, line, and sinker. I've been in business in this neighborhood for thirty-five years. They'd doubt me against that bum? No, sir!" Mr. Canaveslo's eyes lighted with pleasure and victory.

"I saw them hustle him into the police car," Harry said apologetically. "That's not what I'd intended."

"Of course not. You just made a small mistake. And it worked out, didn't it? That's a mistake I'll never regret."

Harry got out the money he had taken and said, "I was using a toy gun."

"Figures."

"Here's your money back, Mr. Canaveslo. I'm sorry."

"Stop being sorry! And put the money back in your pocket. Worth it to me to be rid of that moocher."

"But I can't do that."

"You're going to, or you're in trouble with me. And wait a minute. I'll sack up some cans of limas for you, and some jars of herring, too! I'm a grateful man, Harry!"

"I just didn't plan on things working out this way."

"Well, they did! Here's the sack. And when you get back to your room, sit down and think up a jingle for my daughter—she has a birthday next week. Bring it on in, and I'll have some more limas and herring for you. Enjoy the evening, my boy!" Mr. Canaveslo said, escorting Harry to the door.

Harry sat in his room on a warm day with morning sunlight pouring through the single window that looked out on a temporarily vacant lot where remained some of the rubble of a building smashed to the ground by a giant steel ball. Harry was not hungry—he had breakfasted very well indeed upon marinated herring. His rent was paid. Moreover, by his standards, he would have sufficient funds, as the result of Mr. Canaveslo's generosity, to continue in this relative comfort for perhaps another three weeks.

But after that?

Harry stood and looked out his window, feeling frustration. He'd found reprieve in that robbery attempt. But it remained true that the attempt had been, in its intention, a failure. Could he not even succeed in that? he thought. Could he not even land himself in jail? He gazed dolefully at the litter of the lot below.

He had another idea then, quite suddenly, quite simply.

He picked up the paper sack that had contained the beans and herring, left the room, took the erratic elevator to the lobby, then walked outside and around to the vacant lot. There he selected a brick and placed it in the bag.

He went on toward the business section of the area. As he was moving past a block that was definitely an improvement over the one on which his hotel stood, he saw coming toward him a young woman he had often noticed in his walks.

She was a strikingly beautiful girl with the sort of oval face that had always attracted Harry. It was framed by lustrous dark hair—Harry had always preferred brunettes. She looked at Harry coolly as they met, then away quickly, with disdain.

Well, he thought, he did not blame her for her obvious contempt. He did not know how she supported herself—he saw her often enough to believe she did not work. But perhaps employment was not necessary, with her looks. And perhaps she could rely simply on that beauty to meet the financial difficulties of this world.

So where was his place with a woman like that? he asked himself, stopping, turning, watching her climb the porch steps of a large Spanish-style house now converted to apartments. No, he knew, seeing the calves of her legs flexing nicely as she moved upward toward the front door, there was nothing in her existence for such as he. And nothing in his either, he thought, if he were heading for jail.

He moved on to catch his intended bus, where he sat with the sack containing the brick. When he got out, he walked along streets bordered by homes of such size that they immediately indicated the general wealth of the neighborhood.

He discovered, parked in the drive of an imposing home built above a sloping terrace, a Rolls-Royce. He stopped, considered, then went up the drive toward the car. When he reached it, he could see, behind the house, a large patio with a pool.

Seated there, sunning, was a shirtless, heavy-shouldered man in his mid-forties, browned so that the gray hair on his muscular chest looked totally white; his head was not only bald, but obviously shaved where hair continued to grow. He did not notice Harry.

Harry drew out his brick, positioned himself, shouted, *"Filthy rich!"* and slammed the brick with mighty force into the Rolls's windshield. He dropped the crumpled pieces that now comprised the brick and waited as the large man in the patio jumped to his feet and came running.

"What in the hell have you done?" the man roared.

Harry motioned his hands in resignation.

The man looked at his wrecked windshield, and his face darkened even beneath the tan. "What in the hell did you do that for?" he bellowed like a bull in heat.

"I lost my head," Harry said quietly.

"Do you know how much a windshield for a Rolls-Royce costs?"

"I'm sorry."

"You baboon! I'm going to give you something really to be sorry about!"

"Hit me if you wish," Harry said, "but perhaps you'd prefer to call the police and have them haul me away to jail."

"I'll do both, by God! I'll—" He touched the windshield. "Damn you anyway! Why in God's name did you pick my windshield to do an idiotic thing like that?"

"I was just walking along. I had this brick. And it came over me. Your house is so large. The car is so imposing. I just became overly resentful, I guess. I have no money myself. I'm unemployed, with no prospects whatever. So I took it out on your windshield. I'm terribly sorry. If you want to call the cops, I'll offer no resistance."

"Dummy!" the man said, gazing at the damaged glass again. But he seemed to be regaining control now, and he reexamined Harry. "Out of work, eh?"

"For some time. A real job, that is. I do write poetry."

"What's the sense in that?"

"I sometimes wonder."

The man touched one of the brick fragments with a shoe. "I'll try to put in an insurance claim on this. But they won't . . .

well, now, wait a *minute*. I *do* know something about insurance. This would be vandalism, wouldn't it?"

"I imagine that's what I committed."

"And they'll pay on that. Now look." The man pointed to a part of the glass still intact. "See this pitting? I've had this car for years and that windshield's taken a beating. Have a place in the mountains where we go a lot.

"When it snows, they plow and then lay down cinders, you see? The damned stuff keeps getting kicked up into the windshield. Was getting so when I was driving into the sunrise or sunset, I was damned near blinded." He nodded. "I needed a new windshield."

"I'm sorry," Harry said again.

"What the hell about? You did me a favor! I'll tell you what. I'll call the cops after you leave. I'll tell them I saw someone do it and then he ran away. After that, I'll put in the claim—the broken brick's evidence. You did me a *favor*. So take off now. On the double."

"Sir, I don't think—"

"You heard me. I don't want to get into a heat again, do you understand? Just do what I tell you."

"You're a very understanding man," Harry said, defeated.

"Well, not too many people believe that. But—" He got his wallet from a rear pocket of his slacks and found a bill. "Buy yourself a beer and try to calm down. Coming apart like that isn't going to help anything. All right?"

"Yes, sir."

"Get out of here."

"I will," Harry said, and returned down the drive with the twenty dollars the man had placed in his hand.

It was becoming an obsession, Harry realized, sitting in his room again, to accomplish what he had set out to do. But the means had yet to produce the end, so he thought about it once more as the night deepened. What would really do it? What would get him once and for all in the old slammer?

Then he was visualizing the beautiful girl with the dark hair and oval face he had seen so often on the street. He knew exactly where she lived in that large Spanish-style building. Her apartment was on a side street. He had seen her, now and then, on a small balcony in front of a glass door. He had also seen her passing that door at night and enough of the furniture to know it was her bedroom.

He became more alert as he pictured that part of the building. There was a trellis going up there that just reached the side of that balcony. If he could . . . .

He stood up, his mind made up again. A girl that beautiful? Not your old-maid ugly, who might dream of a nighttime invasion. But a luscious, desirable thing, who would scream her lungs out if it happened.

"Oh, yes," he said aloud and left his room.

There was no moon. Traffic was sparse on that side street. So he climbed right up the trellis, hoping that it would bear his weight. It did. Then he was hauling himself over the railing of the small balcony.

He moved to the door, thinking he would perhaps have to use force to get it open. But it was not locked. He went inside, unable to see anything. Still, he found a chair with his hand and began jiggling it up and down.

"What's that?" a tense voice sounded from across the room.

Harry jiggled the chair again.

"Somebody's there!"

"I'm sorry," Harry said.

"Who *are* you?"

"A stranger in the night."

"What do you want?"

"Nothing . . . now. I've regained my sanity. Things just got out of hand there, so I climbed the trellis. I've seen you a lot on the street, and I knew where you lived. I just couldn't help coming up here. You may scream if you like."

A light on a table beside her bed was switched on, and he looked at her lying in bed with the covers drawn to her pretty chin. 'I"ve seen you on the street, too!"

"Yes, ma'am."

"You looked like nothing at all."

"That's pretty much what I am. I see you've got a telephone on the table by your bed. You're free to pick it up and call the law. I'm not dangerous, I assure you. It's just that I simply belong in the lockup, where I can't do things like this."

But the girl simply stared at him with her lovely eyes. "And you had the nerve to climb up that trellis and open the door and come in here?" Her voice no longer sounded strident, and she appeared to have calmed.

"That's what I did."

"I've never experienced anything like this. Do you do it often?"

"When there's no moon, usually."

"God, and I thought you were nothing."

"That's really all I am—except when I do this sort of thing. Please, ma'am, call the police. I won't cause you any more trouble until they get here, then I'll go peacefully. That's what I deserve—being put in the pokey."

"*Why* did you come up here like this?"

"Because you're so beautiful and desirable-looking."

"Oh, God. And you just climbed the trellis."

"True."

"Risking yourself physically."

"The trellis held up pretty good."

"Taking the chance that you'd land in prison for doing it."

"That's what I deserve."

"Most of them just buy me expensive dinners and things and think they're proving something. I've never been fooled, you know."

"I'm certain you haven't been."

"But you truly proved you mean it. The *risk*!"

"I should be put in solitary."

"Come over here," she said.

"What?"

She switched out the light. "I said, come over here."

"Right now?"

"Faster than that, if you can."

Quite some time later Harry stood looking at her in the light of the lamp on the table. "I don't know what to say," he said.

"Before you leave, get my purse from the bureau."

"Yes, ma'am." She had a way of saying things that seemed to make him want to follow orders. He got the purse and gave it to her.

She found a wallet in it and withdrew currency. "Here."

"I don't expect that."

"Of course you don't. And I've never done it before. But I feel you deserve it."

"I shouldn't."

"I insist."

He took the money and put it in his pocket, feeling defeated again.

She turned the lamp off. "Be careful going down the trellis."

"Yes, ma'am," Harry said. "Thank you, ma'am."

The next day, Harry walked along a sidewalk of his neighborhood's business district. He walked with a slight slouch, hands in his pockets, feeling the continuing pressure of more and more frustration. It was the principle of the thing, he thought angrily —not only had he not achieved his goal, but he was proving his continuing ability to succeed at nothing!

Then he saw, ahead on the street, a uniformed police officer, ambling along in his direction, swinging his billy club as he moved. Behind the officer, down the street, a police car moved slowly in their direction.

Quite suddenly Harry lost his senses.

He ran forward, full-tilt, straight at the astonished officer, and hit the man in the nose.

"What—" the officer managed, raising his billy club.

Harry knocked it out of his hand. He had never before hit anyone. But he had seen fights on television screens. He knew how it should be done. He began pounding at the officer, knowing the man was going down under the barrage.

At the same time, from the corner of an eye, Harry saw the police car come forward with speed and rock to a halt. Two officers flew out of it and ran toward Harry and the fallen victim.

"Here now!" one of them said, grasping Harry from behind and holding him with a steely grip.

The other bent over the downed officer, then turned his head, saying, as a crowd formed around them, "Charley, look! Do you see who it is?"

The man holding Harry looked and whistled. "Him, all right."

"You bet your life it is!" said the other officer, turning the fallen man over to handcuff him from behind.

Harry felt himself released and looked on in bewilderment as one of the officers pulled the fallen man to his feet and marched him through the crowd to the police car.

"I don't understand," Harry said to the remaining officer.

"That was Cop-Beat Andy. He's been pulling that trick for years, all over the country—dressing up like an officer and walking a beat. He'd go into places, without nobody asking any questions, and case the operations. Then hit them later. How'd you know it was Andy?"

Harry felt a pulse beating in his neck. He was unable to answer.

"Knew it wasn't the right cop for this district, eh? Or maybe you saw his mug on a poster somewhere? Doesn't matter. We're just grateful you dropped him for us. Need more people like you, in this world. There's a reward, you know. Or did you?"

"I didn't know," Harry said dimly.

"Fifteen thousand. Well, you deserve it, believe me."

"Attaboy, Harry!" someone called from the crowd. "Didn't think you had it in you. But you did! Atta*boy!*"

It was Mr. Canaveslo.

The weeks and months passed. It was late spring as Harry sat in the office he had created out of a small bedroom of the neat cottage he had exchanged for the crummy hotel room. He was using a desk, a typewriter, and fresh paper now. New clothes hung in the closet. He could see, with pleasure, the shining sports car parked in the drive outside, which he had purchased with a small down payment. He no longer used buses and he had become weary of cabdrivers.

Yes, he felt very good now, because the last months had been rewarding ones. He had sold two poems in just the past ten weeks. They were purchased for a pittance, but that did not matter. His attitude had so changed that any day now true literary success would spring forth at him.

He had simply been negative, and that had been detrimental to the development of his talent. Not now. Not even with his funds dwindling rapidly as the result of his new life-style. He no longer worried about that because he now knew that one's luck *could* shift, as the arrow of a weather vane might swing from one direction to the opposite. He had had nothing but twenty-five years of bad luck. Now that shift was accomplished. So why should he have anything but good luck for the next twenty-five? One could always stick up a grocery store, smash a windshield, climb a trellis, punch an officer in the nose.

He smiled thinking how he would enjoy dinner at a particularly rewarding French restaurant this evening, nurturing the good life he had never known until these past months. He had come a long way from canned beans and bottled herring.

The door chimes sounded.

Harry opened the door to two very neatly dressed men, one tall, the other short. The tall one opened a wallet to reveal identification, as did the other. The tall one said, "Special agent, Internal Revenue Service. Are you Harry Waters?"

"I am." His voice was hesitant. He did not like the looks of these men.

"We'd like to come in."

Harry nodded, and they moved past him into his living room. "Won't you sit down, gentlemen?"

"Thank you."

Both sat on a sofa as Harry eased himself into his reading chair, seeing that they were staring at him coldly. "I, ah, don't know what—"

The tall man opened a briefcase and took out papers. "Did you file an income tax return for last year, Mr. Waters?"

Harry blinked. "Income tax return?"

"That's what I asked."

"Well . . . no, I—"

"Did you not gain a profit of at least fifteen thousand dollars last year?"

"Well, but I didn't *earn* anything like that. I barely earned anything at all."

"Did you receive a fifteen-thousand-dollar reward for the apprehension of a man impersonating an officer of the law?"

"Well, yes. But—"

"That's taxable, sir. And you filed no return. Have you *ever* filed a return?"

"Well, *no!* I never earned much. I didn't think—"

"When the reward was given you, did you not respond by giving the people who presented it to you with a Social Security number? And if so, when did you get that?"

"When I was sixteen, when I worked as an usher in a theater. I just kept the card in my wallet all this time."

"That number must have got lost somewhere in the machinery. Another thing—there has been no trace of any 1099 forms being filed with us at any time, except as the result of that reward. How have you supported yourself, Mr. Waters?"

"A little job here, a little job there. I write poetry, but—"

"And no employer has ever asked for your Social Security number in order to file a 1099 in your name prior to your receiving the reward?"

"Picking grapes? Washing dishes? Working for bums like I have? What do they know about 1099s? I tell you—"

"You're in trouble, Mr. Waters."

"But—"

"Income tax evasion," the agent said coolly. "Fraud."

Harry found himself blinking more rapidly. "I didn't think about that! I'm a *poet*!"

"You're a citizen of the United States. And you've obviously committed two crimes. I'm afraid you're going to have to pay the price."

"Well, what in hell *is* the price! You mean I could be fined? I'm about out of money!"

"I think there's a strong possibility of imprisonment."

Harry sat motionless for a moment, then he threw himself to his feet, face warm, beginning to tremble. And he shouted, "Don't you understand? I don't want to go to jail! Now *now!*"

*One unusual and interesting publishing event of 1977 was the special issue of the literary quarterly* Antaeus *devoted to three genres of popular fiction—western, detective, and science fiction. About one hundred pages were given over to each, containing new short stories and nonfiction pieces. The nine stories and two essays in the mystery section represented a good cross section of writing in the field today, and all nine of the stories were by writers included in this volume or in its two immediate predecessors. For me the best of them was this crime tale by Robert L. Fish, a past Edgar winner in both the first novel and short story categories. Fish is a truly versatile writer whose work ranges from the popular Schlock Homes parodies to tough police novels, like the one that was filmed as* Bullitt *in 1968. Many of his novels concern Captain José da Silva of the Rio de Janeiro police, a city Fish knows well from his work as a consulting engineer to the Brazilian plastics industry. He is the 1978 president of Mystery Writers of America.*

# ROBERT L. FISH
## Stranger in Town

The body lay sprawled against the side of the building, looking like a large rag doll that had been discarded by an exceptionally careless, or perhaps cruel child. Lieutenant Everts shook his grizzled head and looked up at the tall man beside him.

"My guess is whoever hit him had to be doing ninety. They use this block like a goddamn speedway. You got enough light from the patrol car spot, Doc?"

"Plenty," the doctor said dryly and yawned. "I wasn't planning on operating on him here. Do you have your pictures yet?"

"We're all through. We have his ID, too. He's Thomas Middleton the Third."

The doctor grunted and knelt beside the crushed figure. A cursory examination and he straightened up. "You know, Lieutenant," he said evenly, "one thing I'll never understand is the necessity of dragging a medical examiner out of bed at two in the morning just to advise you a man is dead, when anyone with eyes in his head can see he's dead. Did you have any doubts?"

"It's the law, Doc. You know that."

"Yes, I know that. It still doesn't make it any more understandable though." The doctor sighed. "Well, ship him downtown and we'll take a better look at him in the morning."

"Right. And Doc—be careful of the clothes. They go to the lab."

The doctor considered the lieutenant sardonically a moment. "Thanks, Lieutenant. I thought standard procedure with hit-runs was to put the clothes down the incinerator."

Everts reddened. "Well, all I meant was—well, he's Thomas Middleton the Third."

"Oh?" The doctor sounded curious. "Does that make him come before or after Charles the Second?"

"It makes him the son of Thomas Middleton, who happens to be a big shot in this town," the lieutenant said flatly.

"Oh!" The doctor climbed into his car and leaned out the window. "In that case we'll handle him with kid rubber gloves."

He drove off. Sarcastic son of a bitch, the lieutenant thought, and turned to the waiting ambulance attendants. "OK, you can load him up. Joe. You got all the pieces of headlight glass for the lab?"

"Anything big enough to help, Lieutenant."

"Good. Better get somebody from Sanitation to clean up that blood. And then start calling garages. Don't wait until morning."

"We'll get right to it, Lieutenant."

"Good." The lieutenant turned. "Mike, where's that—ah! You the one who called this in? What's your name?"

It was a man in his early thirties, fairly well dressed, but the lieutenant automatically noticed the frayed shirt collar, the worn shoes, and the tight look on the expressionless face.

"George Kennedy, Lieutenant."

"Well, Mr. Kennedy, what happened? Did you see the car? Or the driver?"

"I actually didn't see hardly anything," Kennedy said slowly. "I *heard* it more than I saw it. I was just coming around the corner—"

Lieutenant Everts interrupted, a frown on his face. "By the

way, what were you doing around here at two in the morning? This is a pretty deserted part of town."

Kennedy shrugged. "I was just walking, as a matter of fact. I don't know one part of this town from another. I'm new here."

"Have an address?"

Kennedy smiled. It was not the first time he had heard the question. "Yes, sir. Lincoln Hotel. And I've got fifty cents in my pocket, too."

"No offense," Lieutenant Everts said, and got back to business. "What about the car? Exactly what *did* you see?"

"I was just walking along, thinking, and I came around this corner when I heard this *noise*, like a skid, and then I heard the thud when he hit the man. By the time I got my thoughts together and realized what happened, all I could see was the tail end of a car going around the next corner, practically on two wheels, and that man, there, laying up against the side of the building."

"You wouldn't be able to recognize the driver if you saw him again?"

"I didn't see the driver at all, just the tail end of the car. It was a dark color, is about all I can say—"

"Did you notice what kind of rear window it was? Did the glass have rounded corners or square corners? Was it a convertible, by any chance?" Lieutenant Everts knew from long experience that most people saw far more than they realized.

Kennedy looked unhappy. "I—I didn't see."

Everts sighed. "What about taillights? They must have been on. How many were there? Two? Four? Or almost all the way across, like on a T-bird? And were they more red or more orange?"

"Two, I think." Kennedy suddenly brightened. "In fact, I'm sure there were two, because I remember when he came to the corner, he had to hit the brakes to make it, and the taillights just got larger. And brighter. And they were more red than orange."

Everts nodded and looked at the patrolman beside him. "Got that, Mike?"

"Yes, sir. Two taillights, the kind that get brighter when you hit the brakes. Has to make the car fifteen years old, at least. Dark color, no other ID."

"Good. See that Joe gets that information for the garages." He turned back to Kennedy. "That's all you can tell us?"

"I'm sorry, but that's about it."

"Well," Everts said, "we'd appreciate it if you'd contact us if you happen to remember anything else. And thanks for calling it in. Most people wouldn't have."

Kennedy nodded and turned away, his face expressionless, but with a large inward smile. Most people weren't George Kennedy, he said to himself, and headed back toward his hotel.

Luck! George Kennedy said to himself as he went to bed that night. Luck that he happened to be in this town tonight, whatever its name was. And Luck! he said to himself in the morning, winking at his image in the stained mirror as he knotted his worn necktie. What had his mother always said? She said there was no such thing as luck; it was merely being in the right place at the right time. Well, where the old lady had gone off was in not realizing that the luck came in having enough brains to know what to do when you found yourself in the right place at the right time.

He reached for his jacket, shrugged his way into it, and headed for the door. The call he intended to make was not to be made through any hotel switchboard. People who did things like that were stupid, and one more definition of luck was not being stupid.

A drugstore three blocks away seemed to suit his purpose; the four telephone booths were in the rear of the store and were empty, and from the deserted condition of the run-down place were likely to stay that way. He wedged himself into the last booth, dropped his dime, and dialed a number he could read from the face of the telephone. There was a single ring and a receiver was instantly lifted.

"Police Department. Sergeant Mannering."

Kennedy sounded hesitant, as if not sure he had dialed the correct number. "Is this the number I call if I want to speak with someone in the vehicle registration department?"

"One moment." A switch was pulled, another ring and a second voice was on the line, a woman's voice.

"Vehicle registration. Myra Simon speaking."

Hesitancy disappeared; Kennedy now combined official importance with manly charm. Listening to himself, he had to admit
it sounded good.

"Miss Simon, this is Sergeant Kennedy of the State Troopers,
Troop J. We have a man here apprehended for drunken driving.
He has no driver's license and the vehicle's registration is neither
in the vehicle nor on his person. From his appearance he doesn't
look as if he could afford the car he's driving. We have no record
of a stolen car complaint on the vehicle, but we'd still like a
check on the plates to be sure."

"Of course, Sergeant," Miss Simon said, pleased to be of assistance to the State Troopers. They led a romantic life, while hers
was tied up with papers and files. "What's the plate number?"

"GK-264-S," Kennedy said. It was a number engraved on his
memory from the night before, and one he was no more likely
to forget than the number he had worn at Danbury.

"GK-264-S," Miss Simon repeated dutifully. "And the make
and model?"

"It's a 1974 white Continental Mark Four."

"Thank you. It'll take a few minutes. Would you like to have
me call you back at the barracks?"

"I'm not at the barracks." He made it sound as if working
troopers were seldom at the barracks. "I'll hold."

As he waited, Kennedy congratulated himself on having considered all possible questions and prepared all possible answers.
He suddenly grinned in the privacy of the booth. Who said the
police were never helpful?

Miss Simon came back on the line. "Hello, Sergeant? Here we
are. GK-264-S. White Continental Mark Four, 1974. The owner
is listed as John Coletsos, address 6614 Fayette Boulevard, here in
town." She could not help but add, "Is that any help?"

Kennedy's voice dropped ruefully. "I guess I put you to a lot
of trouble for nothing, Miss. That's the ID of the driver."

"Well," Miss Simon said philosophically, sorry for the man at
the other end of the line who she was sure was single, handsome,
and in line for promotion, "that's what we're here for, Sergeant."

"True," Kennedy said, his tone admiring the young lady's wis-
dom. "Well, thanks again." Luck was still with him, he thought
as he hung up. The Continental might have been from the other

end of the state; or, worse, it might have been a rental, though with a Mark Four that was doubtful.

Sixty-six fourteen Fayette Boulevard was almost an hour's walk from the drugstore, but investigation was necessary; public transportation might possibly lead to future identification, and Kennedy was not a man to take chances. But the walk was worth it, he had to admit, for the house was all he could have wished for: a rambling mansion with a wide, circular drive set in acres of well-tended, landscaped beauty. It smelled of money and lots of it. Kennedy watched the house for some time from the privacy of a stand of trees across the road; then he walked off in search of another telephone.

He found it a mile away on the sidewalk of a discreet shopping center. He consulted a telephone directory, closed the booth door behind him, dropped his dime, and dialed. There was a brief wait; then a questioning voice was in his ear.

"Yes?"

George Kennedy made himself sound completely impersonal. "Mr. John Coletsos, please."

"Who wants to talk to him?"

"Tell him a friend. A very good friend."

"Hang on a second . . . ."

There was a brief wait. Kennedy watched the cars coming into the parking area of the shopping cneter, many chauffeur-driven, all expensive. A fine neighborhood, he thought with a grin, and then heard a second voice on the line. This one was cool, deep, steady.

"Yes? This is John Coletsos. Who is this?"

"This?" Kennedy was surprised at his own calmness. He's been wasting his time all these years in the small time; he had what it took for the heavy suff. "This, mister, is a man who saw you come shooting down Mitchell Street like a bat out of hell at two o'clock this morning, weaving all over the place, drunk as a skunk, and hit and kill a guy crossing the street. And then drive off without seeing if he could help. Now, does that identify me to your satisfaction?"

There was a gasp. "Me?"

"You, mister. Driving a new white Mark Four."

There was a long pause. Then the voice, no longer cool nor steady, said slowly, "I don't know who you are, or what you're after, but you've got the wrong number."

"I don't think so," Kennedy said calmly, now fully in control. "I didn't want to make any mistake, so I waited outside your house, and half an hour ago I saw you drive into your driveway, chauffeur and all, in a big new Caddy. But you're the man I saw early this morning driving that Continental. And you have a three-car garage attached to that big house of yours, and I'll bet ten of mine against one of yours that there's a smashed-up Continental locked up out there right now. Any bets?"

There was a deep breath. "Who *is* this? What's your name?"

Kennedy smiled at the instrument. "Let's keep the conversation serious, shall we?"

There was another pause, longer this time. Kennedy was about to interrupt the silence when the voice came on again, weary. "What do you want?"

"That's more like it," Kennedy said approvingly. "All I want to see is a nice man—a nice, rich man—like you keep out of trouble."

"And what would you expect for keeping me out of trouble?"

"Well, let's consider that point for a minute," Kennedy said thoughtfully. "You have a mansion for a house, plus a chauffeur, plus either a butler or maybe even a male secretary to answer the phone, and probably a cook, not to mention at least two big cars I know of, and probably a third in that garage. I haven't checked out what you do for a living, but it must be pretty profitable. I'd say if you were to donate a small sum to my favorite charity —which admittedly is me—then I'd simply forget the entire matter."

There was a briefer pause. "And if I don't donate this small sum to your favorite charity?"

"Then," Kennedy said firmly, "I'd be forced to go to the police. It would only be my civic duty, you understand." His voice hardened. "And you wouldn't like it."

There was a sigh. "How big a donation were you thinking of?"

"Well," Kennedy said thoughtfully, "I'd say ten thousand. A nice round number. You don't look as if that would hurt you."

"Ten thousand dollars?"

"We have a good connection," Kennedy said.

"And if I should agree," Coletsos said quietly, "where do I meet you?"

Kennedy grinned to himself. Hooked! He straightened his face, almost as if the other could see him. "Do you remember where you had that unfortunate accident this morning? Unless, of course, you were too drunk to even remember."

"As a matter of fact, I don't remember."

"I'm really not surprised," Kennedy said dryly. "Well, it was on Mitchell Street, between Eighth and Ninth, in the middle of the block on the south side of the street under the light. I'll be waiting for you there at two o'clock tomorrow morning."

"And how will I know you?"

"You won't," Kennedy said. "But I'll know you."

"Well," Coletsos said slowly. "Maybe I'll be there."

"I wouldn't leave it to any 'maybe' if I were you," Kennedy said coldly. "Be there with cash in your pocket. I wasn't kidding about the police in this town." He smiled to himself as he thought of a previous thought. "They can be real helpful at times . . . ."

Maxie Kosoff looked across the room. "What did the guy want, boss?"

Coletsos looked at him somberly. "He's trying to blackmail me. Shake me down. For ten grand."

Maxie's eyes almost popped. 'Shake *you* down, boss? Shake down Big John Coletsos? He's got to be a stranger in town!"

"That's still what he's trying to do," Coletsos said heavily. "He claims he saw me driving down Mitchell at two o'clock this morning, dead drunk. He says I was speeding, that he saw me hit and kill a guy. And then drive away without stopping."

Maxie shook his bullet-shaped head as if to rid it of cobwebs. "The guy's gotta have rocks in his head, boss. You ain't had a drink of anything hard since them ulcers, five, six years ago. And as far as where you was at two this morning, you was right here, playing pinochle with Jimmy Griff and the McCauley, remember? You was—"

"Damn it!" Coletsos exploded. "I know where I was this morning!" He pounded the table. "That damn kid!"

Maxie was mystified. "Who, boss?"

"Who else, dummy! John Junior, that's who! I ought to break

his ass! I ought to—" Words failed the big man. He slammed his big fist on the table again.

"But the guy said he seen *you*, boss—"

Coletsos looked at Maxie evenly. "Under a streetlight at night inside a closed car—if they even have streetlights on Mitchell—he saw John Junior, that's who he saw! He also saw him driving a new white Mark Four. Sound familiar? Where is John Junior, by the way?"

"I don't know, boss," Maxie said, feeling helpless. "He ain't home."

Coletsos took a deep breath. "Well, go down to the garage and see if his car's there, at least."

"Right, boss."

Coletsos waited, his thick fingers drumming the table. He had no doubt but that John Junior had done one more dumb thing the night before. But it came at a bad time, when the newspapers were after his scalp for a whole series of things. Dumb kid! He looked up to see Maxie staring at him dolefully.

"I'm afraid the guy could be right, boss. The Four looks like it maybe hit one of our beer trucks, or something."

Coletsos nodded abruptly, his mind made up. "OK, Maxie. Get one of our moving vans over here, one with a ramp. Get the kid's car into it and down to the garage, hear? Tell Eddie I want it in twelve hours, maximum, and I don't care what he has to do. And I want it without a scratch, hear?"

"Gotcha, boss."

"And then I want our garage, here, vacuumed from top to bottom. Better make it the back driveway, too, but nobody's to see. No glass dust, no paint chips, no blood, no anything. Understand?"

"I gotcha, boss." Maxie rubbed one heavy fist into the calloused palm of the other hand. "And then can I take a couple of boys and go down and teach this character a little lesson?"

Coletsos frowned at him. "Good God, no!"

Maxie was properly amazed. "But, boss, you ain't going to pay off no ten grand to no chiseler, are you? Tell him to pound gravel! You got the whole town in your pocket, boss—"

"You don't understand," Coletsos said slowly. "You just take care of getting the car fixed. There's only one way to handle a blackmailer, Maxie; give him his head. He told me if I didn't cough up, he'd go to the police. Well, he's in for one big surprise, because *I'm* the one who's going to the police. Before you go, get me Lieutenant Everts on the line. He owes me a couple of favors."

"Got enough light from the ambulance, Doc?"

"I guess so," the doctor said and looked around. "Where's your trusty patrol car?"

"Me and Joe had a little accident with it a while ago," Lieutenant Everts said. "Got the front smashed, some." He shrugged. "Let's get with it, huh, Doc?"

"Glad to," the doctor said and knelt down. He came to his feet a moment later. "Well, he's dead, if that makes it legal. One thing I'll never understand—a man reports a hit-run one night, and then goes out and gets himself knocked off the same way at practically the same spot the very next night."

"Yeah," Lieutenant Everts said unemotionally. "Some people aren't very smart. I guess he didn't realize just how dangerous some places can be at times. He was a stranger in town . . . ."

*This annual collection would hardly seem complete without a story by Jack Ritchie. No one writes detective and crime tales quite like he does, and this story of a series murderer isn't quite like any others you may have read.*

# JACK RITCHIE
## Hung Jury

I had just returned from my vacation and Ralph began filling me in on the case assigned to us.

"Three members of the jury were murdered," he said.

I nodded wisely. "Ah, yes. I see it all. The jury convicted a felon and he swore he would get his revenge."

"Not quite," Ralph said. "Actually it was a hung jury. Four for acquittal and eight for conviction."

"But of course," I said. "So the criminal promptly proceeded to kill three of the jurors who had voted for his conviction."

"Not that either, Henry. All three of the jurors murdered had voted for his acquittal."

"Why the devil would he want to murder three jurors who voted for his acquittal?"

"He didn't really murder anybody, Henry. He couldn't because he was dead."

"Ralph," I said patiently, "if you keep interrupting, I never will get to the nubbin of this case. Start at the beginning."

"Last year," Ralph said, "one Mike Winkler was arrested for the murder of a Jim Hurley. Both of them had long records for breaking and entering. They had just finished a job and they got into an argument about how they should divide the loot. Winkler pulled a gun and shot Hurley four times, which was enough to kill him. Somebody in a neighboring apartment heard the shots and called the police. They arrived to find Winkler sitting on his couch trying to figure out what to do with Hurley's body. Winkler confessed on the spot that he had killed Hurley and why."

"That should have wrapped it all up."

"Unfortunately, as soon as Winkler got hold of a lawyer, or vice versa, he withdrew the confession. Said he'd been beaten into making it by the arresting officers."

"Was he?"

"No. You know how it is in the department. If one of us does any roughing up, everybody learns about it in time. That doesn't mean that we fall all over ourselves to let the public know. But it's no big secret among ourselves, and nobody laid a finger on Winkler. Anyway, his story was that he went out for a newspaper and when he came back he found Hurley dead and the gun on the floor. But even without the confession, the case against him was still solid as a rock—powder grains on his hands, fingerprints on the murder gun, and so forth."

"But still the jury refused to convict him?"

"It was just one of those things that happen every now and then. You get a balky jury that believes what it wants to believe no matter what the evidence. Maybe it has something to do with the phases of the moon. The jury deliberated for five days without reaching a verdict and the judge finally dismissed it."

"Winkler went free?"

"No. He was taken right back to the county jail while the gears of justice meshed to try him for a second time with a new jury. But there never was a second trial. While Winkler waited, he managed to saw his way out of his cell and steal a car on the street. A squad car spotted him and the chase began. It finally ended when Winkler crashed into another car on a freeway ramp. Both Winkler and the driver of the other car were killed outright."

Faintly I remembered reading about it in the newspapers.

"It happened on the twenty-second of January, this year," Ralph went on. "And now we move on to the twenty-second of the next month, February. One Amos Albee, a bachelor, age thirty-six, accountant, was found hanging by the neck from a rafter in his garage. It was assumed he got onto a chair, slipped the noose around his neck, and then stepped off."

"He didn't leave a suicide note?"

"No. But then many suicides don't. Albee's background indicated that he was a loner, melancholy by nature, and so it looked like he'd got a little more melancholy than usual and decided to end it all. And then exactly one month later, on the twenty-second of March, a Cora Anderson was found dead, also by hanging, in the laundry room of her apartment building. Cora was in her sixties, a widow in bad health, and it appeared that the loneliness of her life and her sickness had got too much for her, and she decided to end her life."

"I gather that both Cora and Amos were members of the hung jury and that they had voted for Winkler's acquittal?"

"Yes, but at the time nobody connected them in any way. Who's to remember the names of the jurors in any of the dozens of trials going on in the courthouse every month? Besides, we get an average of ten suicides a month."

I alertly grasped the situation. "And then a third juror committed suicide, so to speak, and it took place on the twenty-second of the month following? April?"

"Exactly. Gerald Hawkins, a widower, retired, aged sixty-six, was found hanged in his basement. No suicide note either."

"But now somebody finally got suspicious?"

Ralph nodded. "Jurors get paid for their jury duty, but paperwork being what it is, it wasn't until July that the checks went out in the mail. Nine of them were delivered and accepted, but three of the envelopes were returned, addresses unknown. The City Clerk's office sent a man out to the last-known addresses to talk to neighbors and try to come up with some forwarding addresses. He discovered that all three of the jurors had hanged themselves. It seemed like just too much coincidence, so the City Clerk took the whole thing to the police. That was last week, while you were still on your vacation. By the way, where did you go?"

"No place. I stayed home and read and watched the educational channel on television. Also I did some Double-Crostics. Very refreshing and relaxing."

Ralph studied me for a moment and then continued. "We went back to the scenes of the deaths and were able to recover the ropes used on the three jurors—neighbors keep the damnedest things for souvenirs. In our lab we matched the rope ends. In other words, all three of the ropes had come from the same length or coil." He paused a moment. "You stayed in your apartment the entire two weeks?"

I nodded. "Most people travel on their vacations because they feel guilty about having all that free time and doing nothing. But I never feel guilty about having time off." I pondered the case for a moment. "You said that during his escape attempt, Winkler ran into another car and killed the driver."

"James Bellington. Age twenty-eight. A steam fitter and plumber. Married. No children. He was the only one in the car."

I smiled. "Ralph, if you search Bellington's garage or basement, I'll wager you will find a coil of rope whose end exactly matches one end of the rope used on the third juror. My theory is that his wife was so traumatically affected by his death that she systematically hunted down every one of the jurors responsible for the—"

"We searched," Ralph said. "No rope. Besides, Bellington and his wife were separated and in the process of getting a divorce. She was minimum sad about his death, especially since she was still his life insurance beneficiary."

"What about grieving relatives? Brother, sister, parents? Girl friend?"

"None. Bellington's parents are dead and he had no brother or sister. Also no girl friend."

I tried again. "What about the man Winkler shot? Who was unduly affected by his death?"

"Nobody. Hurley ran away from an orphan asylum at the age of fifteen. No relatives and no friends, except for the man who shot him."

I stroked my chin thoughtfully. "And yet it appears that someone has been commemorating the date of Bellington's death by executing a juror on the same day of succeeding months. Clearly someone is saying that if it weren't for the hung jury, Winkler would have been safely stowed in a maximum-security state prison rather than in our flimsy county jail where he had the opportunity to escape and subsequently cause the death of Bellington." I frowned. "Since we cannot find anyone personally devastated by Bellington's death, we must assume that somewhere out there in this city there is a dedicated nut who has taken it upon himself to balance the scales of justice. He could be any one of a million people."

"Possibly," Ralph said. "But on the other hand, looking closer to home, we find that the Winkler jury members were practically at each other's throats after five days of deliberation. The eight who voted for Winkler's conviction felt quite strongly that it was a miscarriage of justice not to find Winkler guilty of murder."

I nodded judiciously. "One of those eight jurors must be our murderer."

"We were able to establish that each of the murders must have occurred between ten and twelve in the evening. And if we assume that one person committed all three of the murders, we can eliminate six of the jurors for one reason or another. They have solid alibis for one, two, or all three of the murders."

I rapidly subtracted six from eight. "Ralph, I believe we've narrowed it down to two persons."

Ralph agreed. "One of them is an Elmer Poulos. Age twenty-eight. Physical culture enthusiast. Works in a florist shop at the Mayfair shopping center. The other is Deirdre O'Hennessey. She's twenty-five and has a job as a secretary in a construction firm."

"Ralph," I said, "when we have a chain of murders like this, the murderer's insufferable ego usually impels him to leave something in the nature of a signature at the scene of each crime. Something more personal than just matching rope ends."

Ralph nodded. "Good for you, Henry. After we decided it was murder, we went over everything again with a fine-tooth comb. We found a small cross, about half an inch in size, scratched on the underside of each of the chairs supposedly used by the suicides."

"Hmm," I said. "What kind of cross was it, Ralph? Latin? Lorraine? Celtic? Maltese?"

"Just a plain ordinary cross." He drew one on a sheet of paper.

"Ah," I said. "The Greek cross. Unless, of course, you tilt it forty-five degrees to either the left or the right. In which case, it becomes a Cross of St. Andrew's."

Ralph and I went downstairs to the police garage where we picked up our car and drove it to the Mayfair shopping center. At the florist shop we talked to the owner who directed us to a room at the rear of the store.

We found Elmer Poulos, a muscular young man in a T-shirt, making a funeral wreath.

Ralph introduced me. "This is Sergeant Henry Turnbuckle. My regular partner. He'd like to ask you a few questions."

I nodded. "I will get directly to the point. I understand that you have no alibi for any of the nights of the murders."

He smiled happily. "Absolutely none. I always go to sleep at nine-thirty and alone. I have to get a good night's rest so that I can lift the weights."

Ralph studied him. "We think that the murderer first subdued his victims, possibly with chloroform, then put a noose around their neck and hoisted them to the ceiling. Which means that our murderer must be quite a strong man."

"Not necessarily, Ralph," I said. "The murderer could have simply pointed a gun at his victims and ordered them to get on the chair and slip the noose around their neck. Then the murderer kicked the chair away."

"Now, Henry," Ralph said, "I find it hard to believe that his victims would cooperate with him to that extent."

Poulos agreed. "I'll bet that ninety-nine percent of the people on this earth would rather be shot than hanged."

"True enough," I said, "*if* the victims were absolutely certain they were really about to be hanged. But I suspect that being human and hopeful, they thought that it might just be some kind of bad practical joke and that the best thing to do was to humor the gun holder by cooperating to a point. They would get on the chair and put the noose around their neck. Having the chair kicked out from under them would come as somewhat of a surprise."

Poulos dissented. "Personally I go with the chloroforming and the hoisting."

I regarded him pointedly. "If that was indeed the method used, then you are certainly our most logical suspect."

Poulos beamed. "I don't mind being a logical suspect. Just as long as you can't prove anything. I'm getting a lot of respect around here now. They think maybe I did it. I mean working in a flower shop isn't all that macho and you need all the help you can get."

A thought came to me. "Ralph, Bellington was killed on the twenty-second of January and then on the twenty-second of each succeeding month—February, March, and April—another juror was hanged. But why wasn't the *fourth* juror murdered on the twenty-second of May? It was certainly his turn. Why did the murderer stop killing? He still had one more juror to go. And yet the twenty-second of May passed and there was no dead fourth juror. Why? Did the murderer forget his name? His address? Who is the fourth juror who voted for acquittal?"

Ralph was about to give me the name, but then he eyed Poulos and changed his mind. "The fourth juror is a woman of thirty. Married with four children, the oldest twelve."

I frowned in cogitation. "Every one of the murdered jurors was single. Alone. In other words their death affected no one but themselves. Is it really too much to postulate that the murderer stopped killing because his heart weakened at the prospect of murdering a woman with four minor children?" I turned to Poulos. "Do you like children?"

He thought about that. "Would it be un-American if I said not particularly?"

I cunningly questioned Poulos for another half hour but gained nothing additional.

When we left Poulos, Ralph drove to an apartment building on the east side. We took the elevator up to the fourth floor.

I glanced at my watch. "Ralph, you said this Deirdre O'Hennessey is a secretary. However, since this is a weekday and therefore a workday, I predict you won't find her home."

"She'll be home," Ralph said. "She's still on her vacation."

Deirdre O'Hennessey had raven hair and extremely violet eyes. She regarded Ralph. "Oh, it's you again."

She let us into her apartment.

I glanced about the room, noticing that she had evidently been working on a Double-Crostic when we rang. I recognized it as one I'd completed several days before.

"Miss O'Hennessey," I said, "I understand you have absolutely no alibi for the nights on which the three jurors were murdered."

She agreed. "None. On the other hand, I doubt very much if I would have had the strength to tie a rope around anybody's neck and hoist him to the ceiling."

I smiled wisely. "We in the department have the suspicion that the hangings might have been accomplished without the need of any strength at all. Do you have a revolver? A threatening weapon of any kind?"

She nodded. "I have a crossbow in the closet. I really don't know what to do with it, but it was on sale and I just couldn't resist it."

I considered the picture. Did she point a crossbow at the quailing? . . .

Deirdre O'Hennessey sat down beside the Double-Crostic. "What is a six-letter word for any of a group of isomeric hydrocarbons of the paraffin series? The second letter has to be a $c$."

"Octane," I said.

She stared at me for a second and then lettered in the word. She looked up. "I have a question. Three of the four jurors who voted for Winkler's acquittal were murdered. Why not the fourth?"

"We don't know," Ralph said.

I found myself chortling.

They looked at me and Ralph said, "Henry, why are you chortling?"

"Ralph, I know who the killer is."

Ralph studied me and then nodded. "All right, Henry, who is the murderer?"

"Well, I don't actually know his name. But it all reminds me of Jack the Ripper."

Clearly I had their undivided attention.

"Why does it all remind you of Jack the Ripper?" Ralph asked.

I smiled. "Well, Jack the Ripper had a pattern too. He murdered a number of women and then as suddenly as the killings began, they stopped. Why?"

"I give up, Henry," Ralph said. "Why?"

"No one knows for certain, Ralph. But there are a number of theories advanced—that he decided the risk was becoming too great, that he finally saw the error of his ways, that he lost interest, and so on. Anyway, to my mind, the theory that holds the most water is that the killings stopped simply because Jack the Ripper died—by natural causes, disease, accident, or whatever.

"What I am saying, Ralph, is that our killer is dead. That is why he did not murder the fourth juror. You said that six of our jurors had alibis of 'one sort or another.'" I smiled broadly. "All right, Ralph, which one of our jurors is dead?"

"None," Ralph said.

I stared out of the window for a few moments. "On the other hand, it is entirely possible that Jack the Ripper emigrated. People did a lot of emigrating in those days. Perhaps his ship was even lost at sea, which may account for the fact that there were no more Jack-the-Ripper-style murders in America, Canada, Australia, or New Zealand."

Deirdre O'Hennessey had been listening to me, obviously impressed. "Why did the murderer go through the bother of making the deaths look like suicide? Why couldn't he just kill his people and leave it at that?"

I had the answer, of course. "Because he didn't want the police interfering before his mission was completed."

I lapsed into thought for a few moments and then chortled again.

Deirdre O'Hennessey tilted her head. "Why are you chortling now?"

"It is my theory that the murderer is off his rocker. Ralph, have head X rays been taken of our suspects?"

"No, Henry."

"Ralph, you must agree that it is a bit unusual for a man to commit three murders for what is basically an abstract, rather than a personal, motive—that is, the desire to achieve justice. Therefore I deduce that the murderer has something wrong with his head and that this accounts for his actions. I believe X rays are in order."

"I don't know about the legal aspects of that, Henry," Ralph said, staring at the ceiling. "It might be considered an invasion of privacy. At the very least, I think we'd have to get warrants. Why couldn't our murderer be just an ordinary run-of-the-mill psychotic?"

"You have a point there, of course," I conceded. "Or perhaps the murderer has a basal metabolism problem. Or low blood sugar. I rather think that if we X-rayed our suspects, or at least gave them a thorough physical examination, it might prove fruitful."

"What is a five-letter word for unearthly, uncanny, wild?" Deirdre asked.

I pondered. "Weird?"

She nodded. "That's it exactly."

I frowned thoughtfully. Strange. I didn't remember that particular word in the Double-Crostic.

I continued my incisive questioning of Deirdre O'Hennessey for another hour and then Ralph and I returned to headquarters.

Assistant District Attorney Orville Jepson came to our desk. "Well, did you come up with anything new on the dead jurors?"

"Nothing yet," Ralph said.

Jepson is considered to be a brilliant dedicated worker and no one has ever failed to notice his Phi Beta Kappa key.

Ralph spoke to me. "Orville handled the Winkler trial."

The memory of it darkened Jepson's brow. "The only case I ever lost. It made no sense at all. He was guilty as hell and I proved it beyond a doubt."

Ralph tried to be consoling. "Maybe Winkler managed to bribe those jurors."

Jepson shook his head. "No. Winkler was broke. The court had to appoint an attorney for him. Besides, even if he managed to get to the jury, all he needed was to bribe one person. Not four." Jepson glowered. "I just had a stinking jury. No wonder people have no respect for our judicial system. As far as I'm concerned, letting a murderer off is tantamount to being an accessory to the act—or anything that follows."

I nodded. "You mean Benninger's death?"

He corrected me. "Bellinger. Edward Slocum Bellinger."

Something clicked in my mind. "You remember his middle name?"

"Of course," Jepson said. "I have a good memory for names."

I studied Jepson and then smiled thinly. "Let me paint a portrait of our murderer. First of all, he is a perfectionist. He is also extremely brilliant. He must be perfect in everything he undertakes. He cannot endure defeat—even one defeat. And what is more, he believes fiercely in justice. The guilty must be punished. And if this can't be done legally, it must be done extralegally."

Jepson cocked his head. "Brilliant, you say?"

"Of course. A twisted, brilliant mind. He feels that if the guilty are not punished, it is a failure on his part and he must make amends. Now, sir, where were you on the night of—"

Ralph sat up quickly. "How did you like Hong Kong, Orville?"

Jepson brightened. "It was great. We all had a swell time."

Ralph turned to me. "Henry, you *do* remember that Orville took a vacation trip to the Orient with his wife and family. Hong Kong, Honolulu, Manila. The works. And they were gone *all* of April."

By George, he was right.

Jepson nodded. "We didn't get back until the beginning of May. Just in time for the funeral."

"Funeral?" I said. "What funeral?"

"Judge Remsford's funeral. He presided at the Winkler trial. Took the hung jury rather hard too, as I remember. His face got quite livid and he had a few choice words for the jury before he dismissed it." Jepson sighed. "The judge was a fine man. Cut down in the prime of his life, you might say."

"Cut down?"

"Yes. Terminal disease. Began acting a bit erratic. His wife finally took him to a doctor. X rays showed that it was inoperable. Died on the first or second of May." Jepson reflected on the death. "Yes, a fine man. Wilbur Cross Remsford."

Wilber *Cross* Remsford?

"Left a wife and three children," Jepson said. He patted Ralph on the shoulder. "Well, keep at it. Let me know if you come up with anything new."

Ralph and I were silent after he left.

Finally Ralph cleared his throat. "Henry, I have the feeling that if we looked in Remsford's garage or basement we'd find a certain coil of rope."

I agreed.

Neither one of us made a move to rise.

"On the other hand," I said, "what would be the point of it all? Remsford is dead. He can't be punished. The only ones to suffer if this came out into the open would be his family."

Ralph and I came to an agreement. The case was officially closed.

Our phone rang and Ralph picked it up. He listened and then turned to me. "She wants to know what's a South African eleven-letter word for a tall acacia on which the giraffe often browses."

That *had* been a difficult one. I smiled. "Kameeldoorn. Literally meaning camel thorn."

Ralph turned back to the phone. "He can't think of the word right now, but he'll have it tonight when he drops in at about seven-thirty. By the way, the only thing he drinks is sherry." Ralph hung up.

"Now, Ralph," I said, "why did you tell her I'd be over?"

"Henry," Ralph said, "she didn't go through the jungle of our headquarters switchboard just so that she could find out what some giraffe—" He stopped and smiled. "Henry, we just can't have her calling day and night and disrupting the department. You go over there tonight and give her all the words you've got."

Deirdre had a bottle of sherry waiting when I arrived that evening.

*Considering the fact that kidnapping, for both political and financial gain, has become one of the most serious crime problems in several European and Latin American countries, it's surprising that so little fiction is devoted to it. Here is a kidnapping story by R. L. Stevens, the pseudonym of a frequent contributor to EQMM.*

# R. L. STEVENS
# The Price of Wisdom

The nightmare began on a Monday in May, when I stepped off the afternoon shuttle flight from Boston and caught a taxi for Martha's third-floor apartment overlooking Gramercy Park. It was a sunny day in Manhattan and my spirits were high. I'd have two nights with Martha before returning home. With luck I might even take care of the business, which was this month's excuse for the trip.

Martha Gaddis was my mistress. It's a word that's rarely used in these liberated times, but that's what she was, nevertheless. I didn't actually support her to the extent of paying the rent on her five-room apartment, but when I made my monthly trips to New York—to check on the diamond merchants along Forty-seventh Street or the antique jewelry at the little shops on upper Madison Avenue—she was always there waiting for me.

Of course my wife, Joan, didn't know about Martha Gaddis. She thought I stayed at the apartment of an old army buddy when I was in New York. Maybe she had her suspicions, but if so she never voiced them. It was probably better that way. Having Martha, after all, didn't mean that I loved Joan any less. Joan was my wife and the mother of our two children. That was one life.

Martha and the apartment on Gramercy Park was another life.

This day she greeted me at the door, as she always did when I phoned from the airport. I could describe Martha by calling her a chic blond, but that was only the surface woman. Actually she was an artist and a poet, merging two ill-paying professions into a sort of livelihood. She never asked me for money, though I insisted on leaving her some each month, if only to pay for the groceries I consumed. I didn't think about what she did in her spare time the rest of the month. If there were other shuttle flights, from Washington or Chicago or Detroit, I didn't want to know about them.

"Jeff, darling," she said in that familiar soft voice, running a hand along my cheek. "It's been so long!"

"Only four weeks."

"It seems a lifetime."

I hung my suitcoat in the front closet and dropped my attaché case on a convenient chair. Then I gave her a long kiss. "It seems a lifetime for me too," I agreed. "How've you been?"

"Fine. Lonesome."

"I wrote you."

"One letter in four weeks! I get that much from Con Edison!"

Traditionally, the first night's dinner was eaten at her apartment. Martha was a good cook, and this night, as we dined by the window overlooking the park, she was filling me in on the history of the area.

"Until 1830 it was a farm belonging to a man named Samuel Ruggles," she said over coffee and dessert. "Then he divided it to form the present park. Most of these houses date from about 1840, and one of them—Number Four—was the home of New York's mayor James Harper in 1844. A few decades later Samuel Tilden, the almost-president of 1876, lived at Number Fifteen. And Edwin Booth the actor was at Number Sixteen."

"You should write a book about it," I told her half in jest. She had a way of going off on subjects like that, pouring out more knowledge than I really cared to hear.

She started to reply but was interrupted by the buzzer. "Who could that be?"

"One of your other lovers," I ventured.

"Some joke!" She spoke through the intercom, asking who was there, but nobody answered. The buzzing kept on. Finally, in exasperation, she unbolted the door. "They probably want one of the other tenants."

Then I heard her scream, not loud, and she tumbled backward through the doorway, landing on the rug. I was out of my chair, crossing the room to her side, when I saw the man in the doorway.

He wore a stocking mask over his head and carried a small revolver. Behind him was a second man, also masked, who held what looked like a sawed-off shotgun.

"What in hell is this? Who are you?" I bent over to help Martha.

"Stay away from her!" the man with the revolver ordered. His voice was brisk and authoritative. "You're Jeff Michaels, right?"

The sound of my name on that man's lips sent a chill through me. This was no random holdup. They were after me and they'd found me. In that wild instant a dozen thoughts crowded my brain. Had Joan learned about Martha and me and sent these people to kill me? No, that was fantastic!

"I'm Michaels," I managed to get out. "What do you want?"

"We're taking you along. Tell the lady not to call the police if she ever wants to see you alive again."

Martha was still on the floor, sheer terror on her face. "Jeff, what do they want?"

"I can't imagine."

The man with the revolver gestured. "You're being kidnapped, mister. Don't struggle, do as you're told, and you won't be harmed. Otherwise, you're dead."

"Kidnapped! I don't have any—"

"Shut up!" While the second man covered me with the shotgun, the first one took out a hypodermic needle. "This won't hurt you and it won't knock you out. It'll just make you a little fuzzy-headed and willing to come with us. It's this or a rap on the head. Take your choice."

"What sort of choice is that?" I mumbled. But I didn't resist when he plunged the needle through my shirt and into my arm.

"Now tell the lady not to call the police. You don't want it all over the papers that you were kidnapped from your girl friend's apartment, do you?"

"I—no." The injection was already beginning to take effect. I turned to Martha. "I'll be all right. Don't call the police."

"Jeff!"

"We won't hurt him, lady, as long as you both behave."

Then they slipped on my jacket and hustled me out the door to the elevator. A part of me was past all caring, but another part still hoped someone would see us and raise an alarm.

They kept me to one side till they saw the elevator was empty, then prodded me in with their guns. We rode down to the basement and they took me out the back door to a waiting car. In the back seat the one with the revolver said, "Now you'll be blindfolded from here on. If you remove the blindfold and see our faces, or see the place where we take you, we'll have to kill you. Understand?"

"Yes."

"Good!"

He fitted some sort of goggles over my face that effectively blocked all vision. Then he ordered me onto the floor of the back seat and covered me with a blanket. We drove for about a half hour, as near as I could tell, but in my drugged state it might have been longer. It was impossible to concentrate on direction, or even to determine whether or not we passed over a bridge going out of Manhattan.

Presently the car stopped and the revolver prodded me once more. "We're here. No tricks now."

They led me inside a building and up several flights of stairs. I tried to listen for sounds but I heard nothing. It was an apartment somewhere in the city, but I could tell no more. The floor was bare, without even a rug, and in the room where I was to be kept there seemed to be no bed. "You'll use that sleeping bag," the man's voice told me. "If your wife pays off, it won't be for long."

The drug was beginning to wear off, and I tried to reason with him. "Look, this diamond ring I'm wearing is worth two thousand dollars. Take it, and my watch and wallet. Then let me go."

"We're after far bigger stakes, Michaels. Pretty soon we're going to phone your wife in Boston and you'll tell her what we want."

"What's that? I'm not a wealthy man."

"You're wealthy enough for us. We know all about your jewelry business."

I realized it had all been carefully planned. "How much do you want?" I asked at last.

"A quarter of a million dollars in uncut rubies."

"Rubies!"

"We have a market for them overseas, and we know they're available through your business. Your wife will phone the manager tomorrow and convey your instructions. If he won't surrender the gems, you may have to phone him too. Your wife will package them as we instruct and fly to New York tomorrow afternoon. The package will be left in a ladies' room at La-Guardia Airport. Your wife will board the next shuttle flight back to Boston. Once the rubies are safely in our hands, without police interference, you'll be released."

A little later they made their call. The telephone was thrust into my hands and I heard Joan's puzzled voice on the other end. "Jeff? What is it?"

Trying to keep my voice calm, I answered, "Don't get excited. I've been kidnapped."

"What!"

"Calm yourself, Joan. I'm in no danger if you do exactly what they tell you. And don't call the police."

"My God, Jeff! What do they want?"

"A quarter million dollars in uncut rubies. You'll have to get them from the company vault and fly to New York with them tomorrow. This man will tell you exactly what to do."

My captor took the phone and spoke distinctly. "We won't contact you again, Mrs. Michaels, so listen carefully." He outlined the procedure to be followed, including the plane she should take the next day and the place where the package should be left. "There's a wastebasket for paper towels. Wrap the package in a couple of paper towels and drop it in. Then leave immediately and take the shuttle back to Boston."

"I—I don't think I can get the rubies that soon," Joan said. I could hear her voice coming from the receiver.

"Your husband will call his manager and take care of that. You just pick them up."

"Can I talk to him again?"

"Do as you're told and he'll be free by tomorrow night. Otherwise he'll be dead."

He hung up, but I could feel his presence near me still. "We'd better call your manager and arrange for the pickup of the rubies. We don't want any slips."

I talked to George Franklin on the phone and told him what had happened, emphasizing he must not call the police. He was a frightened little man at the best of times, and the news of my kidnapping completely unnerved him.

"A quarter million uncut!" he protested. "I don't think we have that much in rubies."

"Then get them! Draw some money out of the special account

and buy them from Craig or Morton. They'll have enough to make up the difference."

"All right." He sounded reluctant.

"These men mean business, George."

"All right," he repeated.

After the phone calls they handcuffed me and gave me another injection, putting me into the sleeping bag for the night. I slept better than I'd expected, helped no doubt by the powerful tranquilizing drug. When I awakened in the morning they brought me a light breakfast—orange juice in a plain water glass and a piece of toast on a paper plate.

I could tell nothing about my surroundings, though occasional street noises penetrated the room. Sitting on the floor with my meager breakfast, I might have been on another planet. I knew that one of the two men was in the room, watching me, and since he didn't speak I suspected it was the silent one with the shotgun.

I found myself feeling for the walls, trying to leave a mark that might be identified later. But they were smoothly painted and any smudges I might make could easily be wiped away. In my hands were a paper plate that would be disposed of and a water glass.

The glass was my only chance to leave some sign, and it was a slim one. I waited till I heard my captor step out of the room momentarily and then I finished the juice and turned the glass upside down. Working quickly, I used my diamond ring to scratch a crude JM on the bottom of the glass. I couldn't see how successful I was, of course. It might not show at all—or it might be so obvious they'd see it at once and throw away the glass. But it was my only chance.

They gave me another injection after breakfast, and I dozed off and on through the rest of the day. With my eyes covered it was impossible to tell when day ended and night began, and once after waking I called out to ask what time it was. The man with the revolver came into the room and answered that it was late afternoon. He said he was waiting for his partners to pick up the rubies.

"You'd better pray there are no cops," he said.

"What good would it do you to kill me?"

I heard him go out of the room without answering.

After a time I lifted my handcuffed wrists and felt the goggles around my eyes. I'd been considering risking a peek at my surroundings, but I discovered that broad pieces of tape had been added. I settled back against the wall, discouraged.

Presently I heard the apartment door open and then the low murmur of voices. I held my breath, half-expecting a bullet at any moment. Or a fatal injection from which I would never awaken. I had a fleeting memory of Martha, huddled on the floor where she'd fallen. And Joan. Had she flown to New York with the rubies? Did she really care whether I lived or died? How hard would it be for her to keep the rubies and only pretend to have made the delivery? She'd be rid of me, and she'd have a quarter of a million dollars to start a new life as the bereaved widow.

If that's what she wanted.

I heard someone enter the room.

It was the man with the revolver, the talkative one. "Your wife delivered," he said. "Right on schedule. This must be your lucky day."

"You mean I can go?"

"We'll wait till it gets dark, then take you out and dump you somewhere. Don't worry, we're not going to harm you."

His words were reassuring, but when you're blindfolded and handcuffed it takes more than reassuring words. Wouldn't he tell me exactly the same thing if they meant to take me out and dump my body in the river?

The next hours passed slowly. They fed me again—a sandwich on a paper plate followed by a cup of instant coffee—and then made preparations to leave. I was taken down the stairs and this time I tried to count the flights. There seemed to be four of them, but I was pretty certain we emerged into a basement. That would mean I'd been kept on the third floor.

"Into the back seat," the man ordered, "and no tricks. We'd really hate to shoot you this close to letting you go."

They drove me around for the better part of an hour, or at least it seemed that long. Finally the car stopped at a curb and I was shoved out. By the time I tore the tape and goggles from my eyes the car was out of sight.

I was somewhere uptown, near Riverside Drive, but I couldn't identify the exact spot. Still handcuffed, I struggled to a corner phone booth. There was a dime among the change in my pocket and I dialed Martha's apartment.

"My God, Jeff—where are you? I've been frantic since last night!"

"I'm free and I'm unharmed. My wife delivered the ransom I'll tell you everything later. Look, call the police and tell them I'm at the corner of"—I glanced up at the sign—"Ninety-eighth Street and West End Avenue."

I waited in the phone booth, oblivious of passersby, until the police car arrived.

My story was that I'd been kidnapped while visiting a client and the police didn't press the matter. Martha was interviewed and the press took pictures, and back in Boston, Joan questioned me about Martha. But if she suspected the truth she didn't pursue it. I was back, all in one piece, and after a week's run in the newspapers the story died down. I had George Franklin checking with the insurance company to see what coverage we carried Certainly it was a theft and certainly they should pay.

Only once, a few weeks later, when I mentioned the need for another trip to New York, did Joan hint that she knew the truth about Martha. "New York again? You'd better stay away from the client this time."

But of course I didn't stay away.

I went back to Gramercy Park, back to Martha's arms, because that's where I'd always belong. The only difference was that carried a pistol now, to guard against any future surprises.

"I'm glad you're back," Martha said, kissing me softly. "I think those two days were the worst of my life, Jeff. Not knowing where you were, afraid to call the police . . . ."

"They weren't much fun for me either," I said, considering for the first time what it might be like to leave Joan and marry Martha. I wondered if men ever married their mistresses.

"What are you thinking about, Jeff?"

"Us, I guess."

"Do you think they'll ever catch the kidnappers?"

"Probably not. Unless they try the same sort of thing again." She patted my arm. "Come on, dear, come to bed."

"Gladly."

I went to the kitchen for a glass of water. I was just setting the glass down by the sink when I noticed the two crudely scratched initials on the bottom of the glass.

*Mysteries and crime stories with an academic setting have a long and noble history, almost as a subgenre, dating back to some of the early Sherlock Holmes tales. (Sherlockians still argue as to whether the university depicted in "The Three Students" was meant to be Oxford or Cambridge.) Since that time we've had Dorothy L. Sayers's* Gaudy Night, *and James Hilton's* Murder at School, *as well as books such as* The Cambridge Murders, Harvard Has a Homicide, *and* The Oxford Tragedy. *The crime involved need not always be murder, and in fact* Gaudy Night *sustained its great length admirably without a killing. Geoffrey Bush, a writer new to our field, uses the academic setting in an innovative and memorable manner in this story, which was an MWA Edgar nominee.*

# GEOFFREY BUSH
# The Problem of Li T'ang

I had a problem. I had sixteen midterm papers from my course on Chinese painting, the first papers from the first course I'd ever taught, and one of them was brilliant.

I'd spent the evening discovering from the first seven or eight of the other papers I'd reluctantly looked into that "Chinese painting is beautiful because—" and "The reason I like Chinese painting is—" The opening paragraph of this one stopped me in my tracks. I woke up, sat forward, began again, and proceeded, with difficulty, through the rest of it.

It could hardly be called easy reading. But important pieces of Chinese painting criticism seldom are. And that's what this was.

It almost certainly ought to be published.

It almost certainly *had* been published.

And there, of course, was the problem. In my first term of teaching, I realized with a growing sense of exhilaration, I almost certainly had a case of plagiarism.

I got up from the sunken coffee table in the living room of

my apartment and mounted the wrought iron steps to the built-in free-form bar. I'd gone to a certain amount of trouble to find quarters with the sort of conveniences I was accustomed to. This overpriced and somewhat overdramatic penthouse had become available when its tenant had been revealed as the central figure in a series of elaborate criminal activities. I made myself a vodka and tonic, sat down on one of his bar stools, and rested my feet on his curved rail. For the first time I began to feel at home there.

I looked out his picture window at his view of midwestern city lights at one o'clock in the morning and considered what to do.

A tricky business. Made trickier by my mysterious position in the art department.

I had a year's appointment at what I shall describe simply as a large state university. It was a decidedly shaky appointment. All that anyone had known about me when I arrived was that James Harris, recent Ph.D., even more recent victim of a slipped disk (the unfortunate young man had bent over to pick a slender scholarly volume out of a bottom shelf and had been unable to stand up), had been hired, without an interview, to teach Far Eastern art this fall on the basis of three letters of recommendation, the book he had made out of his thesis, and his reputation. Since then, thanks to my bad manners, my having changed apartments, and my general inscrutability, no one had found out much more.

Tall, bony, rude, youthful Dr. Harris was on trial. Very much on trial. If he wanted to have his appointment renewed for another year, he was going to have to come through in the clutch.

Good. I felt the familiar symptoms. The blood moving toward the brain. My fingers tapping on my vodka and tonic. One foot jiggling on the rail.

This was the kind of thing I enjoyed.

I had brought the paper with me. I opened it to its title page. "The Problem of Li T'ang," I read. "By Matthew Karp."

I concentrated on Matthew Karp. I summoned up a thin, pale face. I added wild, untidy hair, a dirty T-shirt, crumpled jeans and wire spectacles. I recalled an attitude of intense and, after the first class, nearly wordless attention. "Karp," I heard him saying, as we introduced ourselves to one another. "Matthew Karp. With a _K_." Which was practically the last thing he had said.

Was this the picture of a plagiarizer?

I had no idea. Doubtless plagiarizers, like everyone else in our dubious world, come in all shapes and sizes.

So much for that. It had not got me very far. The next move was to examine the evidence.

I examined it. Binding, inexpensive. Paper, ordinary. Typing, uneven, not to say sloppy. Contents, overwhelming.

It would have been easier, I saw appreciatively, if he had tried to mix in a few sentences of his own, explaining why Chinese painting was beautiful, or why he liked it. The contrast between the true and the borrowed Karp would have been inescapable. Look on this sentence, I would have been able to cry vengefully, and on this.

But he hadn't. He'd been more skillful. He had stolen every phrase in his twenty weighty and intricate pages, word for word. It was going to be difficult to prove that he had committed plagiarism at all. The only way to prove it conclusively was to find out where.

I went to bed and slept deeply and contentedly. The next morning I drove to the university, first to my office and then to the library, to eliminate the obvious possibilities. I looked at Sirén. I checked Sickman. I went through the admirable little book by Susan Bush.

Nothing in them corresponded to "The Problem of Li T'ang." I hadn't expected that anything would.

That afternoon, after an inadequate lunch in the cafeteria, I returned to the library stacks, but no longer to their relatively habitable upper regions; I descended to their gloomy and slightly dank bowels, never visited by the light of the sun and rarely by the foot of man, in search of periodicals. I inspected bibliographies, located references, and pulled down dusty cardboard folders containing forgotten offprints. The one colleague I saw passed by as I was reaching for a journal tucked behind another journal on a top shelf. She produced a faintly worried smile and hurried on. That strange, sarcastic Dr. Harris was going to slip his disk again.

I found out a good deal that day about Li T'ang. What there was, at any rate, to find out. The first sixty years of his life were a blank. Then, at the beginning of the twelfth century, he emerged into the limelight. The occasion was a competition

for admission to the emperor's Painting Academy. The assigned
subject, I learned from a useful five-page summary by Ellen J.
Laing, was "A wine shop by a bridge surrounded by bamboo."
The other competitors obediently submitted paintings of wine
shops by bridges surrounded by groves of bamboo. Li T'ang, with
the sort of imaginative stroke so admired by painting academies
then and now, confined himself to painting the flag of a wine
shop, at the head of a bridge, outside a grove of bamboo.

As he was enjoying the fruits of this triumphant demonstra-
tion that less is more, however, the Painting Academy collapsed,
along with the fabric of northern society in general. The resilient
Li T'ang, now in his seventies, fled south. A second anecdote
illustrated his new adversities. In the mountains a brigand
stopped him, demanding his life or his possessions. These turned
out to consist chiefly of scrolls and paintbrushes. But fortune,
in twelfth-century China, still favored the arts. The brigand, if
not a connoisseur, knew what he liked; overcoming his first dis-
appointment, he enrolled himself as a class of one and followed
his aged teacher south.

In the south Li T'ang's hardships were not finished. In a sar-
donic poem he described the large, gloomy landscapes he would
have liked to paint and their probable effect on customers:

> *I already know that such scenes will not attract*
> *the eyes of today's people.*
> *Most buy cosmetics and paint peonies.*

But the inward resources of this elderly wanderer were not
finished, either. In his eighties, in troubled times, in a new city,
among the cosmetic-buyers and the peony-painters, he resumed
work, caught the eye of the new emperor, and was readmitted
to the new Painting Academy, southern branch. There was his
late masterpiece, to prove that he deserved his success—*Wind in
the Pines amid Myriad Ravines*, which I had looked at that day
in a dozen different reproductions, a vast, dark, brooding, monu-
mental mountain face. And there were the two other landscapes—
light, casual, dreamy—which didn't seem to be in the same style
at all. Which hadn't, according to Matthew Karp, been painted
by the same painter.

And there was I, with no more notion of the source he'd
plagiarized from than I'd had before.

Which was a relief. My instincts had told me from the start

that this was going to be a subtle contest. And my instincts are always right.

The following morning was a class morning. My opponent and I were to meet face-to-face.

I drove to the art department, unaccountably housed in the chemistry building, and parked my yellow Porsche in the lot. I gave a warm greeting to the art department's thin, middle-aged secretary—there is a thin, middle-aged secretary at the heart of every organization, and it is well to be on her good side—and went upstairs to my classroom, temporarily cleared of Bunsen burners.

I did not give one of my better lectures. These required some preparation; my researches of the previous day had not left much time. I found myself relying more heavily than I would have liked on my own sources—Sirén, and when possible, Bush—and observing the third row for signs of guilt and confusion on the face behind the wire spectacles.

Perhaps it was a shade paler than usual. Perhaps the attention it was displaying was a shade more intense. Perhaps.

"Mr. Karp," I said, after the buzzer had sounded.

I had made it clear from the outset that I was not one of your new, matey, with-it teachers, anxious to be my pupils' chum. Our encounters were conducted with classical formality. We were "Mr." or, as the case might be, "Miss." Not even "Ms." Certainly not "Matthew."

It seemed to me that my antagonist jumped a little.

"Sir?"

I regarded him blandly. "Would you be so good as to come to my office for a conference at ten o'clock tomorrow morning?"

It was perfectly proper for him to look nervous at the prospect of a conference. All of my students, at least all of those who had handed in their papers on time, would be conferring with me nervously during the next week or two. But I had picked him out first, a trifle pointedly, and for no evident reason.

It seemed to me he looked a bit too nervous. I was gratified to note, however, as he left the room, that I wasn't sure.

There was one move left. Plagiarism was not a topic to bring up lightly in academic circles. I could not go about asking casually if Matthew Karp was likely to have committed it; it was too grave a sin. But I could inquire of my fellow members of the art department, in the cafeteria, or the men's room, or in our other byways, if they happened to have had a Karp in any of their classes. Matthew Karp, with a *K*.

Several of them, after their surprise at being approached by the unsociable Dr. Harris, admitted that they had.

What sort of a student had he been?

Their eyes brightened. Their voices lost their customary tones of complaint. Fine young man, they said. First-class scholar. Top-grade mind. Reminiscent glows lighted their faces as I turned brusquely away.

Had he been taking in every one of them?

Handing in a succession of fraudulent papers?

Masquerading his way through the art department?

Anything, I was aware, was possible. But as I stretched out that evening in what my real-estate agent had called my conversation pit, it didn't seem probable.

Matthew Karp could hardly have bamboozled so many for so long. Yet he hadn't written that paper. I was almost certain he hadn't. All my instincts told me he hadn't, and my instincts are always right.

I opened it once more. Now that I had untangled most of its Germanic syntax, it was somewhat less difficult going. It even rang a distant bell. As if, somehow, I *did* know something about it.

As soon as I tried to work out where the bell was, its ringing vanished.

I began to feel uneasy.

At 9:55 the next morning I disposed what I liked to think of as my lanky, Ivy League frame behind the desk in my office. From my tweed jacket, on the sleeves of which I had had a tailor sew leather elbow patches, I extracted a pipe, lighter, and pouch containing a black mixture specially prepared at a nearby tobacconist's. Through my window I looked out at the undergraduates perambulating to and fro through the bright October leaves.

How could I have imagined that academic life was dull? How could I have begun to wonder if it was time to move on?

I looked keenly at the closed door, by way of practice. I cleared my throat. "Come in," I said austerely, tuning up.

I glanced at the small traveling bag I kept packed in the
orner, just in case.

There was a knock on the door.
I looked keenly at it. I cleared my throat. "Come in," I said
usterely.
He came in.
There was no question about it. His face was paler. His hair
ooked wilder, his T-shirt dirtier, and his jeans more crumpled.
Ie was in a state of controlled agitation.
"Sit down," I said.
He sat down on the only other chair, which I had positioned
incomfortably close to the corner of my desk. He attempted to
ind room for his legs, without success. He looked up, with a
aze that was not only intense but squinting. Light flashed off
is wire spectacles.
"Sun in your eyes, Karp?" I inquired.
No "Mr." this morning. I sat forward, an inch or two, in the
nsulting fashion of someone offering to get up and pull down a
vindow shade with no intention of actually doing so.
"That's all right, sir," he said.
I sat back. The inch or two I had sat forward. "Ah," I said
rrelevantly. I allowed an empty silence to grow, more and
nore pointlessly, in which he was free to twitch, or bite his lip,
r exhibit other indications of cracking under the pressure of
ncreasing meaninglessness.
He did not move. Neither did his somewhat magnified eyes.
nstead, under his continuing regard, I felt a desire of my own
o change position, or cough, or do something or other, no mat-
r what. I checked the impulse. But it was a warning.
"I asked you to see me, Karp," I said, "about your paper."
t was lying in front of me on my desk. I pushed it away from
ie slightly with the tip of my finger, the first suggestion that
here might be something offensive about it.
He did not speak.
" 'The Problem of Li T'ang,' " I quoted. I paused. "Tell me
bout the problem of Li T'ang."
He took a deep breath.
"I tried to, sir," he said, "in my paper."
I tested the ring of those words, silently, on instant replay.

Apprehension, yes. But not the panic I was listening for.

"Tell me again."

He took another deep, and slightly ragged, breath.

"Li T'ang was a landscapist. The most celebrated of all the Sung landscapists."

"What do we know about him?"

"He was born in the 1050s. He died in the 1130s."

That much was right, anyway.

"Go on."

"When he was in his sixties he was accepted into the Painting Academy. The assigned topic was 'A wine shop—'"

"Yes," I interrupted. "What else do we know?"

"After the fall of northern Sung, when he was in his seventies, he went south. During his journey through the mountains he was held up by a—"

"Yes," I said. "What else?"

"He died in his eighties."

"And that's all we know about him?"

"We have a poem he wrote about—"

"A curious figure."

"Yes, sir."

"Elusive."

"Yes, sir."

"But one who landed on his feet."

"On his feet?"

"Wherever he jumped. In difficult times."

"I suppose so, sir."

I picked up my pipe. I put it down again.

"Tell me about his work."

"His style became the model for two generations of southern Sung painters. And that's the problem."

"What is?"

"What is his style?"

I regarded him.

"You tell me, Karp."

"On one hand, there's his great mountain landscape in the Palace Museum in Taiwan, *Whispering Pines in the Mountains.*"

My ears pricked up.

"*Wind in the Pines amid Myriad Ravines?*"

"That's another translation, sir."

I relaxed. "Ah."

"On the other hand, there are two more landscapes attributed to him in a monastery in Kyoto. And they're completely different."

"In what ways?"

"They're airier. Freer. The brushstroke is different, the conception, everything."

All that was right, too.

"In that case," I said, "why not attribute them to someone else?"

"Because one of them seems to have his signature. The first character of his name may be visible, and the second character appears to show up in infrared photography."

" 'Appears to'?" I repeated.

"Yes, sir."

" 'May be'?"

"Yes, sir."

"Not exactly conclusive evidence."

"No, sir."

I shifted gears, to a slightly slower and more significant delivery.

"And a signature doesn't prove anything, does it?"

"No, sir."

"Anyone can take someone else's work and attach his name to it."

"Yes, sir."

"Can't he, Karp?"

He gazed at me, sitting rigidly in his chair.

"Yes, sir."

"Hm," I said. I toyed with a pencil. "What's your view?"

"I think that's what happened."

"What?"

"I think they were painted by someone else."

"Hm." I was beginning to repeat myself. I'd been waiting for him to give himself away with phrases from his paper, learned by rote. But he hadn't. He'd explained the question in his own words, so far as I could tell, and just as succinctly as I could have explained it. Perhaps more so. "Why?"

"I don't think they could be by the same painter as the landscape in Taiwan."

"They couldn't?"

"They're too different. I don't think they could be by the

same *person*."

"Why not?"

"I don't think it's possible for a painter—for anyone—to turn into a different person."

"You don't?"

"No."

Ah, I thought, the certainties of youth.

"Even if he had to?"

"Had to?"

"To start again? In a new place?"

"If he could change that much—"

"Yes?"

"Like a chameleon—"

I thought I heard a quaver in his voice.

"Yes?"

"I'd feel sorry for him."

"You would?"

"Really sorry."

At last he was beginning to look upset. Somehow I had got through to him. I wondered how.

"Because he was able to adapt himself?"

"Because—"

"Yes?"

"Because he had so little self to adapt."

"But isn't that," I inquired, not wholly grammatically, "what an artist is?"

"What an artist is?"

"What all of us are?"

"All of us?"

"Chameleons?"

He clenched his hands.

"I don't think so, sir."

Somewhere I had touched a nerve. Where? But this was not the time for a discussion of identity crises in the modern world. It was time to come to grips with the situation, and the problem, *my* problem, was that I didn't know what to do next. I could not continue this interrogation much longer without its becoming apparent that that was exactly what it was, and at that point he would have every right, or *almost* every right, to get up, announce that he was not required to listen to any more of this, and walk out. Leaving matters twice as snarled as when he had walked in.

He unclenched his hands. I observed that he bit his fingernails.

I looked up.

"Why did you take this course, Karp?"

I meant the question to be unsettling. It wasn't. He had the fixed, desperate air of someone preparing himself for a last stand.

"I admired your book."

"You did?"

"Yes, sir."

I felt an inner tremor. If he admired that book, perhaps he *could* have written this paper. "You embarrass me," I said, waving a hand. "It was unreadable."

"Not at all."

"Ph.D. theses always are."

"Not that one."

"I looked at it myself, last summer, and could scarcely get through it."

"You couldn't, sir?"

"No."

"Really?"

"No."

"You're joking, sir."

"Certainly not. I never joke." I gave him a penetrating look. "And that's the reason you took this course?"

"That and my cousin, sir."

I stiffened slightly. Why was this new character being introduced into the drama?

"Your cousin?"

"Andrew Karp. He's in the art world, too."

I had been drawing something with the pencil on a sheet of paper. I saw that it was an airplane. A jet, in flight. I wondered what it meant.

I glanced up. "Have I met him?"

"I don't think so, sir." I looked down. That was a relief. "He's an assistant curator at the Met."

"He is?"

"He's a few years older than I am."

"About my age?"

"Yes, sir. But he doesn't look like you."

I glanced up again. Sharply. Why had he said that? "Why did you say that, Karp?"

"He looks more like me."

I continued to scrutinize him. Closely. There were hairs, I noticed, growing out of his nose. I decided not to probe the question any further. "Hm," I said.

"He's going to Taiwan this summer, and he's invited me to go with him."

"To the Palace Museum?"

"To arrange for the loan of three of their scrolls."

"I see."

"I wanted to be ready for the trip."

"I see."

"To know something about what I was going to look at."

I began a wiggly line underneath the jet. It looked like waves the jet was flying over. Perhaps my unconscious was trying to tell me something.

"So you'll have a chance to examine *Wind in the Pines amid Myriad Ravines*."

"Yes, sir."

"Or, if you prefer, *Whispering Pines in the Mountains*."

"Yes, sir."

"An opportunity to settle the problem of Li T'ang."

"Yes, sir."

Our conversation seemed to be losing direction. I decided to get it at least partly back on the rails.

"You've never been there?" I asked carelessly.

"No, sir."

"But your cousin Andrew has," I added lightly.

"No, sir."

"They're acquainted with him, though."

"No, sir."

"They're not?"

"They've never met him."

Andrew Karp, about my age, the Met, Palace Museum, never met him. I filed it all away.

"I envy you." I had finished the waves the jet was flying over. I began a round-cheeked wind, blowing it westward. "I'd like to go there myself."

"You've never been to Taiwan either, sir?"

I thought rapidly. "Once. To do research."

"There must be nothing like seeing the real thing."

He sounded almost unhappy. Why?

"The real thing?"

"The paintings themselves."

"Oh."

"Instead of reproductions."

"I suppose so."

"Reproductions aren't the same, are they?"

"No."

"Even the best ones."

"No," I said. "I suppose not."

"May I ask you something, sir?"

I leaned back.

"That depends."

"When you were appointed to the art department, last summer, sir—"

I sat without moving.

"Yes?"

"Without being interviewed—"

"Yes?"

"Because of your slipped disk—"

"Yes?"

"Were you in a hospital, sir?"

"Yes."

"Would you mind telling me which one?"

I let a moment pass.

"Yes. I would mind."

He didn't speak. Neither did I. I let several moments pass, while we both sat without moving.

"Is that all?" I said.

"Yes, sir."

"Is there anything else you'd like to know?"

"No, sir."

"You're sure?"

"Yes, sir."

"Very well. There's something I'd like to know."

"Yes, sir?"

"About this paper."

"Sir?"

"This paper is magnificent. Almost impossible to read, of

course. Because of its wretched writing. And arriving, in my judgment, at the wrong conclusion. But superbly researched, splendidly argued, and authoritatively presented."

I paused.

"Thank you, sir."

I leaned forward.

"Who wrote it?"

He leaned forward, too. That wasn't right.

"You did, sir."

That certainly wasn't right.

"I beg your pardon?"

"It's Chapter Seven of your book."

"Ah."

I stood up. I began to put pipe, lighter, and tobacco pouch into my pockets.

"I'm sorry, sir." He was still addressing me as "sir." Good. "I didn't think you were real from the beginning. With that pipe that you never smoke, and that tweed jacket with the elbow patches, and the whole old-fashioned, Ivy League bit." Ah, well. At least it hadn't been my lectures. "And your lectures. They were just paraphrases. Of Sirén and Bush." I stopped listening and started calculating. No time to go back to the apartment. Leave the Porsche in the parking lot. It wasn't paid for, anyway. The nearest form of public transportation was a Greyhound bus. And then—

Why not? A few letters, a passport, a discreetly trendy New York suit, and I'd be equipped.

He was still talking, more and more anxiously. "I couldn't ask you about it. I couldn't ask anyone about it. It was too—too awful." He halted. "But I had to find out. And this seemed like the only way." He seemed increasingly distressed. "I couldn't let you get away with it, could I, sir?"

"Of course not, Karp," I said soothingly.

"I think if I knew which hospital the real Dr. Harris was at, and called them up, I'd find out that he's still laid up somewhere with a slipped disk."

"Very likely." I looked around the office. "We weren't able to do much for him."

"I think that's how you got this impossible idea of coming here in his place."

"Yes." I picked up my traveling bag. "Good-bye, Karp."

"I think you need help."

"Help?"

Was this an offer of assistance?

No. He was standing barring the door.

"I think you were a patient at that hospital."

"What?" I was stung. "A patient?" I couldn't let that go by. "Certainly not. I was the head surgeon."

"You were?" His voice faltered slightly.

"Certainly." Perhaps a little more accuracy was called for. "For three weeks." I reached past him for the doorknob. "And I don't need help. You do."

"I do?"

"You're wrong about the problem of Li T'ang." I turned the doorknob. "It's not only quite possible to turn into a different person." I opened the door. "In these uncertain times—" I stepped through. "It's essential."

I closed the door behind me and walked briskly down the empty corridor.

"Karp," I said to it, smiling cordially, striding forward, gripping my traveling bag, feeling the familiar rush of blood to my head, on my way to the Palace Museum in Taiwan, a few months ahead of time, to arrange for the loan of three of their scrolls. Perhaps more. Six. A dozen. "Andrew Karp. With a *K*."

Who has been, I may say, a very pleasant, amiable, undemanding person to be.

Until the day before yesterday, at the end of the second week of my visit, when the Palace Museum received word that another Andrew Karp, no doubt alerted by his cousin Matthew, is to arrive this afternoon to make sure that the eighteen scrolls to be loaned to the Met are delivered to the real Andrew Karp.

If there can be said to be such a thing as the "real" Andrew Karp.

Or "reality."

But that is hardly a topic I can touch upon when I disclose, to the rather excitable director of the Palace Museum, half an hour from now, my current, challenging, and possibly extremely brief assignment as an agent of the U. S. State Department sent from Washington to try to clear the problem up.

# The Yearbook of the Detective Story

Abbreviations: *EQMM* —Ellery Queen's Mystery Magazine
*AHMM*—Alfred Hitchcock's Mystery Magazine
*MSMM* —Mike Shayne Mystery Magazine
*MM*   —Mystery Monthly

## BIOGRAPHY
## JOHN D. MACDONALD

John Dann MacDonald was born in Sharon, Pennsylvania, July 24, 1916. At the age of twelve he moved to Utica, New York, and attended high school there. He received a Bachelor of Science degree from Syracuse University in 1937, and at about the same time he married an artist, Dorothy Mary Prentiss. They have a son, Maynard J. P. MacDonald, who now resides in New Zealand.

Following his marriage, MacDonald pursued his studies at the Harvard School of Business Administration, where he received a Master's degree in Business Administration shortly before the outbreak of World War II. By 1940 he had entered the United States Army; he served with the Office of Strategic Services in Ceylon and received a separation promotion to lieutenant colonel. When army censorship restricted his letters home to his wife, he wrote her a short story, "Interlude in India," which she promptly sold to *Story* magazine for twenty-five dollars.

After his discharge from the army in 1946, MacDonald took up the career of magazine writing, selling articles and stories to *Cosmopolitan, Esquire, Good Housekeeping, Liberty, Collier's, Ladies' Home Journal, Redbook, McCall's,* and others. At the same time, his stories were appearing in a variety of pulp magazines under his own name and such house names as Scott O'Hara, John Lane, Peter Reed, John Wade Farrell, Robert Henry, and Henry Rieser.

With the decline of the pulp magazines, he turned to writing paperback novels, beginning with *The Brass Cupcake* in 1950. This has been followed by sixty-three books to date in paperback or hardcover, notably *Wine of the Dreamers* and *Ballroom in the Skies* (1951 and 1952, science fiction), *The Damned* (1952, was a paperback best seller when reissued in 1974), *Dead Low Tide* (1953, highly praised in Barzun and Taylor's

*A Catalogue of Crime*), *Murder in the Wind* (1956), *Soft Touch* (1958, filmed as *Man Trap*), *The Executioners* (1958, filmed as *Cape Fear*), *The Girl, the Gold Watch, and Everything* (1962, a fantasy now being filmed in France), *A Key to the Suite* (1962), *The Last One Left* (1967, nominated for an Edgar Award), *No Deadly Drug* (1968, fact crime, about the Coppolino case), and *Condominium* (1977, a best seller).

MacDonald's major contribution to the mystery field has been the creation of Travis McGee, a Fort Lauderdale-based detective who lives on a houseboat and operates outside the law to recover stolen property. To date McGee has starred in sixteen novels: *The Deep Blue Good-by, Nightmare in Pink, A Purple Place for Dying, The Quick Red Fox* (all 1964); *A Deadly Shade of Gold, Bright Orange for a Shroud* (both 1965); *Darker than Amber, One Fearful Yellow Eye* (both 1966); *Pale Gray for Guilt, The Girl in the Plain Brown Wrapper* (both 1968); *Dress Her in Indigo* (1969); *The Long Lavender Look* (1970); *A Tan and Sandy Silence* (1972); *The Scarlet Ruse, The Turquoise Lament* (both 1973); and *The Dreadful Lemon Sky* (1975). The seventeenth McGee novel, *The Empty Copper Sea,* will be published in 1978. Travis McGee was first portrayed in film in 1970, when Rod Taylor was featured in *Darker than Amber,* and negotiations are under way for a new McGee movie.

MacDonald edited the 1959 Mystery Writers of America anthology, *The Lethal Sex.* He served as president of the organization in 1962, and MWA honored him with its Grand Master award in 1972. Two collections of his short stories have been published: *End of the Tiger* (1960) and *Seven* (1971).

About his work, Kurt Vonnegut, Jr., has written: "To diggers a thousand years from now . . . the works of John D. MacDonald would be a treasure on the order of the tomb of Tutankhamen." Anthony Boucher, commenting on his unequalled ability to portray American society and mores, called him "the John O'Hara of the crime-suspense story." And Richard Condon summed it all up by calling MacDonald "the great American storyteller."

This year marks MacDonald's sixth appearance in *Best Detective Stories of the Year.* Further proof of his vast popularity can be seen in the fact that he is one of very few living writers to have a continuing publication devoted to his works: The *JDM Bibliophile* has been published regularly by Len and June Moffatt, since 1965.

John MacDonald was prompted to move to Florida in 1949 because he loves boating; he presently resides at Sarasota.

BIBLIOGRAPHY

I. Collections

1. Aiken, Joan. *The Far Forests*. New York: Viking Press. A mixed collection of fifteen stories of romance, fantasy, and suspense.

2. Ashdown, Clifford. *From a Surgeon's Diary*. Philadelphia (Box 1891, Zip 19105): Oswald Train. Six medical mysteries from *Cassell's Magazine* (1904–1905), by the collaboration of R. Austin Freeman and John J. Pitcairn.

3. Bloch, Robert. *The Best of Robert Bloch*. New York: Ballantine/ Del Rey. Twenty-two fantasy and science fiction tales (1943– 1974), many of them criminous. Introduction by Lester Del Rey and afterword by the author.

4. ———. *Cold Chills*. New York: Doubleday. Fourteen stories, some supernatural, from various magazines.

5. ———. *The King of Terrors*. Yonkers, N.Y. (Box 334, East Station, Zip 10704): The Mysterious Press. Fourteen stories of mystery and the macabre from various magazines (1956–1967), with an introduction by the author.

6. Brennan, Joseph Payne. *The Chronicles of Lucius Leffing*. West Kingston, R.I.: Donald M. Grant. Eight stories, five from magazines and three newly published, with an introduction by Frank Belknap Long.

7. Collins, Wilkie. *Little Novels*. New York: Dover Publications. First U.S. edition of an 1887 collection of fourteen stories, some criminous.

8. Doyle, Arthur Conan. *Tales of Terror and Mystery*. New York: Doubleday. A new selection of thirteen tales from prior collections (1908–1921), introduced by Doyle's daughter-in-law.

9. du Maurier, Daphne. *Echoes from the Macabre*. New York: Doubleday. Nine stores, some fantasy, chosen from prior collections.

10. Fletcher, David. *Raffles*. New York: G.P. Putnam's Sons. Published as a novel but actually seven short stories adapted from a British television series. For a better collection of Raffles stories, see number 15 below.

11. Gilbert, Michael. *Petrella at Q*. New York: Harper & Row. Eleven short stories from *EQMM,* plus a new novelette and an introductory essay about Petrella.

12. Grant, Maxwell. *Norgil the Magician*. Yonkers, N.Y. (Box 334,

East Station, Zip 10704) : The Mysterious Press. Eight pulp stories about a magician detective (1937–1940) by the creator of The Shadow.

13. King, C. Daly. *The Curious Mr. Tarrant.* New York: Dover Publications. First U.S. edition of a highly regarded 1935 collection of eight detective stories from the pulps.

14. Macdonald, Ross. *Lew Archer, Private Investigator.* Yonkers, N.Y. (Box 334, East Station, Zip 10704): The Mysterious Press. The first collection of all nine Archer short stories, with a new introduction by the author.

15. Perowne, Barry. *Raffles of the Albany.* New York: St. Martin's Press. Eleven stories from *EQMM* and *The Saint Magazine.*

16. Post, Melville Davisson. *The Complete Uncle Abner.* Del Mar, Calif.: Publisher's, Inc. All twenty-two Uncle Abner mysteries together for the first time, with an introduction and bibliography by Allen J. Hubin. Volume 4 in the continuing Mystery Library series.

17. Queen, Ellery. *The Ellery Queen Casebook.* New York: Reader's Digest Press. Five stories from prior collections with a new introduction by the author; a forty-eight-page booklet published to accompany a two-volume set of condensed mystery classics.

18. Quinn, Seabury. *The Horror Chambers of Jules de Grandin.* New York: Popular Library. Six occult detective stories from *Weird Tales* (1927–1934).

19. Shiel, M. P. *Prince Zaleski and Cummings King Monk.* Sauk City, Wisc.: Mycroft & Moran. The three original Zaleski stories (1895), plus a fourth written for *EQMM* and published in 1955, combined with the three Cummings Monk episodes from a 1911 collection.

20. Simenon, Georges. *Maigret's Christmas.* New York: Harcourt Brace Jovanovich. Nine short stories and novelettes (1939–1950) in new translations by Jean Stewart.

21. Stout, Rex. *Justice Begins at Home.* New York: Viking Press. Sixteen early stories (1913–1918) collected for the first time and introduced by Stout's biographer, John McAleer. For more on Stout see also numbers 4 and 12 under Miscellaneous Nonfiction.

22. Symons, Julian. *How to Trap a Crook.* New York: Davis Publications. Thirteen stories from *EQMM* (1957–1972), introduced by Ellery Queen.

23. Theroux, Paul. *The Consul's File.* Boston: Houghton Mifflin. Twenty stories, a few criminous, about an American consul in Malaysia.

II. Anthologies

1. Ashley, Leonard P. N., ed. *Tales of Mystery and Melodrama.* Woodbury, N.Y.: Barron's Educational Series. A mixed collection of twenty Victorian tales of mystery and adventure, designed for school use.

2. Clarke, Stephen P., ed. *Crimes and Clues.* Englewood Cliffs, N.J.: Prentice-Hall. A high school textbook containing a dozen classic mystery short stories, plus essays, poems, and study aids.

3. Hitchcock, Alfred, ed. *Alfred Hitchcock Presents: Stories That Go Bump in the Night.* New York: Random House. Twenty-four stories, mainly reprints from various magazines.

4. ———. *Having a Wonderful Crime.* New York: Dell Publishing. Fourteen stories from AHMM (1960–1975), paperback.

5. Hoch, Edward D., ed. *Best Detective Stories of the Year—1977.* New York: E.P. Dutton. Sixteen of the best mystery-crime stories published during 1976.

6. Kittredge, William, and Krauzer, Steven M., eds. *Great Action Stories.* New York: New American Library/Mentor Books. Seventeen stories, mainly criminous but including some adventure and fantasy.

7. Maling, Arthur, ed. *When Last Seen.* New York: Harper & Row. Sixteen stories about mysterious disappearances; the annual anthology from Mystery Writers of America.

8. Page, Gerald W., ed. *The Year's Best Horror Stories: Series V.* New York: DAW Books. Fourteen stories, mainly fantasy but including three selections from mystery magazines.

9. Pronzini, Bill, ed. *Midnight Specials.* New York: Bobbs-Merrill. Nineteen suspense stories about railroads, some fantasy, plus an extensive bibliography.

10. Queen, Ellery, ed. *Cops and Capers.* New York: Davis Publications. Six stories from prior Ellery Queen anthologies; a Dale Books paperback edition.

11. ———. *Crimes and Consequences.* New York: Davis Publications. Six stories from prior Ellery Queen anthologies; a Dale Books paperback edition.

12. ———. *Ellery Queen's Anthology, Spring-Summer 1977.* New York: Davis Publications. Seventeen stories from *EQMM;* semi-annual softcover anthology. A hardcover edition, *Ellery Queen's Champions of Mystery,* is distributed by Dial Press.

13. ———. *Ellery Queen's Anthology, Fall-Winter 1977.* New York: Davis Publications. Eighteen stories from *EQMM;* semiannual softcover anthology. A hardcover edition, *Ellery Queen's Faces of Mystery,* is distributed by Dial Press.

14. ———. *Ellery Queen's Searches and Seizures.* New York: Davis Publications/Dial Press. The thirty-first annual hardcover anthology from *EQMM,* containing twenty-seven stories published during 1975.

15. ———. *Masterpieces of Mystery: The Golden Age: Part One.* Des Moines, Iowa (1716 Locust St.): Meredith. Twelve stories featuring authors and sleuths popular in the 1920s and 1930s. Volume 4 in a mail-order series that also includes numbers 16 and 17 below.

16. ———. *Masterpieces of Mystery: The Golden Age: Part Two.* Des Moines, Iowa (1716 Locust St.): Meredith. Volume 5 in a mail-order series; contains sixteen stories.

17. ———. *Masterpieces of Mystery: Detective Directory: Part One.* Des Moines, Iowa (1716 Locust St.): Meredith. Volume 6 in a mail-order series; contains seventeen stories about sleuths in various occupations.

18. ———. *X Marks the Plot.* New York: Davis Publications. Nine stories from prior Ellery Queen anthologies; a Dale Books paperback edition.

19. Ruhm, Herbert, ed. *The Hard-Boiled Detectives.* New York: Vintage Books. Fourteen stories from *Black Mask* (1922–1949).

20. Sullivan, Eleanor, ed. *Alfred Hitchcock's Anthology, Spring-Summer 1978.* New York: Davis Publications. Twenty-nine stories from 1976 issues of *AHMM.* A hardcover edition, *Tales to Take Your Breath Away,* is distributed by Dial Press.

21. Watson, Hilary, ed. *Winter's Crimes 8.* New York: St. Martin's Press. Ten new stories by British writers in the first of this annual anthology series to appear in America.

## III. Miscellaneous Nonfiction

*1978 Calendars.* An increasing number of calendar items in the mystery field: Davis Publications brought out their third *EQMM* calendar, entitled *Ellery Queen's 1978 Mystery Art Calendar.* From Universe Books came *The Mystery and Suspense Engagement Calendar 1978,* and both Doubleday and Drake offered a *Sherlock Holmes Calendar.*

1. Aldrich, Pearl G., ed. *The Popular Culture Scholar, Winter 1977.* Frostburg, Md.: Frostburg State College. A special issue of this journal devoted entirely to essays on mystery and suspense fiction.

2. Barzun, Jacques, and Taylor, Wendell H., eds. *Fifty Classics of Crime Fiction, 1900–1950. A Book of Prefaces.* New York: Garland Publishing. Collected prefaces from the fifty-volume edition published during 1976.

3. Beaman, Bruce R., ed. *Sherlockian Quotations.* Culver City, Calif. (3844 Watseka Ave.): The Pontine Press. A chapbook of almost four hundred sayings of Sherlock Holmes, arranged by subject.

4. Bourne, Michael, ed. *Corsage: A Bouquet of Rex Stout and Nero Wolfe.* Bloomington, Ind. (Box 1431, Zip 47401): James A. Rock & Co. The first book publication of a 1940 Nero Wolfe short novel, *Bitter End* (which Stout adapted from his non-Wolfe novel *Bad for Business*), plus an interview with Stout, an article by "Archie Goodwin" on Wolfe's liking for orchids, and a checklist of Stout's mysteries about Wolfe and other characters.

5. Burack, A. S., ed. *Writing Suspense and Mystery Fiction.* Boston: The Writer, Inc. Thirty-five essays, mostly new, on various aspects of mystery writing, plus a glossary of legal terms and a brief guide to law and the courts.

6. Campbell, Frank D., Jr. *John D. MacDonald and the Colorful World of Travis McGee.* San Bernardino, Calif. (Box 2845, Zip 92406): The Borgo Press. A sixty-four-page booklet examining each of the sixteen McGee novels in detail. One of the Milford Series on Popular Writers of Today; most of the other volumes are devoted to science fiction authors.

7. Champigny, Robert. *What Will Have Happened: A Philosophical and Technical Essay on Mystery Stories.* Bloomington, Ind.: Indiana University Press. A book-length study of American, British, and French detective stories.

8. Christie, Agatha. *An Autobiography.* New York: Dodd Mead. Dame Agatha's own life story, written between 1950 and 1965.

9. Harmon, Robert B., and Burger, Margaret A., eds. *An Annotated Guide to the Works of Dorothy L. Sayers.* New York: Garland Publishing. The first complete bibliography of her work. For a late addition to it, see number 21 below.

10. Keating, H. R. F., ed. *Agatha Christie: First Lady of Crime.* New York: Holt, Rinehart & Winston. A collection of thirteen new essays by mystery writers and critics.

11. Mallowan, Max. *Mallowan's Memoirs.* New York: Dodd Mead. Informal memoirs by the husband of Agatha Christie.

12. McAleer, John J. *Rex Stout.* Boston: Little, Brown and Company. The first full-length biography of Nero Wolfe's creator.

13. McCormick, Donald. *Who's Who in Spy Fiction.* New York: Taplinger. Brief biographies of more than one hundred authors of spy fiction, with an introductory history of the genre and a glossary of espionage terms.

14. Millikin, Stephen F. *Chester Himes: A Critical Appraisal.* Columbia, Mo.: University of Missouri Press. Covers all of Himes's

work, including his Grave Digger Jones and Coffin Ed Johnson novels.

15. Norris, Luther, ed. *The Pontine Dossier*. Culver City, Calif. (3844 Watseka Ave.): The Pontine Press. The 1977 edition of this annual; articles and stories relating mainly to the Solar Pons adventures created by August Derleth.

16. Pate, Janet. *The Book of Sleuths*. Chicago: Contemporary Books. An illustrated guide to forty famous detectives from books, films, television, and comic strips. For a similar but better book see number 18 below.

17. Pearsall, Ronald. *Conan Doyle: A Biographical Solution*. New York: St. Martin's Press. A new biography of Sherlock Holmes's creator.

18. Penzler, Otto. *The Private Lives of the Private Eyes*. New York: Grosset & Dunlap. The lives of twenty-five great fictional detectives, with bibliographies, filmographies, and brief biographies of their creators. Included are "private eyes, spies, crime fighters, and other good guys."

19. ———, Steinbrunner, Chris, and Lachman, Marvin, eds. *Detectionary*. New York: Overlook Press/Viking Press. Revised trade edition of a biographical dictionary of leading characters in mystery fiction, first published in a private edition in 1971.

20. Pohle, Robert W., Jr., and Hart, Douglas C. *Sherlock Holmes on the Screen*. Cranbury, N.J.: A.S. Barnes & Co. A study of all the Holmes films since 1903.

21. Sayers, Dorothy L. *Wilkie Collins—A Critical and Biographical Study*. Toledo, Ohio: Friends of the University of Toledo Library. An unfinished manuscript, edited and introduced by E. R. Gregory.

22. Shulman, David, ed. *An Annotated Bibliography of Cryptography*. New York: Garland Publishing. More than three thousand entries, including many works of fiction in the mystery field.

23. Tepper, Ruth Lake. *The Sherlock Holmes Crossword Puzzle Book*. New York: Crown Publishers. Puzzles based on twenty-two of the Holmes stories, included in summarized versions.

24. Tracy, Jack W. *Encyclopedia Sherlockiana*. New York: Doubleday. More than 3,500 entries on people, places, and things that occur in the Sherlock Holmes stories.

25. Winn, Dilys, ed. *Murder Ink: The Mystery Reader's Companion*. New York: Workman Publishing Company. A massive anthology of some 150 articles by mystery writers and crime experts on nearly every aspect of real and fictional crime.

26. Wolfe, Peter. *Dreamers Who Live Their Dreams: The World of*

*Ross Macdonald's Novels.* Bowling Green, Ohio: Bowling Green University Press. A critical study with plot summaries of all the novels.

## AWARDS

*Mystery Writers of America*

Best novel—William H. Hallahan, *Catch Me: Kill Me* (Bobbs-Merrill)
Best American first novel—Robert Ross, *A French Finish* (Putnam)
Best short story—Thomas Walsh, *Chance After Chance* (*EQMM*)
Best paperback novel—Mike John, *The Quark Maneuver* (Ballantine)
Best biography and criticism—John McAleer, *Rex Stout* (Little, Brown)
Special award—Dilys Winn, editor, *Murder Ink* (Workman Publishing)
Special award—Allen J. Hubin, editor, *The Armchair Detective*

*Crime Writers Association* (London)

Gold Dagger—John le Carré, *The Honourable Schoolboy* (Hodder & Stoughton/U.S.: Knopf)
Silver Dagger—William McIlvanney, *Laidlaw* (Hodder & Stoughton/ U.S.: Pantheon)
John Creasey Memorial Award (for the best first crime novel)—Frank Parrish, *Fire in the Barley* (Constable)

## NECROLOGY

1. Appel, Benjamin (1907(?)–1977). Author of a half-dozen gangster novels beginning with *Brain Guy* (1934).
2. Bonnecarrere, Paul (1925(?)–1977). French war correspondent, co-author (with Joan Hemingway) of a political kidnap thriller, *Rosebud* (1974).
3. Cain, James M. (1892–1977). Famed author of *The Postman Always Rings Twice* (1934), *Double Indemnity* (1936), and *Mildred Pierce* (1941), all made into successful motion pictures. He wrote more than a dozen other crime novels and was a winner of MWA's Grand Master award.
4. Carr, John Dickson (1906–1977). Master of the locked-room mystery, he published forty-five novels and four short story collec-

tions under his own name (1930–1971), notably *The Three Coffins* (1935) and *The Crooked Hinge* (1938), both about Dr. Gideon Fell. Under the pseudonym Carter Dickson he published twenty-five novels and one collection (1934–1956), notably *The Judas Window* (1938) and *The Curse of the Bronze Lamp* (1945), both about Sir Henry Merrivale. Carr was a past president of Mystery Writers of America and winner of its Grand Master award. He also produced two notable works of nonfiction, *The Murder of Sir Edmund Godfrey* (1936) and *The Life of Sir Arthur Conan Doyle* (1949).

5. Dresser, Davis (1904–1977). Under the pseudonym of Brett Halliday he authored more than sixty novels about famed private eye Mike Shayne. One of the founders of Mystery Writers of America, he also edited the sixteenth and seventeenth annual collections of *Best Detective Stories of the Year*. He published mystery fiction under his own name and more than a dozen pseudonyms, including Asa Baker, Matthew Blood, and Hal Debrett.

6. Durham, Philip (?–1977). Professor of English at UCLA; produced one of the first academic studies of Raymond Chandler, *Down These Mean Streets a Man Must Go* (1963).

7. Elston, Allan Vaughn (1886(?)–1976). Western writer; authored a number of mystery-crime short stories for the early pulp and slick magazines. Seven were reprinted by *EQMM* (1945–1955).

8. Erskine, Laurie York (1894–1976). Authored ten novels about Renfrew of the Royal Mounted and two mystery novels.

9. Fairman, Paul W. (1916–1977). Author of many paperback mystery and science fiction novels under his own name and several pseudonyms. Managing editor of *EQMM* from 1959 to 1963.

10. Fosburgh, Hugh Whitney (1916–1976). Newspaperman; author of one mystery novel, *The Drowning Stone* (1958).

11. Gibbs, Henry (1909–1975). British author of twenty suspense novels under his own name (1943–1963), but better known for some forty spy novels published under the pseudonym of Simon Harvester (1943–1972).

12. Hamilton, Edmond (1904–1977). Well-known science fiction writer and author of a single mystery novel, *Murder in the Clinic* (1946).

13. Jones, James (1921–1977). Best-selling novelist and author of one mystery novel, *A Touch of Danger* (1973).

14. Kantor, MacKinlay (1904–1977). Pulitzer Prize-winning writer who produced a single crime novel, *Signal Thirty-two* (1950), in addition to scores of mystery short stories for pulp and slick magazines. Eleven were reprinted by *EQMM* (1944–1952).

15. Kendrick, Baynard (1894–1977). Creator of blind detective Duncan Maclain who starred in twelve novels (1937–1961). A founder and first president of Mystery Writers of America.

16. Laing, Alexander Kinnan (1903–1976). Author of *The Cadaver of Gideon Wyck* (1934) and other mysteries.

17. Litvinov, Ivy (1889(?)–1977). Widow of the Russian ambassador to Washington during World War II, and author of one mystery novel, published in America as *Moscow Mystery* (1943).

18. Mainwaring, Daniel (1902–1977). Author of twelve mystery novels (1936–1946) under the pseudonym Geoffrey Homes.

19. Masterman, Sir John (1891–1977). A leading figure in British Intelligence during World War II; author of three mystery novels (1933–1956) unpublished in America.

20. Matschat, Cecile Hulse (1894(?)–1976). Author of two novels, *Murder in Okefenokee* (1941) and *Murder at the Black Crook* (1943).

21. McDaniel, David (1939–1977). Author of seven paperback "Man from U.N.C.L.E." books, novelized from the television series.

22. O'Keeffe, Patrick (1900(?)–1977). Short story writer, contributor to the early pulp magazines and, more recently, to *AHMM*.

23. Phillifent, John T. (1916–1976). Science fiction writer under the name John Rackham, and author of three "Man from U.N.C.L.E." novelizations under his own name.

24. Reamy, Tom (1935–1977). Science fiction writer and SFWA Nebula award winner whose novelettes sometimes combined elements of detection and fantasy. (See the Honor Roll.)

25. Samson, Joan (?–1976). Author of a single crime novel, *The Auctioneer*, published shortly before her death.

26. Sanders, Marian K. (?–1977). Collaborator with Mortimer S. Edelstein on a mystery novel, *The Bride Laughed Once* (1943).

27. Smith, David Frederick (1888–1976). Radio pioneer and author of *The Broadcast Murders* (1931) by "Fred Smith."

28. Wheatley, Dennis (1897–1977). British author of some sixty mystery-suspense novels, known in the 1930s for his elaborate "Crime Dossier" series containing facsimiles of documents and clues. Best known today for his novels of Satanism and black magic, beginning with *The Devil Rides Out* (1935).

29. Willis, George Anthony Armstrong (1897–1976). British author of ten suspense novels (1927–1957) under the name Anthony Armstrong.

30. Wormser, Richard (1908–1977). Author of a dozen hardcover and paperback mysteries (1935–1972), notably *The Hanging Heiress* (1949) and his final novel, *The Invader* (1972), which was an MWA Edgar winner.

## HONOR ROLL
(Starred stories are included in this volume)

Amoury, Gloria, "The Cat's Paw," *AHMM*, January

Backus, Jean L., "Last Rendezvous," *EQMM*, September

Ball, John, "Virgil Tibbs and the Cocktail Napkin," *EQMM*, April

Bankier, William, "The Final Twist," *EQMM*, January

——, "Wednesday Night at the Forum," *AHMM*, August

Biery, Janet, "The Revenoor," *AHMM*, November

Blankenship, D. G., "The Waters of La Fleur," *EQMM*, October

Block, Lawrence, "A Candle for the Bag Lady," *AHMM*, November

——, "Collecting Ackermans," *AHMM*, July

*——, "Gentlemen's Agreement," *EQMM*, April

——, "Nothing Short of Highway Robbery," *AHMM*, March

Brand, Christianna, "Upon Reflection," *EQMM*, August

Brashler, Anne, "The Empty Chair," *EQMM*, March

Breen, Jon L., "The Clara Long Case," *AHMM*, July

Brennan, Joseph Payne, "The Case of the Mystified Vendor," *Chronicles of Lucius Leffing*

Bretnor, R., "The Accident Epidemic," *EQMM*, December

Brittain, William, "The Second Reason," *EQMM*, February

Buchanan, Donal, "Death on the Move," *MSMM*, November-December

Burke, J. F., "I'll Kill You in the Morning," *AHMM*, October

*Bush, Geoffrey, "The Problem of Li T'ang," *The Atlantic Monthly*, August

Callahan, Barbara, "Don't Cry, Sally Shy," *EQMM*, April

——, "The Man with the Yellow Hair," *EQMM*, December

——, "The Pinwheel Dream," *EQMM*, July

*——, "To Be Continued," *EQMM*, January

*Colby, Robert, "Paint the Town Green," *AHMM*, October

Dahl, Roald, "The Hitchhiker," *The Atlantic Monthly*, August

Darling, Jean, "The Seventh Son," *AHMM*, May

de la Torre, Lillian, "The Spirit of the '76," *EQMM*, January

Dudley, William J., "On Death Row," *EQMM*, November

Eckels, Robert Edward, "Account Settled," *EQMM*, May

——, "Lang and Lovell Go Legit," *EQMM*, November

Ellin, Stanley, "The Family Circle," *EQMM*, December

Ely, David, "The Looting of the Tomb," *EQMM*, December

Fick, Alvin S., "A Shroud for the Railroad Man," *AHMM*, October

Fish, Robert L., "The Adventure of the Animal Fare," *EQMM*, October

*——, "Stranger in Town," *Antaeus*, Spring-Summer

Fremlin, Celia, "A Case of Maximum Need," *EQMM*, March

———, "Etiquette for Dying," *EQMM*, January
Garfield, Brian, "The Glory Hunter," *EQMM*, September
———, "Hunting Accident," *EQMM*, June
*———, "Jode's Last Hunt," *EQMM*, January
Garve, Andrew, "A Glass of Port," *EQMM*, February
Gilbert, Michael, "Captain Crabtree," *EQMM*, July
———, "The Happy Brotherhood," *EQMM*, May
———, "Rough Justice," *EQMM*, March
*Godfrey, Peter, "To Heal a Murder," *EQMM*, August
Gottlieb, Kathryn, "Life Sentence," *AHMM*, October
Graham, Janet, "The Follower," *EQMM*, June
Hamill, Pete, "The Men in Black Raincoats," *EQMM*, December
Hamilton, Dennis, "The Regression of Jason Guiness," *MM*, January
Hamilton, Nan, "Incident at the Bridge," *MSMM*, July
Harrington, Joyce, "Grass," *EQMM*, March
*———, "The Old Gray Cat," *EQMM*, December
———, "The Thirteenth Victim," *Antaeus*, Spring-Summer
———, "When Push Comes to Shove," *AHMM*, November
Hoch, Edward D., "Captain Leopold Looks for the Cause," *EQMM*, November
———, "The Problem of the Voting Booth," *EQMM*, December
———, "Second Chance," *AHMM*, July
———, "The Theft of Nothing at All," *EQMM*, May
Holding, James, "Dumb Dude," *Antaeus*, Spring-Summer
Kelly, Mary, "Life the Shadow of Death," *Winter's Crimes 8*
Lutz, John, "One Man's Manual," *AHMM*, March
———, "Something for the Dark," *AHMM*, November
Lyon, Dana, "Chains," *MSMM*, October
———, "The Empty House," *MSMM*, September
*MacDonald, John D., "Finding Anne Farley," *Chicago Sun-Times*, began May 22
Mahoney, Mick, "Sixty Seconds Delay," *MSMM*, April
Maling, Arthur, "The Attack," *AHMM*, April
Malzberg, Barry, "Getting In," *AHMM*, March
Markham, Marion M., "The Ultimate Weapon," *Buffalo Spree*, Fall
Marx, Olga, "The Calendar of Death," *AHMM*, December
Masur, Harold Q., "Framed for Murder," *EQMM*, June
Maybury, Florence V., "The Grass Widow," *EQMM*, August
Mayers, Carroll, "Thicker Than Blood," *AHMM*, July
*McKimmey, James, "The Crimes of Harry Waters," *MSMM*, May
McMullen, Mary, "Her Heart's Home," *EQMM*, May
Nevins, Francis M., Jr., "Fair Game," *AHMM*, May
———, "A Picture in the Mind," *AHMM*, February
Nussbaum, Al, "Korda," *AHMM*, June

# About the Editor

Edward D. Hoch, winner of an Edgar award for his short story, "The Oblong Room," is a full-time writer, mainly of mystery fiction, and his stories appear regularly in the leading mystery magazines. He is probably best known for his creation of series-detective Nick Velvet, whose exploits have even been dramatized on French television. A collection entitled *The Thefts of Nick Velvet* was published by The Mysterious Press. His first novel, *The Shattered Raven* (1969), has recently been reissued. He is the author of *The Transvection Machine, The Fellowship of the Hand,* and *The Frankenstein Factory,* and is presently at work on another novel. Mr. Hoch is married and lives with his wife in Rochester, New York.